"Did you think we wouldn't recognize you?"

"I may look like him, but I'm not your father," Joe said to the two children gazing at him as if he were the villain in a horror movie. "My name is Joe Smith."

"That sounds like a made-up name," the boy accused.

"It's not. If you wait just a minute, I'll go inside and get my wallet. It has my driver's license in it."

"It's probably fake."

"If you're not going to accept my license as proof, what will satisfy you?"

The little girl whispered something to her brother, who then turned and said, "Take off your shirt. Or are you chicken?"

Joe almost chuckled at the absurdity of the request. Two kids were accusing him of being their deadbeat dad—and demanding that he remove his shirt to prove it. He decided to humor the kids rather than argue with them. He'd do pretty much anything to show them he wasn't their father. He pulled the bottom of his T-shirt from his pants and lifted it over his head, leaving him bare chested and the object of their wide-eyed stares.

"It *is* you!"

Dear Reader,

What is it about fathers?

Alex, the ten-year-old boy in this story, wants one so badly that he goes to great lengths to find his missing dad. That's because a father holds a very special place in his child's heart. I know mine does, and it's been a while since I was ten. My father was my first hero, chasing away the monsters under my bed at night and carrying me on his shoulders to keep my feet from getting stuck in the snow. He taught me how to ride a bike, to drive a car and above all, how a woman should expect to be treated by a man.

I'm no longer a little girl, but I haven't stopped looking at my father as a hero. He has no medals of honor or commendations for bravery, but he is kind, gentle, honest and dependable. Most important, he's given his children a great gift. He's loved their mother for more than sixty years.

Alex's search for his father leads him to an important discovery. He finds a hero who holds a special place not only in his heart, but in his mother's, too. I hope you'll enjoy their story.

Sincerely,

Pamela Bauer

P.S. You can write me c/o MFW, P.O. Box 24107, Minneapolis, MN 55424 or visit me via the Internet at www.pamelabauer.com.

TWO Much Alike

Pamela Bauer

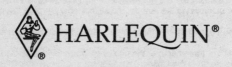

HARLEQUIN®

TORONTO • NEW YORK • LONDON
AMSTERDAM • PARIS • SYDNEY • HAMBURG
STOCKHOLM • ATHENS • TOKYO • MILAN • MADRID
PRAGUE • WARSAW • BUDAPEST • AUCKLAND

ISBN 0-373-71007-0

TWO MUCH ALIKE

Copyright © 2001 by Pamela Muelhbauer.

This edition published by arrangement with Harlequin Books S.A.

Visit us at www.eHarlequin.com

Printed in U.S.A.

For two very special sets of twins:

My dad, Clifford Ronning, and his brother, Clarence
and
Marilyn and Marlene Muehlbauer,
two dear friends who introduced me
to my real-life hero, their brother Gerr

PROLOGUE

"DID YOU GET IT?"

"Yeah, but it wasn't easy." Alex Harper unzipped his backpack and pulled out a photograph. "My mom threw out most of his pictures. I found this one in a box in the basement." He gave the photo to Josh Gallivan, who studied it closely.

"He's a sailor?"

"He *was* a sailor. Now he's a bum."

Josh glanced at the photograph, then at Alex and then back at the photo again. "He looks normal."

"He's not. I'm just glad I don't look like him. I don't, do I?" Alex's tone dared his best friend to disagree.

Again Josh looked from the picture to Alex. "Naw, you don't look like him at all. He could be a total stranger."

He *was* a total stranger as far as Alex was concerned. With each passing birthday, Alex's memories of his father had dimmed, until now—at the age of ten—his father was simply a face on a piece of paper, a man who smelled like cigars and didn't like to get his pants wrinkled.

As Josh slipped the photo into the scanner, Alex turned his attention to the monitor, waiting for the image to appear on the screen. He wasn't nervous, yet his stomach felt funny—the same way it had that time he'd fallen out of the big oak tree in the back-yard.

"Here it comes," Josh said, as the image appeared on the screen in startling clarity. "Okay, we've got it. Now all we have to do is cut and paste it to your poster." Josh moved the mouse with a familiarity Alex envied. Known as the biggest computer geek in the fourth grade, Josh knew more about computers than some adults. Most kids thought it was because his dad was a programmer and Josh had had his very own computer since he was big enough to sit on a chair. Alex, however, knew the real reason. Josh was super smart.

"Done," he boasted proudly.

Alex gazed at the monitor. At the top of the screen in large letters were the words "Have You Seen This Man?" Occupying the rest of the space was the picture Josh had just scanned. A shiver rippled through Alex.

"What happened to the stuff at the bottom?" he asked.

"It's there." Josh scrolled down the page until the message typed in capital letters appeared. Then he read aloud, "His name is Dennis Harper. He's a deadbeat who deserted his family. If you see him, call me immediately." He rattled off the digits of Alex's phone number. "Well?"

"It's okay…I guess," Alex said tentatively.

"I think it'd be better if we put your picture on it, too," Josh suggested. "My mom's in advertising and she says that if you want to get people's attention, you should use pictures of kids. You do want people to take a good look at the poster, don't you?"

Alex thought for a moment. "You really think it would help?"

Josh nodded, then reached across his desk to a cork bulletin board where push pins held half a dozen wallet-size photos in place. He grabbed the one Alex had given him at the start of the school year and placed it in the scanner.

A few moments later, he said, "Now we'll print." He hit another key and almost immediately a paper emerged from the printer. He pulled it from the tray and handed it to Alex. "What do you think?"

Alex thought it was weird to see his picture on the same paper as his father's. A deadbeat dad and a searching son. They weren't exactly the typical father and son.

Not that Alex cared. He didn't need a dad and he didn't care if his ever came back. He just wanted to find him so the judge could make his dad pay what he owed his mom. Then she wouldn't have to work so much. If she had someone to help pay the bills, she could take some time off to spend with him and his sister and brother this summer. They might even get to take a vacation. And get some new clothes instead of having to wear the stuff his mom found at garage sales. Maybe he could even get his own computer and show the other kids at school that he was just as smart as Josh.

"Well, is it okay or isn't it?" Josh asked. "You want me to make copies?"

With his father's face staring at him, Alex found that suddenly he wasn't sure. For so long he'd wanted to find his dad, yet now that there was a possibility he might just do it, he found the prospect a little scary. What if his mom was right? What if they were better off without Dennis Harper in their lives?

He looked at Josh. "This isn't a dumb idea, is it?"

"Uh-uh. When Billy Carson's cat was missing, he found it by printing up posters and putting them all over town. If it'll work for a cat, why wouldn't it work for a person?"

Alex realized that Josh thought he was questioning the wisdom of printing the posters, not his attempt to locate his father. It shouldn't have surprised him that his friend wouldn't understand why he might have second thoughts. After all, Josh had a father. It was true his parents were divorced, but his dad came every other weekend to pick him up and take him places. He also played catch with Josh and helped coach his little league team. He hadn't abandoned his kids after the divorce. He wasn't anything like Dennis Harper.

"Do you want me to print them or not?" Josh asked a bit impatiently, when Alex still hadn't given him the go-ahead.

Alex hesitated only a moment before saying, "Yeah. It's about time somebody found that deadbeat."

CHAPTER ONE

JOE SMITH WAS ON HIS WAY into the hardware store when he heard a voice behind him say, "Someone's looking for you."

For a moment Joe felt trapped. It was an instinctive reaction caused by a fear that the identity he'd worked so hard to conceal might be exposed. It didn't matter that during the two years he'd lived in northern Minnesota, no one had suspected that he was anyone but Joe Smith, a man looking for a quiet life along the shores of Lake Superior. He knew, however, that the past had a way of catching up with a person, especially when that past contained secrets.

Hoping today wasn't that day, he forced himself to turn around. Standing behind him was the owner of Whispering Pines, a resort on the outskirts of the small town of Grand Marais.

"Hey, Pete. How's it going?" Joe greeted him with a handshake.

"It's going good. How about yourself?"

"Can't complain." Joe knew he needed to get right to the point. "Did you say someone's looking for me?"

"Yup. One of the guests at the lodge," the older man responded. "Says he wants to talk to you about a fly-in."

The muscles in Joe's body began to uncoil. He

should have known that it would be someone wanting to go fishing, not a snoop asking questions.

"Did you tell him to contact Blue Waters?"

"Sure I did, but I suspect they told him what they tell most tourists about this time of year. If you don't book ahead, you're out of luck. And you know how these rich folks are. They think they can get whatever they want by flapping a few extra bills in someone's face."

"How big of bills?" Joe asked with a sly smile.

"Big enough to turn my head," Pete admitted with a chuckle. "Seriously, it could be a nice little side job for you," he said, lowering his voice and glancing around to make sure they wouldn't be overheard. "I know you have a loyalty to Blue Waters, but you really should think about being your own boss."

Joe looked out at Lake Superior and squinted as the sun bounced off the glistening water. "It's a lot of work running your own business."

"You don't need to tell me," the other man said with an understanding shake of his head. "But you're a good pilot, Joe. And as for the responsibility and hard work...well, you're practically running Blue Waters right now."

"I appreciate the vote of confidence, Pete, but I'm content to leave the problems behind when I go home. Blue Waters has been good to me."

It was true. Joe had worried that with a new identity he'd have trouble finding work as a pilot. Although he'd logged a considerable number of hours in the air while in the Navy, they were hours he'd been forced to leave behind, along with his name, when he'd moved to Minnesota. Not wanting to risk being traced because of his license, he'd started over, taking flying lessons and passing all the requirements of a new pilot. If anyone at Blue Waters thought it was odd that he appeared to be a much better pilot than his experience indicated, they didn't comment on it. He was able to work in relative anonymity, without any questions about his past, without any enquiries into his personal life.

It was the way Joe wanted it and the way he needed it to be. It would have been nice to run his own flying service, but it was a risk he couldn't take. Running a business meant regulations and regulations meant red tape and inspectors. What he couldn't afford was to leave a paper trail that would allow the wrong people to come looking for him. He'd made a new life for himself, deliberately choosing Smith as a surname because it was common and hard to trace. There was no point in taking a chance that someone would discover that he'd once been somebody else.

"Besides, with my dad's health being what it is…" He let the sentence trail off, knowing perfectly well the lodge's owner would deduce that Joe worked for someone else because he needed to take care of his father.

Which wasn't a lie. A head injury and subsequent stroke had forever changed his father. Joe hadn't anticipated that the strong, imposing man who had run his home with the same discipline he'd used when commanding his naval troops would ever need to lean on anyone—and especially not his son. The man who had been the epitome of authority now found himself dependent.

"I understand what you're saying, Joe," Pete said,

his eyes as sympathetic as his tone. "How is the Admiral?"

"He's doing all right," he answered honestly.

Pete shook his head. "The brain's a complicated thing, isn't it?"

Joe nodded. "It is. He can tell you exactly what he paid for every car he ever purchased, yet he has trouble making change for a dollar."

"How's Letty been working out for you?"

Letty was a retired nurse Joe had hired to look after his father whenever he was gone. "She's been great. She certainly has made my life a lot easier."

"I knew she would." Pete nodded toward the hardware store. "You going in or coming out?"

"In. Need to get a washer for a faucet. What about you?"

"I'm on my way to get my ears lowered," he said, glancing in the direction of the barbershop down the street. "But I'm glad I ran into you. About this fella that's looking for you…should I tell him to stop by?"

What Joe didn't want was people coming to his place. His home at the lake was his sanctuary. The fewer people who visited there, the less complicated his life would be. "I'll tell you what. How about if I give him a call when I get back to the house?" he suggested.

"Good enough." Pete gave him the man's name, then bid Joe goodbye, leaving him with a "You take care now."

Joe certainly would do just that. He'd taken a lot of care from the very first day he'd arrived in northern Minnesota. He'd been careful to mind his own business, careful not to raise anyone's curiosity about his or his father's past, and especially careful not to give anyone a reason to believe he was anything but a concerned son who'd brought his ailing father to spend what was left of his life in the peaceful woods near the Canadian border.

No question—Joe would take very good care not to let his past catch up with him.

"I WISH I COULD GO WITH," ten-year-old Emma said on a sigh as she watched her mother apply mascara to lashes that were already long and lush.

"You wouldn't enjoy yourself," Frannie Harper told her daughter.

"Yes, I would. Auntie Lois is so much fun."

Lois *was* fun, Frannie thought as memories of their last night out together filtered through her mind. Latin music, salsa dancing, Corona beer, handsome men.

"Sorry, love, this is a night for grown-ups only."

And there weren't many of those in her life, Frannie acknowledged as she put aside the mascara and went to the closet. Being a single parent, she'd had little time for anything except work and taking care of her family. Nor did she have the money for going out with the girls—something she was reminded of when she opened her closet door.

She grimaced as she pushed aside hangers holding garments that should have been relegated to the rag bag years ago, but still constituted her wardrobe. She didn't have a single thing that could be classified as trendy. Practical yes, trendy no. She knew the kind of places her sister frequented, and they were filled with people wearing the latest styles.

She sighed, knowing she really had only one

choice: Old Faithful. It was a black sheath with a touch of glitter, a dress she figured she must have worn at least a hundred times. ''Timeless'' was how the clerk who'd sold it to her had described it. ''Boring'' was how Frannie had come to look at it. She dragged it from the hanger and went to stand in front of the full-length mirror.

''One hundred and one,'' she mumbled to herself as she tugged the dress over her head.

''One hundred and one what, Mommy?'' Emma asked.

''Nothing, sweetie. I was wondering if I've worn this dress a hundred times yet,'' she said as she straightened the hemline.

''I'd wear it a million times if it were mine. It's so pretty,'' Emma said with a childlike sincerity.

Frannie sighed. ''It's old.''

''You said there's nothing wrong with old,'' Emma reminded her.

Frannie smiled. *So my words come back to haunt me.* ''You're right. Old is comfortable.''

When Frannie spritzed her neck with a cologne Lois had given her for her birthday, Emma said, ''You never wear perfume. Are you going looking for men?''

She put her hands on her hips and clicked her tongue. ''You know better than to even ask that question. I have all the men in my life that I need.''

Emma slipped her feet into Frannie's high-heel sandals and walked over to the mirror where she pirouetted on wobbly legs. ''I'm never getting married.''

As much as Frannie was tempted to say, ''Smart girl,'' she simply said, ''Never is a long time.''

"I know, but I hate boys. They're stupid. That's why I'm never getting married," Emma insisted. "I'm glad you don't have a boyfriend. They're too messy."

Curious, Frannie asked, "Messy how?"

"Ever since Ashley Wilcott's mom got a boyfriend, their life's been messed up. They don't get to dog-sit for the humane society anymore, Ashley can't eat her dinner on a TV tray and if she leaves even one little sip of milk in her glass he tells her she's wasting food and makes her do extra chores. Ashley says he's always at her house butting into their business, too."

Frannie felt a wave of sympathy for Ashley's mother. She knew firsthand how difficult it was for a single mom to have any kind of personal life. When Lois had finally convinced Frannie she should start dating again, it hadn't taken long for her to realize that whether or not the kids were with her physically, they were always with her emotionally. And the few men she had brought home had been put through an inquisition no human should have to endure. Frannie had decided a long time ago that life was complicated enough without adding romance to the picture.

Just then the doorbell rang, and Emma kicked off the shoes and exclaimed in delight, "Auntie Lois is here!"

"Tell her I'm not quite ready, but I'll be there in a few minutes."

As Frannie ran a brush through her blond hair, she could hear the commotion her sister's presence generated. It had always been that way. Her kids hovered around their aunt like bees around a flower.

By the time Frannie went into the living room,

however, the bees and the flower were nowhere in sight. She poked her head inside the boys' room and, as she'd expected, saw her children gathered around Lois. She held a bright yellow piece of paper in her hands that Alex snatched away when he noticed his mother.

Normally Frannie would have asked what it was they'd been looking at, but her sister's appearance had her mouth agape. Lois's short hair, which normally fell in soft blond layers, was the color of a red pepper, sticking straight out from her head like porcupine quills. She had on black leather pants, a matching leather bandeau top that revealed more of her midsection than it covered and platform shoes that added three inches to her already tall figure. More than trendy, Frannie thought.

"Like my new look?" she asked Frannie with a crooked grin.

"If you open your mouth and I see metal, I'm not going anywhere with you," Frannie warned.

Lois grinned, then stuck out her tongue. There were no rings of any sort piercing it. "You know I hate pain. The hair's cool, isn't it?" she asked, then stuck out her hands. "Look. My nails are the exact same color as my hair."

"They are!" Emma exclaimed. "Cool!" She examined her aunt's long, slender fingers carefully.

"Is it permanent?" Frannie asked, nodding toward her sister's red head.

"Heavens, no. It washes out. I have to be in court tomorrow morning."

"Is it a murder case?" Alex asked, his eyes widening.

"No, just someone who needs help," Lois answered.

"I'm going to be a lawyer and help people when I grow up, too," Emma said, gazing at her aunt with adoration.

"Me, too," said three-year-old Luke, who often repeated everything his older sister said.

Lois ruffled her nephew's hair affectionately. "I thought you were going to be a cowboy."

"I think he's going to be a demolition man. He destroys everything," Alex said dryly.

"He's not that bad," Emma chastised her twin.

Their conversation was interrupted by the arrival of the baby-sitter.

After going over a list of instructions with the teenager, Frannie gave each of her kids a kiss and hug, then headed out the front door with her sister.

"Is that for us?" Frannie asked when she saw a taxi at the curb.

"Yes. I figured you wouldn't want to take your car, and you know how much I hate driving downtown. Besides, someone wanted to do me a favor," she said as she ushered her sister toward the cab.

"And this is the favor? A chauffeur?" she asked, as a thickset man hopped out of the taxi to get the door for them.

"Yes. This is Lenny." She tossed a smile at the man who fussed over them as if they were celebrities.

Lenny, Frannie discovered, was the brother of a woman Lois had counseled through a domestic crisis. Relieved that the man who'd made life so miserable for his sister had been put behind bars, Lenny had insisted on showing his appreciation by giving Lois free taxi service on his night off.

"It will be nice not to have to worry about traffic and parking," Frannie said as she settled into the back seat.

"Yes, it will," Lois agreed. As soon as the taxi had pulled away from the curb, she said, "You didn't tell me that Alex is trying to find Dennis."

Frannie sighed. "You know how he feels about money. He thinks we don't have enough and that getting Dennis's child support payments would make our lives much easier."

"It would," Lois said candidly. "That's why you were looking for him, too. Remember?"

She shook her head. "Please, don't remind me."

"Frannie, he *should* pay. He's their father."

"At one time I felt that way, but not now. I don't want his money and I certainly don't want him back in our lives." She hated the bitterness that always managed to creep into her voice at the mention of her ex.

"Well, Alex does, and he's printed up a couple of hundred posters with Dennis's picture on them. He's going to put them all over town."

A knot formed in Frannie's stomach.

When she was silent, Lois asked, "You do know about the posters, don't you?"

"I knew he was thinking about doing them. We talked about it a couple of weeks ago, but I thought I'd convinced him it wouldn't accomplish anything." Unsure if she needed to persuade her sister, she added, "It won't, you know."

To her relief, Lois said, "I didn't say it would. If he hasn't been found by now, I doubt anyone's going to locate him. We know Dennis Harper's not in the

Twin Cities and chances of him being anywhere in the Midwest are next to none.''

''Which means it's just a waste of time,'' Frannie concluded.

''Not to Alex it isn't.'' She shot her sister a sideways glance. ''That's what's really bugging you, isn't it? The fact that Alex still thinks about his father.''

''Of course it bothers me,'' Frannie admitted, knowing there was no point in denying it. ''My kids have spent more time with their dentist than they have with their own father. Dennis was never a dad to them, just a man who drifted in and out of their lives when it was convenient for him. He doesn't deserve to have *any* of their thoughts and he certainly isn't worthy of a son like Alex. Believe me, if I had it in my power to make Alex forget Dennis ever existed, I would do it in a minute.''

''But he did exist. And it's something Alex needs to deal with in his own way.''

''Why?'' she cried out in frustration, although she already knew the answer. So did her sister, who chose not to say anything.

After a few moments of silence, Frannie said, ''I hate knowing Alex even thinks about the man.''

''It's normal, Frannie,'' Lois said, putting a hand on her sister's arm.

She chewed on her upper lip as she nodded. ''It just seems as if every time I think I've managed to let go of my anger, I realize I'll probably always be angry at Dennis. Not because of what he did to me, but because of what he continues to do to my kids.''

''Your kids are going to be just fine,'' Lois insisted. ''They're bright, well-adjusted, and happy—

and that's because of you, not Dennis. So put him out of your mind. He's not worthy of your thoughts—not even the nasty ones,'' she said, grinning.

Frannie didn't return the smile, prompting Lois to ask, ''Hey, you're not going to let this spoil our evening, are you?''

She shook her head, although the enthusiasm she'd felt earlier had waned. ''I do wish Alex had shown me the poster himself.''

''I think he wanted to test the waters with me first,'' Lois remarked. ''And I'm glad he did. That poster has your phone number on it.''

Frannie groaned. ''Tell me that doesn't mean I'm going to have creeps calling my house in the middle of the night.''

''You won't,'' Lois stated confidently. ''I suggested Alex use one of my office numbers, instead. I told him it was much safer to do that, and he said he'd have Josh redo the posters.''

''Thank you. That means that if by some strange twist of fate someone does call with information, you'll be the first to know and you can tell me.''

''He's not going to hear anything.''

Frannie hoped her sister was right. It had been a long, painful struggle, but she'd put her life back together after Dennis had done his best to ruin it. She'd made a good life for her children, and she wasn't about to let him disrupt it again.

For the rest of the taxi ride, Lois talked about the place where they were meeting several of their friends. It was a new club that had become popular among singles. Frannie listened and made appropriate responses, but her thoughts weren't on the evening ahead. She stared out the window at the passing scenery, watching trees and houses and storefronts disappear in a blur and thinking how her life with Dennis had been like a car ride.

They'd started a journey together and reached a destination, but everything in between had been of little consequence. All the places they'd been, the things they'd seen were gone, just like the passing scenery. There was nothing memorable about that journey—except for the children—and that was the part of the ride Dennis wanted to forget.

"This is it." Lois's announcement interrupted her musings. The taxi stopped in front of an old brick building in the warehouse district. The only indication there was a club inside was the line of people waiting to gain admission. "Come on. We need to find Shannon and Misti."

Frannie wasn't sure how they'd find the other two women in the crowd, but she was glad when they did; being with her women friends was exactly what she needed to push all thoughts of Dennis Harper out of her mind. They moved from club to club, each one a little bit noisier than the previous one, all of them perfect backdrops for the laughter they shared. It felt good to have fun, and when it was time to go home, not even fatigue could stop Frannie from wishing the night wasn't over.

Their final stop was a twenty-four hour deli where they ate chocolate desserts and rehashed the encounters they'd had that evening. Frannie couldn't remember when she'd laughed so much, and made a promise that she wasn't going to let so much time pass before she went out with them again.

She and Lois were both grateful they had Lenny

to drive them home. After saying good-night to her sister, Frannie dragged her feet up the walk to the front door. She paid the baby-sitter, then stood on the front porch until the teen was safely in the house next door.

Then she went inside the place that had been home for the past five years. A quick peek into Emma's room assured her the little girl was asleep. Next she went to the boys' room and poked her head in to make sure everything was all right. She was about to leave when she remembered the posters. Unable to resist, she tiptoed over to the desk and opened the top drawer.

A small night-light in the shape of a baseball was just strong enough for her to see the stack of flyers. In the near darkness, Dennis's face stared up at her. She squeezed her eyes shut and didn't open them again until she'd pushed the drawer shut. Angry for letting her curiosity get the better of her, she quietly left the room.

Later, as she lay in bed, all thoughts of her night out with the girls had vanished. There was only one thing on her mind: Alex's deadbeat father.

"MOM, LUKE'S BEEN MESSING with my baseball cards again," Alex cried out in frustration as he stormed into the kitchen, his faux-leather album spread wide so she could see the empty pockets.

"No, I didn't," the three-year-old denied.

"Yes, you did," Alex said, then turned back to his mother.

"I told you to keep them out of his reach," Frannie said absently, her attention on the negatives she held up to the light.

"They *were* out of reach," Alex said in exasperation. "I had them on top of the dresser, but he's like a monkey, climbing all over the place. You either need to put him in a cage or give me my own room."

She clicked her tongue in reprobation. "He's not a monkey, he's your brother—he doesn't belong in a cage. And you know you can't have your own room."

"So what am I supposed to do? Watch all my stuff get ruined?"

"They're only dumb old trading cards," Emma said, standing at the counter buttering her toast.

He shot her a look of disdain. "Go ahead and call them dumb. They're gonna be worth a lot of money someday."

Emma grunted in disbelief.

"They are! Trading cards are big business. I heard a guy got a thousand dollars for a Cal Ripken."

Frannie raised one eyebrow. "Do you have a Cal Ripken?"

"No, but some of my cards will be worth something someday if they're not all wrecked. Mom, you've got to do something. He's always into everything…my homework, my cards…everything. Can't I please have my own room?"

"That would mean putting Luke in with Emma," Frannie said, telling him with her tone what a bad idea that was.

"He can't. He's not a girl," Emma said.

"It's not fair," Alex said, slamming his album down on the table. "Luke's a monster." It was a comment that caused the three-year-old to chuckle with delight.

"It's just a stage he's in," Frannie said consolingly. "It won't be long before you're the best of friends."

Alex made a sound of disbelief.

"You should read *Tales of a Fourth Grade Nothing*," Emma suggested. "Peter has the same problem with his brother Fudge that you have with Luke."

"I don't want to read a book. I want my cards," Alex demanded.

"Luke, did you take your brother's baseball cards?" Frannie asked.

Luke giggled again, then ran from the room. When he returned, he clutched two trading cards in his fists. Alex grabbed them from him.

"Books are make-believe," Alex said to Emma. "This isn't." He held up two dog-eared cards for their inspection. "Look! Chuck Knoblauch and Derek Jeter ruined!"

He grabbed his album and was about to stamp out of the kitchen, when Frannie said, "Alex, I'd like to talk to you after you've had breakfast."

"I'm not hungry."

"Well, when you are hungry, let me know. I'll make you some pancakes and you and I will have a heart-to-heart."

Alex grunted, then slipped out of the kitchen. As he left, Emma called out, "If you want my *Tales of a Fourth Grade Nothing*, I'll loan it to you."

Frannie didn't think Alex wanted anything but to be left alone. When Luke would have followed him, she grabbed him by the waist and set him on a chair. "Time to eat."

"He's mad, you know," Emma commented.

"He just needs some time alone," she told her

daughter, but she knew that as soon as she'd fed Luke, she'd see if there wasn't something else she could do for Alex.

ALEX HEARD HIS SISTER'S VOICE echo through the hallway as he headed for his room. He didn't care if *Tales of a Fourth Grade Nothing* was the best book in the whole wide world. He didn't want to read about some kid named Peter who had a little brother who messed with his things.

It was bad enough that *he* had a little brother who messed with *his* things. And the title of his sister's favorite book was enough to make him want to bury it at the bottom of his closet. Why would anyone want to read about a kid who thought he was a nothing?

If the title was Tales of a Fourth Grade Somebody, he might read the book, but a fourth grade nothing? No way. He already felt like a big fat nothing when he thought about his dad.

There was knock on his door, and then Alex heard his mother's voice: "Can I come in?"

He knew she wouldn't go away until he said yes. Mothers never did. "All right," he mumbled.

She came in and closed the door behind her, then sat down next to him on the bed. "I'm sorry Luke ruined your cards. Can I buy you new ones?"

He shrugged. "If you can find them."

"I saw in the paper there's a trading card show next weekend at the junior high. Would you like to go?"

"You'll take me?"

"If you want. And you could bring Josh, too."

"All right."

"Alex, there's something else I want to talk about with you." He could tell by the look on her face that it was serious. "Lois told me you've made up the posters you hope will help you find your father."

He'd figured his aunt would tell her, so he went over to his desk and pulled open a drawer. He removed a single sheet of paper and showed it to her. "Are you mad?"

He thought it was probably a dumb question. She'd already told him a while back that she didn't think the poster was a good idea.

"You call him a deadbeat." Her voice was quiet, not angry.

"Because he is. You don't need to pretend with me, Mom. I heard you and Auntie Lois talking. I know he's a deadbeat."

"Then, why look for him?"

"To make him pay. He owes you money. It's not right that you have to work so much just to pay the bills he should be looking after."

She slid her arm around his shoulder and squeezed him. "It's sweet of you to worry about me, but I can take care of the four of us just fine. Are you sure there isn't another reason why you want to find him?"

"Like what?"

"Maybe you think there's a possibility that when you find him, things will be different. That your father will want to be a father again."

"No! That's not it. I'm not doing this for me, Mom. I told you that. It's for you and Emma and Luke."

She gave him another squeeze and said, "Oh, Alex. You really are a very special boy."

He wanted to believe her. And most of the time he did, but there were those times when he had his doubts. "If I'm so special, why did dad leave?"

As soon as he'd asked the question, he wished he hadn't, because his mom's eyes got all watery.

Then she pulled him even closer to her, resting her chin on his head as she said, "It's nothing you or Emma or Luke did. Your father left because he was missing something inside himself. And it was a big something. It was what tells us that the greatest treasure anyone can ever have is a family to love. So don't ever think you aren't special. You were just unfortunate to have a father who wasn't smart enough to recognize what special is."

This time she didn't just give him a hug, but a kiss, too. Right on his forehead. Then she said, "Now how about coming out and letting me make you some pancakes?"

He *was* hungry. "Oh, all right." He tried to make it sound as if he really didn't care about breakfast.

Before they could cross the living room into the kitchen, the doorbell rang. Emma raced to the front window to push aside the curtains so she could see who was standing on the step.

With a screech she cried out, "Oh, my gosh! It's Gramma!"

CHAPTER TWO

WHAT FRANNIE DIDN'T NEED today of all days was to have her former mother-in-law drop in. "This is a surprise," she said, although it really shouldn't have caught her off guard. After all, Arlene Harper had a way of showing up when she was least expected. If there was one word Frannie would use to describe Arlene, it was *unpredictable*.

"Did you take a taxi from the airport?"

"Oh, I didn't fly," Arlene answered. "I drove."

"By yourself? Where's Harry?"

Harry was Arlene's fiancé—or at least he was the last time Frannie had seen her. She glanced at Arlene's left hand and saw the ring finger was bare. It looked as if Harry had gone the way of the rest of the men in Arlene's life.

"I'm afraid that didn't work out."

"Oh, I'm sorry to hear that," Frannie said, although she really should have told Arlene how lucky she was to be rid of the moocher. From the very first time Frannie had met Harry she'd had her suspicions that he was all charm and no substance. But then, in the eleven years she'd known Arlene, that's all there had been in her mother-in-law's life—men with charm but little substance.

Arlene's next words indicated that she'd finally figured out Harry, too. "It's for the best. He wasn't

the man for me,'' Arlene said without any bitterness.
"He thought work was for other people. But let's not
waste our time talking about me. I want to hear
what's been happening to my beautiful grandchildren,'' she said, wrapping her arms around Luke and
Emma.

"As you can see, they're fine,'' Frannie answered.

"We only have one more week of school and then
we're on summer vacation,'' Emma stated joyfully.

"I know. That's why I came. I want to spend lots
of time with you this summer.''

Frannie gulped. "You're staying for the summer?''

"This is going to be so cool,'' Emma gushed, giving her grandmother another hug.

"Yes, it is,'' Arlene agreed with a smile. "You
won't have to have a baby-sitter while your mother's
at work.''

As much as she appreciated Arlene's offer, the
thought of her mother-in-law staying with them in a
house that was already too small did not put the glee
in her eyes that it did in her children's.

"It's very generous of you to offer, but I've already contracted for day care,'' she said, trying not
to sound ungracious.

Alex, who'd been standing in the background,
stepped forward. "We hate going to day care. It's all
little kids. Why can't Gramma take care of us?''

"Because it'll cost me money if we back out
now,'' Frannie explained.

"But it's going to cost you money anyway,
right?'' Arlene asked.

"Can't we please stay home with Gramma?''

Emma begged, giving her mother a look that was just as dramatic as her plea.

"What about summer camp? The bus is supposed to pick you up at the day care center," Frannie reminded them.

"That's not until August," Alex answered.

"Oh, by then I'll be gone," Arlene told them.

Frannie hoped no one heard her sigh of relief.

Emma's face dropped. "I thought you said you were staying the whole summer."

"Just for part of the summer, dear. But I will be here all of June and part of July."

"What about your job?" Frannie asked.

"Oh, I quit," she said with a flap of her hand.

"You quit?"

"Yes. Don't look so alarmed, Frannie. I'll find another," she said nonchalantly, then turned to the twins and said, "Wait until you see what I brought for you."

"Did you bring us cards with the holes in them?" Alex asked, moving closer to the couch.

"I most certainly did," Arlene said proudly. "Two decks for each of you."

"And the teeny bottles of shampoo and lotion?" Emma wanted to know.

Arlene nodded. "They smell just heavenly. Wait until you see."

Because she worked as a cashier at a hotel casino in Atlantic City, Arlene often brought playing cards as well as complimentary bottles of lotion and shampoo.

Her glance moved between Emma and Alex. "Now, what should we do today? Gramma wants to take you someplace fun." Arlene looked at Frannie and asked, "You don't have plans for today, do you?"

"Actually, I do." She was assigned to cover a charity walk-a-thon. She'd planned to put Luke in the stroller and let Emma and Alex push him, as they walked with the rest of the participants and she took photos.

Alex groaned. "We don't have to go to that, do we?"

"Go where?" Emma asked.

"Some stupid walk-a-thon," Alex answered.

"It's not stupid. It's for a good cause," Frannie chastised him.

"We can always do something tomorrow," Arlene suggested, which provoked groans from the twins. Then she looked at Frannie and said, "Or I could take the children today and then you'd be free to concentrate on your work."

It was a tempting offer. The children would be a distraction while she tried to work. On the other hand, Frannie knew her children could be a handful, especially Luke. The memory of her son throwing a temper tantrum the last time she'd had him at the mall made her hesitate. As much as Frannie wanted to say yes, she wasn't sure she could do so with a clear conscience.

Finally, after much cajoling by the twins, she agreed to let them stay with their grandmother, but extracted the promise that they would help their grandmother with Luke. They also needed to complete their Saturday chores, which would give Arlene a chance to rest before their adventure.

Alex didn't protest the later start. "That means I can go over to Josh's and get my posters done."

That raised his grandmother's curiosity. "What posters are those?"

"I'll show you," he answered, then disappeared into his room.

Frannie thought about stopping him, but knew it would only be a matter of time until Arlene found out about his campaign to find his father. When Alex returned with the flyer, he held it up for his grandmother's inspection.

"I'm trying to find my dad. Me and my friend Josh made this, but I have to change the phone number. That's why I have to go to his house. He has a computer," he explained.

Arlene looked first at the poster, then at Frannie, her eyes filled with questions. Frannie didn't know how to answer them, so she simply lifted her brows and shrugged.

"I'm going to put them up all over Minneapolis, and some of my friends are going to take them when they go on vacation this summer," Alex continued. "Will you take some back to Atlantic City with you, Gramma?" He looked at his grandmother expectantly.

Arlene placed her hand on his shoulder. "If it's important to you, of course I will, but I don't know if it will do any good. I doubt he's anywhere close. If your father were living near me, he'd call."

"But there are lots of people who come to the casinos and hotels. Maybe a tourist will see the poster and recognize his picture," Alex argued.

Frannie could see how unsettling it was for Arlene to have such a discussion with her grandson, and decided to change the subject. "Okay, kids, get your chores done."

That got Alex to table the discussion of his missing father. Frannie knew, however, it was a subject that wouldn't be left for long. Sooner or later she and Arlene would have to talk about Dennis's disappearance and Alex's quest.

That's why she wasn't surprised when later that evening, after the kids had gone to bed, Arlene joined her in the kitchen. Frannie offered to make her a cup of tea, but the older woman said she just wanted to sit for a bit and talk.

Seeing her yawn Frannie said, "The kids can wear you out, can't they."

"It's a nice kind of tired. Alex, Emma and Luke are good kids, Frannie. You're doing a fine job with them," she said, taking a seat at the table where Frannie sat folding the laundry.

Frannie smoothed the wrinkles out of a small undershirt. "Thank you, Arlene. I do my best."

"I know you do. And it shows. Of course, Luke does have quite a temper," she remarked.

Frannie gave her a smile. "He had a tantrum?"

"I didn't know kids could arch their backs that way," she reflected with a weary chuckle.

Frannie grimaced. "I'm sorry if he was a handful."

"There's nothing to be sorry about. I'm a mother, too. I know what kids are like." She picked up one of Luke's socks that had fallen out of Frannie's basket. "I'd forgotten how tiny they make these things."

Frannie smiled in understanding and continued to fold the clothes. "I appreciate your help with the kids today. They didn't want to go to the walk-a-thon."

"And you shouldn't have to take them with you

when you work,'' Arlene said as she reached inside the laundry basket for the matching sock.

''Most of my assignments are during the week, and I can drop the kids off at day care if necessary, but on weekends I have to rely on the girl next door. When she's busy, it means I either have to find someone to cover for me at the paper or bring the kids along.''

''That can't be easy,'' Arlene commented, adding the pair of folded socks to Frannie's pile.

''No,'' she said. ''That's why I'm grateful for what you did today.''

Arlene blew off Frannie's gratitude with a wave of her hand. ''It was nothing. Actually, I'm the one who should be thanking you. You've always made me feel welcome here, Frannie, despite everything that's happened.''

''That's because you *are* welcome here,'' Frannie said sincerely.

''Thank you. It's nice to hear you say that, especially when I know you wouldn't say it if you didn't mean it. I hope you don't mind that I want to spend some time here with the children.''

Frannie wasn't sure how she felt about it, but she didn't admit her uncertainty. ''You said you quit your job?''

''Yes. I wanted to see what it would be like to be footloose and fancy free.'' She smiled reflectively. ''I discovered I like it. Now I know why women marry money.''

''Money isn't everything.'' Frannie recited the familiar refrain she'd used hundreds—maybe thousands—of times in the past few years.

"No, but it makes life a bit less stressful," Arlene said.

"Is that why you're looking so relaxed? Because you've come into some money?"

A self-satisfied grin spread Arlene's lips. "I'm here because I've had some very good luck recently and I want to share it with you and the children."

"What kind of luck?"

"Do you remember me talking about Martha Ball?"

"That sweet little old lady who lives down the hall from you?"

Arlene nodded. "I used to pick up her groceries for her, take her to the beauty shop once a week...you know, those kinds of things. She had such bad arthritis that it was difficult for her to get around."

"Had?"

A sadness came into Arlene's eyes. "She passed away a couple of months ago."

Frannie placed a hand on Arlene's arm. "I'm so sorry. I know you were fond of her."

"Yes, she was a dear. And a bit of a gambler. She used to look forward to me coming over so we could play penny-ante poker." Arlene shook her head, a nostalgic twinkle in her eye. "All those years we played for pennies...I had no idea how much she was actually worth."

"She had a lot of money?"

"Oh, yes, and no family to share it with. That's why when she died she left everything to the people she said had been the kindest to her."

"And you were one of them?"

Again she nodded. "There weren't many people

who took the time to visit her. Just a handful of us who stopped in to play cards. None of us expected to get anything. Heck, we all thought she was one step from poverty. We'd often let her win just to give her a few extra bucks.'' She chuckled at the memory.

''Then it must have come as a surprise to learn you had an inheritance.''

''Oh, my goodness, yes! I had no idea she had money in the bank. Every month when I'd help her write out her checks to pay the bills, there barely seemed enough for her to get by. She would say she had a little bit put away for a rainy day—which I thought meant thousands, not hundreds of thousands.''

''Hundreds of thousands?'' Frannie's eyes widened.

''You can imagine my shock. I've lived payday to payday my entire life.''

''Most of us do,'' she said soberly.

''*You* shouldn't have to.''

Frannie really didn't want to be having this conversation with her ex-mother-in-law because she knew where it was leading. And she didn't want to talk about her ex-husband.

Arlene, however, would not be swayed. ''I want to give some of this money to you and the kids…you know, to try to make up for what Dennis hasn't done.''

''You don't need to do that,'' Frannie began, only to have the other woman cut her short.

''I know I don't have to. I want to. What good is inheriting money if you can't share it with the ones you love?''

It was a very generous gesture, yet Frannie

couldn't let her do it. She knew that Arlene had worked hard all her life and had very little to show for it. Forever bailing Dennis out of trouble, she'd never hesitated to spend her money to help her son. Now she wanted to give away what could be her retirement nest egg because of obligations he'd failed to meet.

"If you want to put a little money aside for college for the kids, that's fine, but you don't need to help us out, Arlene. We're doing all right." It wasn't exactly the truth. Frannie was tired of there never being enough money, but she also knew that until she no longer had the expense of day care, she'd continue to scramble for money.

Arlene's face fell. "You don't want my help?"

"You shouldn't have to sacrifice your future because of Dennis's irresponsible behavior. That money should be used for your retirement, not for raising your grandchildren." Frannie didn't like the awkwardness that the subject of money had introduced into their conversation. "Look, I think it's best that we don't talk about Dennis."

"No, you're probably right," Arlene agreed. "It's how we've managed to stay friends, isn't it? By not talking about him?"

Frannie knew there was no need for her to answer.

"I just have one question," Arlene said.

Reluctantly, Frannie asked, "About Dennis?"

She nodded. "Do you think there's any chance that Alex's posters might succeed in finding him?"

Frannie shook her head. "We've hired private investigators who haven't been able to come up with any leads."

"That's true."

"And if Dennis was going to contact anyone, it would be you."

"I don't think so, not after I threatened to turn him in to the authorities." Arlene sighed. "I'm not proud to call him my son, Frannie. You ought to know that. And it hurts me to see Alex struggling with all of this. If there was some way I could make that son of mine behave like a man, I would have done it by now."

Frannie felt a rush of sympathy for the older woman. She could imagine how painful it would be to be estranged from one of her children. "I don't think we should be talking about this, Arlene."

She nodded. "You're right. I'm sorry, Frannie."

"It's all right. He's still your son, Arlene, no matter what happens."

"And the father of Alex, Emma and Luke," her ex-mother-in-law added.

As much as Frannie wanted to argue that Dennis had given up the right to be a father, she knew it would be wise to say nothing. If Arlene planned to stay for part of the summer, Frannie needed to keep a tight rein on her feelings about Dennis.

And she would. For her children's sake.

"It's working out better than I thought it would," Alex told Josh the following Monday on their way to school. "Now that my gramma's staying with us, I won't have to go to day care next week when school's out. And you know what that means."

"You'll be home to answer the phone when someone calls with information about your dad," Josh supplied. "Aren't you worried your mom's gonna get mad when she finds out you left your phone number on the flyers?''

"Only on half of them. The ones I put up around here all have my aunt's office number on them." He kicked a rock in his path and it went rolling across the street.

"You think your aunt will tell you if someone calls about your dad?"

"I'm not sure. She says it's better for society if deadbeats like him drop out…at least, that's what I heard her tell my mom one night when they didn't know I was listening."

"Hey, I heard Jamie Richards is going camping in the Boundary Waters as soon as school's out. You should have him put some posters up there."

"Good idea. And Angela Martin is going to the Wisconsin Dells."

"You asked *her?*" Josh wrinkled his nose in disgust. "She's a dork."

"It doesn't matter. She said she'd take my posters with her."

"How many out-of-town ones does that make?"

"Seventeen. Before summer's over, my posters will be all over the country."

"Cool. I bet you're going to find him."

"Maybe" was all Alex said, remembering all the times he'd heard his mom and his aunt discuss his father. He knew it wasn't easy finding a deadbeat.

TRUE TO HER WORD, Arlene did her best not to mention her son's name during her stay. Alex, however, asked every day if his auntie Lois had called with any information. And each day Frannie would give him the same response. No, not yet.

As days turned into weeks and there were still no leads as to Dennis's whereabouts, Frannie expected Alex to become discouraged. He didn't. He just kept sending the posters with his friends as they left on vacation.

Frannie viewed Arlene's presence as a mixed blessing. It was wonderful to see how warm and loving she was with her grandchildren, but it also made Frannie realize how much easier her life would be with another person sharing the responsibilities of child rearing. Having another adult in the house meant Frannie actually had some time to herself, and she discovered she liked it.

When she expressed this sentiment to her sister as they lunched at an outdoor café, Lois said, "You sure don't sound like the same woman who only a few weeks ago was bemoaning the fact that her ex's mother would be a houseguest for the summer."

Frannie took a sip of her iced tea. "I did have my apprehensions at first, but it's worked out remarkably well. I'm actually going to hate to see her go, even if she does occasionally get on my nerves."

"When does she leave?"

"Next week. She's going out to California for her high school reunion, where she's meeting up with some friends. Then they're all going on a road trip."

"A road trip?"

Frannie nodded. "Apparently they want to see the western part of the United States, go to some of the national parks, stop in and see friends along the way. You know Arlene—she has friends all over the country. I suppose it'll be months before we hear from her again."

"Do you think she'd ever consider moving here?" Lois asked as she stuck her fork into her salad.

Frannie shook her head. "I don't know. She has wanderlust. It's why she moves so often—and why she didn't mind life in the military."

"She must have family."

Frannie reached for her napkin. "A couple of older sisters and some cousins."

"What about the Harper side?"

She shook her head. "Never talks about them. Dennis never did, either."

"There's probably a good reason why they didn't."

Frannie shrugged. "All I know is that it's been good for the kids to have a grandmother around. They're going to miss Arlene."

"By the end of the year Mom will be back," Lois remarked.

"We hope."

Lois frowned. "Why wouldn't she be back? Richard's contract was only to work overseas one year."

"That's true, but the last time I talked to Mom, she told me Richard was doing such a terrific job that the company was thinking about extending their stay."

"Mom's not going to like that."

"I'm not so sure. Obviously it's a great opportunity for them. I mean, what Minnesotan wouldn't want two years working in a warm climate with beautiful sand beaches?"

"But she misses her grandkids." Lois took one last sip of her iced tea, then reached for the check. "I'd better get back to the office. Oh, one other thing

I should mention. We did get a call in response to one of Alex's posters.''

Frannie's heart skipped a beat. ''And?''

''It wasn't legit. Some kid thinking it was funny to place the call.''

Frannie breathed a relieved sigh. ''You're sure?''

''Yes. Caller ID told us it was a call placed in South Minneapolis, not Los Angeles, which is where the kid said he was. Technology can be such a time-saver, can't it?''

ARLENE'S DEPARTURE was a solemn occasion at the Harper house. Frannie, Alex, Emma and Luke all waved at her as she pulled out of the driveway in her shiny new minivan. Frannie understood the reason for her children's tears. Even she had to choke back sadness as she said goodbye.

Seeing their faces as Arlene's van disappeared from sight, Frannie was grateful that there was a summer arts festival going on in a nearby park. It would give them something to take their minds off their grandmother's absence. As well as arts and crafts, there were street vendors and musical entertainment with a small outdoor stage production.

While she was putting together a picnic lunch for them to take along, the phone rang. She heard Alex call out that he'd answer it. A few minutes later, he came bursting into the kitchen, his eyes wide. In his fist was a slip of paper.

''I got it!''

''Got what?'' Frannie asked, as he stood wiggling before her.

''I got the name of the place Dad is!''

Frannie was stunned. After six weeks of getting

no responses to Alex's posters, she'd assumed that nothing would come of his efforts.

"Was that Auntie Lois?" she asked weakly.

He shook his head. "Uh-uh. It was some lady. She gave me her name but I didn't write it down. I think it was Margaret or something with an *M*..." He trailed off, his face showing his bewilderment.

Frannie took the piece of paper from his hands. On it Alex had printed, "Gran Moray. North Shore. Fishing. Nice, helpful."

When she didn't say anything, he added, "It's where Dad is...in Gran Moray."

Gran Moray had to be Alex's spelling of Grand Marais, the small Minnesota town located on the North Shore of Lake Superior. Frannie's heart hammered relentlessly in her chest.

"The lady said she saw someone who looks just like Dad when they were fishing in one of the streams," Alex continued. "They talked to him and everything."

It couldn't be, Frannie told herself, taking several calming breaths. "Your father doesn't like to fish," she told him. "And you heard your grandmother say that she doesn't think he's living nearby. It's not him," she said with a confidence she wasn't feeling.

"How do you know? This lady said he looked just like the guy on the poster. It could be him, Mom. It could be." There was a plea in her son's voice that tore at Frannie's heart.

"I'm going to call Lois and see what she thinks." Frannie started to walk out of the room, but Alex stopped her with a hand on her arm.

"Auntie Lois doesn't know about this."

Frannie frowned. "What do you mean she doesn't

know? She must have given that woman our number…"

Guilt made his eyes dart back and forth nervously.

"Alex, you didn't put up the posters with *our* phone number on it, did you?"

She could see by the look on his face, that was exactly what he'd done.

"Alex!"

"I wanted to be the one to get the calls, not Auntie Lois. He's *my* father," he said on a note of frustration.

Frannie pushed an errant curl away from her forehead. "Oh, good grief! *Our* phone number's out there for all the world to see?"

"You don't need to get upset. No one's even called except for this one lady. And she was really nice, Mom."

Again, pain knifed through Frannie's heart. She could see how much Alex wanted this strange woman to be the connection to his father. She closed her eyes momentarily, trying to find the words to tell her son that the man this woman had seen couldn't possibly be Dennis.

"It can't be him, Alex," she began.

"Why not?" he demanded.

Because I don't want it to be. She pushed aside that thought and said, "I told you. Your father doesn't know how to fish."

"Maybe he learned."

"He hates cold weather. Why would he live in northern Minnesota?"

He shrugged. "I don't know, but we need to go find out. Will you take me?"

Frannie stifled a groan. "I wish you'd let me talk

to the woman who called and gave you this information."

"She said she lives in Minneapolis."

"You should have written down her phone number."

"You can call her. All you have to do is press star sixty-nine, and you can get it."

Frannie realized he was right. Why hadn't she thought of that? Because she'd been too upset over the fact that there was even the tiniest of possibilities that the man spotted along the North Shore might be her ex-husband.

The woman who had phoned Alex was named Margaret, just as he'd said. She was also very nice and helpful, as he'd written on the slip of paper. Only, Frannie soon discovered that Alex hadn't written those adjectives about the woman who'd phoned. They were the words Margaret had used to describe the man she'd seen at the North Shore.

As well as repeating what Alex had already told Frannie, the woman told her that this man didn't seem like the type to abandon his kids. By the time the phone call ended, she had told Frannie enough about the man's personality to convince her it couldn't have been Dennis.

Frannie knew her ex-husband would have no patience for fishing or for helping a couple of senior citizens change a flat tire on their car—which is what the man had done for Margaret and her husband.

"Are we going to go there?" Alex asked as soon as she'd hung up the phone.

Frannie wanted to again say, "It's not him," but she stifled the words. "I'm going to call Lois and see what she thinks."

Alex groaned. "Do you have to?"

"Yes." Frannie dialed her sister's number. As soon as she heard the voice-mail recording, she remembered that her sister was out of town for the weekend. "I forgot. She's in Chicago and won't be home until Tuesday."

"What does that mean? That we have to wait for her to get back before we can do anything?" he asked, obviously hoping that the answer to his question wasn't yes.

"There's no point in driving all the way to the North Shore without first investigating whether the possibility exists that it is your father," Frannie answered patiently. "If—and I say *if*—there's a chance it is your father, then it's up to the authorities to investigate, not us."

"You mean we're not going to go?"

Frannie tried not to let the devastation on his face tug on her emotions. It wasn't easy.

"I'm sorry, but that's my final word on the subject. We wait until we talk to Auntie Lois before we do anything," she said firmly.

"Do what?" Emma asked as she entered the kitchen, backpack slung over her shoulder.

"It's none of your business," Alex said, stomping out of the room.

"What's wrong with him? Aren't we going to the arts festival?" Emma asked.

"Yes, we're going. Just give me a few minutes," Frannie replied. "Watch Luke for me, will you?"

Frannie found Alex in his room, lying on his stomach on his bed, his elbows supporting him as he played a video game.

"I know you're disappointed, Alex, but you don't

need to take it out on Emma.'' Her words were met with silence. ''Get your stuff together and we'll go to the arts festival at the park.''

''I don't want to go,'' he grumbled.

Frannie put her hands on her hips. ''You wanted to earlier this morning.''

''I changed my mind.''

Frannie could see the stubborn set to his shoulders. If there was one thing she knew about Alex, it was that when he made up his mind about something, he didn't change it. ''Alex, I can't leave you home alone.''

He sat up then and said, ''I'm ten, not two. I'll keep the door locked and won't let anybody in. Satisfied?''

She wasn't. She knew that some parents did leave their kids home alone for short periods of time, but she wasn't one of them. She didn't doubt that Alex would be fine on his own for a couple of hours, yet she wasn't ready to set a precedent. If she left him today, then he'd want to stay home alone the next time she had to go somewhere that was of no interest to him.

''Come on, Mom. I'm almost eleven,'' he pleaded. ''I'm responsible. Didn't I prove that to you that time you had the flu and I had to take care of Luke because you couldn't get out of bed?''

''But I was still in the house.''

''You couldn't even lift your head off the pillow,'' he reminded her. ''I did a good job taking care of everything. Even you said so. Please, let me try it just once,'' he pleaded. ''I won't answer the door, and if the phone rings I won't say you're not here.

I'll say you can't come to the phone, like I'm supposed to do.''

Frannie could feel her resolve weakening. She knew Alex wouldn't enjoy the arts festival as much as Emma and Luke would. And then there was that look of devastation on his face when she'd told him they weren't going to go looking for his father. It tugged at her heart in a way that made her fall back on emotion rather than logic.

"Please, Mom?" he begged. "Don't make me go with you."

The park was just at the end of the block, and if Alex did have a problem he could call on any one of the neighbors. Finally Frannie caved in. "All right, you can stay home."

It was a decision that left her feeling uneasy, however, as she wandered later through the various exhibits. It was also the reason why, despite Luke and Emma's groans of protest, she packed up their things as soon as they'd finished lunch.

A feeling of relief washed over her as she returned home and saw that the house looked exactly as it had when they'd left. The front door was still shut, the drapes closed, the yard empty of kids. Using her key, she let herself in and called out, "Alex, we're home."

When there was no answer, she repeated the call. Then Emma handed her a piece of paper. "I found this on the kitchen table."

Frannie read the note written in her son's handwriting: "Mom, I'm going to look for Dad. I'm taking the bus. Don't worry about me. I'll be fine. Alex."

CHAPTER THREE

ALEX WAS ON A BUS headed for the North Shore!

"Do you think he really found Dad?" Emma's voice was a pin bursting the bubble of panic that held Frannie motionless.

"No." She reached for the phone and dialed 911. When she was told her son would be considered a runaway and that a police officer would be sent to her home to ask her more questions, she told the dispatcher, "No, don't do that. I'll find him myself."

"Are you mad at the police?" Emma asked, as Frannie slammed the receiver down.

"No."

"You look like you're mad."

"I'm not. I'm worried.

She rubbed her fingers across her forehead. She couldn't think. She *had* to think. She took several more calming breaths, then grabbed the phone book and searched for the number to the bus depot.

She vented her frustration at the faceless person on the other end of the line. "I don't understand how you could let a ten-year-old on the bus without an adult."

Frannie didn't like the answer she received. Alex hadn't been alone. A woman had purchased the ticket for him, saying he was going to visit his father in Grand Marais and would be met at the bus stop there.

What woman would buy a bus ticket for a ten-year-old boy? Frannie asked herself, as panic again bubbled up in her throat. She closed her eyes momentarily and tried not to think the worst. Alex easily could have cried a bucket of tears and concocted a story that would have had any compassionate woman offering to buy him a ticket.

Frannie couldn't waste time wondering about what had already happened. Her son was on a bus headed for a small town in search of his father. She needed to be calm and she needed to be rational.

She turned to Emma and said, "We need to go find Alex, so I want you to gather a few things for Luke to play with in the car...some books, his blanky," she said as she mentally made a list of what she needed to bring along.

With her usual systematic approach, she loaded the car. Bottled water, juice boxes, munchies for the kids, change of clothes for Luke in case he had an accident. Luke was toilet trained most of the time, but whenever she least expected it, an accident occurred.

Frannie couldn't believe how long it took to pack up two kids and get on the road. By the time her station wagon pulled out of the drive, it was mid-afternoon, which meant they would be lucky to reach the North Shore before evening.

Once they found Alex, they'd have to eat dinner. And by the time they made the journey home again, they'd be fortunate to get to bed by midnight. She gripped the steering wheel tightly, trying not to think about anything but staying calm and finding Alex.

Never had the drive from Minneapolis to Duluth seemed so long. Although Emma read stories and kept Luke entertained for most of the journey, three hours was a long time for any child to spend in the car. Even Emma found it difficult to be still and asked if they could take a break.

"There's a park down there. Can we go down by the water?" she asked as their journey took them past the harbor.

"You know we can't stop."

"But we've been in the car forever. And it looks like it's really fun." She gazed longingly out the window toward Canal Park.

"I'll bring you and your brothers back for a visit some other time. Right now we need to get to Grand Marais."

"Oh, look! That bridge is going up so the boat can get through." She sighed. "Can't we stop for just a few minutes?"

Frannie ignored her and continued following the highway along the shoreline of Lake Superior. It being the height of tourist season, traffic moved slowly as motor homes and pickup trucks pulling trailers leisurely made their way to recreational parks.

She glanced at her watch. It was almost six. The bus should have arrived in Grand Marais by now. She wondered where Alex was and what he was doing.

Frannie's heart rate increased. What if she couldn't find him? What if Dennis Harper was in the small resort town? What if Alex had found him and he— She pushed such thoughts from her mind. She needed to keep a clear head if she was going to find Alex. She couldn't allow what-if's to distract her.

Finally she saw the green road sign: Grand Marais. Frannie's adrenaline kicked into a higher gear. As she drove into the business district, she kept one eye on the road, the other on the sidewalks in search of her son.

It only took a few minutes to locate the bus stop. When she saw no sign of Alex, she parked her car, then grabbed Luke by the hand and ordered Emma to stick close by.

"I'm looking for my son. He's ten, dark hair, a couple of inches shorter than I am, wearing a pair of jeans and a blue shirt," she would say to each of the shopkeepers she met. Each gave her the same answer. No one had seen him.

"When are we going to eat? I'm hungry," Emma asked as they approached a diner. The aroma of beef grilling wafted on the air, and Luke echoed his sister. "I want to eat, Mommy."

Frannie pulled open the door to the diner and motioned for Emma to step inside. Her daughter hadn't taken but a couple of steps when she said, "He's in here!"

Relief washed over Frannie at the sight of her son sitting on a stool at the lunch counter. In front of him was a half-eaten hamburger and a plate of French fries, and he held a fountain glass in his hand. Seeing his mother, his eyes widened. He slammed the glass down on the counter.

"Mom!"

Hours of pent-up emotion came spilling out. Instead of throwing her arms around him and telling him how relieved she was that he was safe, she scolded him. "Alexander Harper, what do you think you're doing? Do you know how worried I've been about you?" It was only as she noticed the heads turned in her direction that she realized how loud her voice was.

"You're in big trouble," Emma said, taking the stool next to his and grabbing a French fry from his plate. "You're gonna get grounded."

Seeing the food in front of Alex, Luke squirmed and wriggled, trying to be free of Frannie's arms. "I'm hungry!" he cried, fingers clawing the air in hopes of reaching Alex's fries.

"Can I have a hamburger?" Emma asked.

Frannie knew she needed to feed her children. She looked around the small diner for a place for them all to sit.

The waitress behind the counter, a teenage girl wearing a red chef's apron over her jeans and T-shirt, said, "Why don't you take that table next to the window?" She gestured to a booth directly behind Frannie. Alex didn't look as if he wanted to leave his spot at the counter, but the young girl picked up his plate, saying, "Come on, big fella. You'll have more room over here."

She led Alex over to the booth, stopping at the end of the counter to pick up a booster seat for Luke. Frannie noticed that on the upper-left corner of her apron was a small white patch with the name Rosie embroidered in black letters.

As soon as they were all seated, she set four paper place mats on the table, each one a map of the area showing local tourist attractions. Then she added silverware and four glasses of water, finishing with menus.

"The kids' menu is on the back," she announced, then asked, "Can I start you off with something to drink?"

"I'll have a Coke," Emma answered.

"She'll have milk," Frannie amended.

Emma made a sound of indignation. "Alex has pop."

As if suddenly realizing that indeed his brother did have a soda, Luke climbed out of his booster seat and reached across the table for the straw in Alex's glass. "Pop!"

Frannie pulled Luke off the table and returned him to the booster chair. "Bring two more Cokes, and I'll have an iced tea," she said to the waitress, then looked at Luke and said, "You have to sit down like a good boy if you want the nice lady to bring you pop."

To Frannie's relief, the waitress returned with not only their drinks, but a small square block of wood holding half-a-dozen crayons and an activity sheet for Luke. While Emma helped her brother connect the dots on a puzzle, Frannie spoke to Alex.

"Do you realize how worried I've been?"

Alex didn't answer, but stared down at the French fries on his plate.

"You shouldn't have come up here, Alex. Not only is it dangerous for someone your age to ride the bus alone, you have no real proof that your father is even here."

"I'm gonna find him," he said stubbornly, still not lifting his gaze.

"You're going to come home with me," Frannie said, her voice stern.

"It's not fair. What if he *is* here?" He looked up at her then, his eyes full of something Frannie didn't want to see. Hope.

"He's not here, Alex," she said quietly but firmly.

"You don't know that for sure."

They were interrupted by the waitress. "Are you ready to order?"

Without even looking at the menu, Frannie ordered hamburgers and fries for the three of them, although she didn't have much of an appetite. It seemed that Alex didn't, either. His food hadn't been touched since they'd arrived.

"Don't you want to know if he's here?" Alex asked a few minutes later, his face full of youthful innocence and curiosity.

"I told you. He's not here," Frannie replied.

"How do you know?"

"Because he hates Minnesota."

"But that lady who called said she saw him."

"Alex, the picture on that poster is eleven years old."

"It could be him," he argued, refusing to be persuaded.

There was a short silence, then Emma said, "I don't know why you want to find him anyway. He doesn't want to be with us."

It was said so matter-of-factly, with so little emotion, that Frannie felt her heart break. "I think it would be a good idea if we didn't discuss your father."

Alex didn't say a word, but leaned back against the padded cushion of the booth, his arms folded across his chest.

"Aren't you going to finish eating?" Emma asked.

"I'm not hungry," he mumbled between pinched lips.

"Can I have your fries?" his twin asked.

He shoved the plate in her direction. Emma

reached for the bottle of ketchup and poured a generous serving on the plate. "Was it fun riding on the bus?"

Alex simply shrugged, not that Emma seemed to mind. She carried on with her chatter. "Wasn't that big rock tunnel cool? And the lake is so huge! We saw a really long ship in the harbor in Duluth. Can we please stop at that park on the way home?" Emma asked her mother as she happily devoured Alex's fries.

"We have a long way to go before we get home, Emma," Frannie answered.

"That means no," she said, obvious disappointment in her voice.

"We didn't come up here to visit the parks," Frannie reminded her. "We came to find Alex."

That broke Alex's silence. "You didn't have to come. I can take care of myself."

"I know you can buy a bus ticket without my help, but where did you plan to sleep tonight?" Frannie demanded.

"At a campground. Rosie's cousin has one and she said I could stay there."

"You don't have a tent." Frannie eyed his backpack, which was exceptionally fat yet couldn't possibly hold a tent and sleeping bag.

"I don't need one. I brought a blanket. I like sleeping on the ground. Me and Josh did it a whole bunch last summer."

"It's one thing to sleep outside in your best friend's backyard in the city and quite another to be in the wilderness," Frannie said.

He puffed up his chest. "I'm not afraid."

Just then Rosie came hustling toward them with a

tray full of food. "Okay, we've got two regular burgers and fries and one kiddie-size," she said as she cheerfully set the food on the table. Noticing that Alex had shoved his half-eaten meal aside, she put a hand on his shoulder and said, "Hey, a big kid like you ought to be able to finish that burger. You feeling okay?"

"I was until my mom said I have to go home without finding my dad." He turned his brown eyes on her, looking very much like a puppy in need of a scratch behind his ears.

Frannie could see the look produced the desired effect. The teen's face softened in sympathy; she turned to Frannie and said, "If you need a place to stay for the night, my cousin has a resort and campground not far from here. I could call and see if he has any empty cabins."

Frannie watched Alex's eyes brighten at the possibility. "Can we?"

Frannie knew her son wasn't going to like her answer. She stared out the window briefly, trying not to let the look on his face tug so strongly on her emotions.

"I appreciate the offer, Rosie. It's very kind of you," she said. "Unfortunately, we're not prepared to spend the night away from home."

The waitress shrugged. "If you change your mind, just let me know. Can I get you anything else?"

Frannie couldn't help but warm to the genuine caring in the young woman's eyes. It made her realize that her son had been fortunate to stop in this particular diner.

"I think we're fine for now," she replied, then

turned her attention to Luke, who needed help getting more ketchup on his fries.

To her relief, Alex didn't force the issue. He sat in silence, occasionally taking a bite of his hamburger, but mostly sipping his pop. Just as Rosie returned to ask if they needed refills on their beverages, Alex jumped up.

"Look! There he is!"

Frannie immediately turned around to see who had captured her son's attention, but all she saw was the back of a man getting into an SUV.

"It's Dad! Mom, it's him! I know it is!" Alex could barely contain his excitement, bobbing up and down like a jack-in-the-box. "Can't you see him?"

Frannie couldn't. The SUV was across the street, and traffic moved at a busy clip in front of it.

"That's your dad?" Rosie asked with an incredulous lift of her brows, but Alex didn't answer her.

"He's going to drive away. I have to stop him. Move!" he ordered his sister, pushing her out of the way so he could get out of the booth.

"Alex, wait!" Frannie called after him, but he didn't stop. She slid out of the booth, following him outside onto the sidewalk. They saw the SUV pull away from the curb and travel down the street.

"He's gone!" Alex stood on the corner, his shoulders sagging.

Frannie gently put a hand on his. "Come back inside."

He shrugged off her hand. Frannie didn't try to take his arm again, but let him stand there for a few moments before she again said, "Come back inside."

Finally, he did as he was told. As soon as he sat

down, Rosie came over to the table. "Did you see him?" he asked the waitress. "Do you know who he is?"

"That was Joe Smith. Are you sure he's your father?" she asked uneasily, then looked at Frannie, who shook her head gently.

Alex unzipped his backpack and pulled out one of the yellow flyers. "See? Doesn't he look like that guy in the SUV?"

Rosie studied the photograph, her eyes narrowing. "It sure does look like Joe, but he wears his hair different."

"What I've been trying to explain to Alex is that there are men who look like his father. You know, they have the same color hair, the same nose, similar smiles," Frannie said to the waitress. "I'm sure that's the way it is with this Joe Smith. He's simply someone who resembles Alex's father."

The waitress nodded in agreement. "And to be honest, Joe doesn't seem like the kind of guy to lie about who he is. He's a pilot. If you want, I can give you directions to his place. It's on the Gunflint Trail."

Alex said yes at the same time Frannie said no. He looked at his mother and asked, "Why not?"

"Because he's not your father. Your father isn't a pilot," Frannie reminded him. *Joe Smith isn't Dennis Harper,* she told herself, and to take a trip up the Gunflint Trail would only make the day more frustrating for all of them. Alex's eyes were filled with a false hope that Frannie had no doubt would be replaced by disappointment if he were to meet this Joe Smith.

When Luke indicated he needed to go to the bathroom, Frannie gave the twins strict instructions. "Don't either of you move from this booth. Understand?"

Both nodded. As much as Frannie hated leaving Alex alone for even five minutes, she knew she needed to tend to Luke. As she walked past Rosie, she said, "Would you do me a favor and let me know if Alex tries to leave?"

The young woman smiled. "Sure."

When she and Luke emerged from the rest room, Frannie was grateful to see that Rosie had followed her request. Emma and Alex were still seated in the booth. Alex's face was animated, and it was only as Frannie returned that she saw the reason why. In his hands was a crudely drawn map on a white paper napkin.

"What is that?" she asked, eyeing the map suspiciously.

"Rosie told me how to get to the Gunflint Trail," Alex answered.

"We're not going there," Frannie said as she helped Luke back into the booster seat.

"Why not?" It came out as a whine. "Mom, please! I spent all of my can money to buy that bus ticket."

Frannie felt even worse. She knew how hard Alex worked to collect cans. Every week he'd go from house to house in the neighborhood, gathering aluminum cans so they could take them to the recycling center where he'd receive a small amount of cash. Every cent he made went into a locked box he kept under his bed because he had a goal: to buy his own computer.

Now he'd spent that money on a bus ticket to go

in search of a man who didn't want to be found. A man who didn't care that Alex even existed.

"We're already here," Alex continued to plead with her. "Can't we at least go see him?"

It seemed as if two hands had a hold of Frannie's heart and were tugging it in opposite directions. She briefly closed her eyes, hoping that when she opened them she'd discover this entire day was a bad dream.

It wasn't.

Alex could see she was weakening and pushed even harder. "Can't we, Mom, please?"

"I need to pay the bill. Sit here," she ordered the three of them, then went up to the cash register near the door. Rosie immediately hurried over to help her.

"Is everything all right?" she asked, glancing back to where Alex sat slouched in the booth, frowning.

"It will be. Thanks for keeping an eye on Alex. I appreciate the kindness you showed him today." She handed the girl several bills.

"It wasn't a big deal." She counted out the correct change into Frannie's hand. "He still thinks Joe Smith is his father, doesn't he."

Frannie nodded. "How far is it to this Gunflint Trail?"

"Not very far at all. It wouldn't take but maybe half an hour to find the Smith place. Then at least Alex would know for sure…" She let her voice trail off, giving Frannie an understanding smile that indicated she was more mature than her age indicated.

"Yes, he would," Frannie said with an answering smile. "Thank you, Rosie."

When Frannie got back to the booth, Alex was

silently sobbing. She knew how much he hated to cry.

Frannie's emotions were near the breaking point as well, yet she knew there was only one way for any of them to have peace of mind. She said a silent prayer that she wouldn't regret what she was about to do.

"All right. We'll drive up to this Joe Smith's place."

"I'M HOT," Emma complained.

So was Frannie. When she'd left Grand Marais, she'd turned off the car's air-conditioning because of the road's steep grade. She felt the engine needed all of its power just to get them up the incline. Although the windows were down, the air inside the car was hot and sticky.

"Are you watching the signs?" she asked.

"There should be a lookout point coming up soon," Alex told her, acting as navigator. "There it is—" His arm shot out to the right. "Now we just keep going straight on this road."

Apprehension crept down Frannie's spine just as beads of perspiration trickled down her forehead. Because of the tall trees, what little there was left of the sinking sun vanished as she drove deeper into the forest. As often as she told herself that this Joe Smith was not Dennis Harper, she knew that her anxiety wasn't only due to what effect meeting this man would have on Alex. No matter how hard she tried, she couldn't ignore the tiny voice that asked mercilessly, *What if it really is him?*

"We should be getting close," Alex said, when

she expressed her concern that they had gone a long way without seeing the next landmark.

"There! On the right!" he said excitedly.

Frannie glanced to the side of the road and saw a small sign: Nature's Hideaway.

"Stop!" Alex called out.

Frannie turned onto the dirt road and encountered a wrought-iron gate barring the entrance. "It says Private and No Trespassing."

Alex hopped out of the car and went to investigate. Within minutes he had pushed opened the gate and was motioning for his mother to drive through. When he got back in the car, she said, "We shouldn't be doing this. It's private property."

"But the gate was open. If he didn't want anyone coming in, he would lock it," he reasoned.

The hair on the back of Frannie's neck rose as she continued down the winding gravel road. The sun had completely disappeared, and if she hadn't glanced at her watch, she would have thought it was much later. Having difficulty seeing the road, she switched on her headlights.

"How come everything's such a funny color?" Emma asked, calling Frannie's attention to the green pall that seemed to surround them. "Is it going to storm?"

Frannie's apprehension doubled. "I sure hope not." Frannie turned on the radio but found the static was so bad that it was impossible to hear. With an impatient sigh, she turned it off again.

"The sky's a funny color, too," Alex observed. Frannie wondered how he could even see the sky through the heavy foliage.

"I see something," Alex called out. "I think it's a house."

It *was* a house, Frannie discovered as she pulled into a clearing. A beautiful log home sitting on the shore of a lake. She parked the car next to the SUV they'd seen in town. As she turned off the engine, she found herself short of breath, her uneasiness creeping into her throat. She didn't want to let go of the steering wheel for fear her hands would tremble. She looked toward the house, wondering if anyone had heard their arrival. If they had, they weren't in any hurry to come out and greet them.

The sudden buzzing of a chain saw starting up told her why.

"He's over there," she heard Alex say, then she looked behind them toward a shed where a man was sawing a fallen tree into logs.

In the blink of an eye, Alex was out of the car and sprinting toward him. "Stay with your brother," Frannie barked at Emma, then went after Alex.

She was no match for her son's youthful speed. She watched him run up to the man, who wore a denim shirt and jeans. The chain saw stopped.

With his back to her, Frannie couldn't see whether the man was Dennis Harper. He appeared to be the same height, and he had the same dark brown hair as her ex-husband. But when he turned and looked in Frannie's direction, she felt as if someone had delivered a swift blow to her stomach. He did look like Dennis, even with the plastic goggles over his eyes. She paused, suddenly feeling as if her knees might buckle beneath her.

It can't be him. She stared at the man, not wanting

to believe she could be looking at her ex-husband. *It can't be,* she repeated to herself.

"Are you lost?" he asked, the question directed more at her than at her son.

Not only did he look like Dennis, but he sounded like him, too. Frannie's limbs shook so much, she thought she might fall to the ground. With great difficulty, she swallowed against the dryness in her mouth and walked toward him. This time she moved slowly, but her mind raced. How could it be him? Why would he be here?

When he removed the protective goggles and let them dangle around his neck, she saw that his eyes were brown—the same as Dennis's—yet these eyes were looking at her as if she were a perfect stranger.

Again he spoke, "Do you need directions?"

She didn't answer. She couldn't. All she could do was stare at him.

Alex, however, had no trouble finding his voice. "You thought we wouldn't find you, didn't you?"

"I think there's been some mistake," he began, only to have Alex cut him off.

Like a preacher in a pulpit, the boy wagged his finger to emphasize his words. "Yeah. You're the big mistake. Mom never should have married you. You're a deadbeat. It's bad enough that you didn't want to stay married to Mom and be our dad, but you don't even have the decency to be any kind of dad at all—not even a rotten one. You just hid so you didn't have to pay anything."

Frannie found her voice. "Alex, that's enough."

"No, it's not." He defied her, continuing on with his sermon. "He needs to know that you had to work two jobs most of the time to pay the bills. When

Luke was sick, we had to go to the food bank to get stuff to eat. But Dad didn't care. All he wanted was to forget about us.'' He turned back to the man who looked so much like his father. ''Well, I'm not going to let you forget. I'm going to go to the police and tell them who you really are, and they'll make you pay.''

Alex's cheeks were red and his chest was heaving by the time he'd finished his tirade. Frannie knew he was close to tears, yet he stoically stood his ground, his head held high. Frannie thought it was strange that not even a bird chirped or an insect buzzed. All she could hear was Alex's breathing. She wanted to wrap him in her arms and squeeze away all his heartache. She knew she couldn't.

Alex finally broke the silence. ''Well, aren't you going to say anything?''

The man looked at Frannie, and she knew what his next words were going to be. She wasn't surprised when he said, ''I'm not your father.''

''YOU LOOK LIKE HIM.'' A female version of the boy who'd just verbally blistered him approached Joe with curiosity in her eyes, but not hostility.

''Emma, I told you to wait in the car,'' the woman said to the girl. ''Where's Luke?''

''He fell asleep. I left the windows down.''

That information had the woman hurrying back to the battered old station wagon parked next to his SUV. ''Are you two brother and sister?'' he asked the pair now standing before him, gazing at him as if he were the villain in a horror film.

''As if you don't know,'' the boy said with derision.

"We're twins," the girl said.

"Do you think we wouldn't recognize our own dad when we saw him?" the boy continued.

"I may look like him, but I'm not him," he replied, as the pair continued to scrutinize him. "My name is Joe Smith."

"That sounds like a made-up name to me," the boy said.

"It's not. If you wait just a minute, I'll go inside and get my wallet. It has my driver's license in it," he told them.

"It's probably a fake," the boy countered.

"If you're not going to take my driver's license as proof, what will satisfy you?"

The little girl whispered something to her brother, who then said, "Take off your shirt."

"What?" Joe almost chuckled at the absurdity of the request.

"I said, take off your shirt," the boy repeated.

"Look, I told you I'm not your father," Joe said, trying not to lose patience with the kids.

"Then take off your shirt and prove it," the boy challenged him. "Or are you chicken?"

Joe could hardly believe what was happening. He was being confronted by two kids who were accusing him of being their deadbeat dad and demanding that he take off his shirt. "No, I'm not chicken, but I'm not your father, either," he said evenly.

"Then, why won't you take off your shirt?" the boy persisted.

Joe decided to humor the kids rather than stand there arguing with them. If it took revealing his bare chest to convince these two that he wasn't their father, he'd do it. He unbuttoned his shirt and took it off, leaving him bare-chested and the object of their wide-eyed stares.

"Oh my gosh! It *is* him!" The little girl stared at him as if she'd seen a ghost, then went running back to the car.

"And you said you weren't him!" the boy accused him before racing after his sister. They met their mother, who was coming toward them with an even younger child in tow. The two jumped up and down excitedly and pointed in Joe's direction. Joe couldn't hear what they were saying, but it was enough to stiffen their mother's shoulders and put a frown on her face.

She approached him cautiously, carrying a sleepy child in her arms. She looked like a mother hen about to do battle for her chicks.

He put his shirt back on, unsure what it was that had triggered such a response in the kids. "If these are your biological children, you must know that I'm not their father."

From her expression, he could see that she didn't.

"Dennis, if you're playing some kind of joke with these kids, it's not funny." A shadow in her eyes told him that whoever this Dennis was, he'd hurt her badly.

"I'm not Dennis and I wouldn't play such a cruel trick on any children," he answered a bit impatiently. "My name is Joe Smith. I don't have any kids. If I had, I wouldn't deny their existence. Surely you, their mother, must see that I'm not the man they think I am."

"Stop lying!" she shouted. He could see that she was close to losing control. "You've been running and lying all your life. Just for once tell the truth."

He ran a hand over his hair in exasperation. "I'm not their father. Whatever it was they saw when I took off my shirt…it doesn't mean I'm their father."

Her eyes narrowed as she stared at him. "They saw your tattoo."

Suddenly he realized the reason behind the children's demand. It had been to see if he had a tattoo on his upper arm. He wasted no time in explaining. "You can't possibly think I'm their father because I have the same tattoo as he does on my arm. Do you know how many sailors get tattoos while they're in the Navy?"

"Let me see it," she said quietly.

This time he didn't take off his shirt, but pushed up the sleeve until the anchor with the letters *USN* could be seen. She took one glance, then looked away, her teeth tugging on her upper lip.

"If it's the same as your husband's—"

"My *ex*-husband," she corrected defiantly, as if reminding him she couldn't stand to be around him. "Ex-husband," she repeated like a warning.

"If it's the same tattoo, it's a coincidence." He stared into deep blue eyes. What he saw in them was contempt, and it annoyed him that those beautiful eyes contained such venom toward him because of what another man had done. "Look. All you have to do is come inside and I'll show you proof of who I am."

"Now *that* is something I will not do," she said through clenched teeth.

Thunder rumbled in the distance. Joe glanced at the sky, then said, "I think you'd better come inside just the same. There's a storm moving in. You're welcome to stay until it passes."

"I will not stay anywhere with you. All I want is to get as far away from here as possible," she said, her voice breaking with emotion. She called to her kids, "We have to get in the car. It's going to rain."

"Are we going to call the police?" Joe heard the boy asked.

Police. Joe knew he needed to convince this woman that he was not her ex-husband. What he didn't need was for some kid to mistake him for a man who was in trouble with the law. He had his own past to haunt him. He didn't need another man's.

"Would you people listen to me?" he said in frustration as big raindrops began to pepper the earth. "I am not the man you're looking for."

A gust of wind sent the boy's baseball cap sailing through the air. He went chasing after it, but it kept tumbling on the wind.

"Don't worry about the hat, Alex. Just get in the car," the woman said, as a sudden downpour pelted them. She herded her kids toward the station wagon.

Joe watched them struggle to reach the car, the gusty winds impeding their progress. Then he took another look at the sky and knew he couldn't let this woman and her children leave. He caught up with her and grabbed her by the arm.

She flinched when he touched her, and he immediately let go. "You can't drive in this," he said as large raindrops stung his cheeks and dampened their clothing. "Please. Come inside. Your children will be safer in the house."

As if emphasizing his words, lightning lit the sky and thunder cracked around them. Even with rain plastering her blond curls to her head and running down her face, she looked as if she were about to refuse.

Then the boy hollered, "It's starting to hail!"

"Are you coming inside or not?" Joe asked.

To his relief, she didn't protest. "Yes, we're coming." Then she turned to her children and said, "Emma, Alex...follow this man."

Joe noticed she didn't call him their father. He wanted to see that as a good sign. As he led them toward the house, however, the only thing that kept going through his mind was that he hoped he wouldn't regret being a good Samaritan.

CHAPTER FOUR

"I'LL GET YOU some towels," Joe said, then disappeared down a hallway.

Alex tugged on Frannie's shirtsleeve. "It's him, Mom, isn't it?"

"I'm not sure," she answered, which was the truth. Joe Smith *looked* like her ex-husband, but it had been almost four years since she'd seen Dennis. And even though they'd been husband and wife and had had three children, they'd spent less time together than most married couples. The U.S. Navy had seen to that. During their short marriage, overseas duty had taken him away from his family, leaving Frannie alone with two kids. At one time she'd believed him when he'd told her he volunteered for overseas duty because he wanted the training provided on those assignments. Now she knew it was because overseas he could forget all about the wife and children who waited for him back home.

"It *is* him," Alex insisted. "I know it is."

"Why is he pretending to be somebody else?" Emma asked.

"I'm not pretending to be anybody else—"

Joe Smith's return startled Frannie. He handed her a stack of towels, his eyes pinning hers with a look that warned her he didn't appreciate their accusations.

"My name is Joe Smith."

She searched those dark brown eyes, hoping to find some truth in them, some explanation for what was happening right now, but they revealed nothing. She wondered if Dennis Harper could be so cruel as to deny his own children's existence, then realized that's exactly what he'd done when he'd left them. She dropped her eyes and gave her attention to her children, handing each of them a towel.

As she ran the soft terry cloth over Luke's head, his tiny feet danced on the floor and he clutched his shorts. "I have to go potty."

Frannie hoped he hadn't already done the deed, as his only pair of dry training pants was in the car.

"The bathroom's the first door on your left," Joe told her, motioning toward the hallway.

"Thank you." She turned to the twins and said, "Just stay here and don't touch anything."

"They might as well come in and sit down," Joe suggested.

"No. Their shoes are wet." Frannie didn't want her children making themselves comfortable in this man's house. "They can wait there."

She took Luke into the bathroom, but not before giving the twins a look that said if they dared to move from that spot, they would have to answer to her. It did no good. By the time she'd returned, both were seated on wooden stools at the island counter in the kitchen.

Alex was quick to leap to his own defense. "He told us to come away from the door because of the glass." The "he" to whom her son referred was not Joe Smith, but a silver-haired man at the kitchen sink. He wore a pair of dark slacks and a white dress shirt, as if he'd just come home from the office.

"It's not safe to be near windows when there's lightning," the older gentleman said without turning around.

Frannie looked at the twins and mouthed, *Who is he?*

They both shrugged. Emma whispered, "He just came out here and starting peeling a potato."

Frannie wondered what had happened to their host. Noticing her perusal of the room, Alex said, "Dad went to make sure all the windows are closed."

Although Frannie didn't like the fact that he had called Joe Smith "Dad," she didn't correct him.

The man at the sink turned around. "You know what they call this?" he asked the twins, holding up the pared vegetable.

"A potato?" Alex answered, as if he were seated at his desk in school and his teacher was the one posing the question.

"A poor man's apple," the silver-haired man corrected him with a grin. Then he took a bite of the raw potato, relishing its taste as he chomped on it. He walked past the island, shuffling his slippered feet. As he passed Alex, he paused, his eyes narrowing. "Have you done your homework?"

"We don't have homework. It's summer vacation," Alex answered.

"That doesn't mean you stop learning," he said, wagging his finger. "The smarter you are, the better you'll do in the Navy."

Alex looked at his mother, his eyes wide and full of questions. Frannie doubted she had the answers to any of them.

"You are going to enlist in the Navy when you grow up, right?" The old man stared at Alex, waiting for an answer.

Before Alex could utter a word, Luke discovered the aquarium in the living room. "Fishies!" he cried out in excitement, running across the wood plank flooring to press his nose to the glass.

The old man followed him. "Aren't they pretty?" He bent down beside Luke, pointing out the various fish by color rather than by name as he, too, pressed his face close to the glass. "See? There's a blue one and a purple one…"

Emma joined them at the tropical display, but Alex stayed at the counter.

Nature was putting on its own show in the stormy sky, with lightning flashing as rapidly as a strobe light.

Alex turned to his mother. "It looks pretty bad out there, doesn't it."

Frannie watched the trees bend in the wind and a curtain of rain move across the lake. When thunder clapped around them, its force so great it seemed to reverberate in the walls, Luke let out a yelp and came scurrying back to his mother's side.

"I think we should go into the basement," Joe announced as he came into the room. He went straight to the older man's side. "Come with me, Dad. We're going to go downstairs until the storm passes."

Dad. Frannie realized they were father and son, which only added to her confusion. As far as she knew, Dennis had been estranged from his father ever since he'd been a teenager. Frannie supposed it was possible they'd been reunited, yet judging by the comments she'd heard her ex-husband make about his father, she thought it unlikely. Still, the possibility existed, which meant that this elderly gentleman could be her children's grandfather.

She wasn't the only one thinking such thoughts. "Is he our grandpa?" Alex asked, as Frannie shepherded her kids down the stairs.

Joe heard his question and said, "No, he's not your grandfather."

"I think he's lying," Alex whispered to his mother.

She didn't respond, but led her children into the basement. A couple of bare bulbs dangled from the wooden beams. Concrete walls and floor made the room cool and damp. Like most basements, its function was utilitarian. In one corner was the furnace and water heater; in another, old furniture and household items. Along the walls were stacks of boxes and storage containers.

"There's no place to sit," Emma remarked as she eyed her surroundings cautiously.

Joe pulled out a couple of folding chairs and set them up in the middle of the room. He was about to get two more, when the lights went out.

Emma shrieked. So did Luke. Frannie lifted her youngest child into her arms and whispered in his ear, "It's okay. Mommy's here."

One of the metal folding chairs clanged as it toppled to the cement floor, and the older man cried out, "Joe? Joe, where are you? I can't see! You're not going to leave me here, are you?"

"No, I won't," the strong, reassuring voice filled the air. "It's scary when the lights go out, isn't it,

Dad. You stay right where you are, and I'll get a lantern. I have one on the shelf next to the furnace.''

"This is spooky," Emma said, her voice shaky.

"So the power went out. Big deal." Alex tried to sound bored, but Frannie knew better. He was as close to her side as Emma was.

"Big deal yourself," Emma retorted. "When you can't find the bathroom you'll think it's a big deal."

"I don't have to go to the bathroom, so there," he snapped back.

"Both of you stop," Frannie demanded. "This isn't helping matters."

The next voice she heard was Joe's, as a beam of light cut a path through the darkness. "Dad? You okay?"

Frannie watched him fuss over the older gentleman. He set up a folding chair, then helped his father sit down, offering words of comfort and reassurance to the trembling senior.

"Who's on command?" the old man asked.

"I am, Dad. Everything will be fine," Joe said. "You just sit here and let me do my job, okay?"

"You know I don't like the dark, Joe." The voice wobbled with the same fear Frannie had heard in her children when the lights had gone out.

"I know you don't, Dad."

"You won't leave me, will you?"

"Only for a few minutes until I get the generator going. I'll tell you what. I'm going to let you use the lantern until I can get the electric lights back on." He handed him the battery-operated light. "How's that?"

"You're not going to leave me alone, are you?" he asked for the third time.

''No. This nice lady and her children are going to stay with you,'' Joe answered, crooking a finger in Frannie's direction and motioning for her to come closer to his father's chair. ''You're going to have to share the light with the little ones, Dad. They get scared in the dark.''

''Not me,'' contradicted Alex.

Joe looked at him and said, ''No, I don't suppose much scares you, does it.'' Then he turned to his father. ''We have one brave kid and two not as brave ones, Dad. They need you to look out for them.''

Frannie looked at Joe Smith. In the shadows cast by the lantern, he looked even more like her ex-husband, yet she was certain he wasn't the man she'd married. How could he be? Her ex-husband wouldn't have treated his father with such patience and understanding. The Dennis she knew cared for no one but himself and certainly wouldn't accept responsibility for an aging parent.

Frannie blinked as the beam from the lantern shone on her face.

''What's her name?'' she heard the older man ask.

She didn't hesitate to answer. ''It's Frannie.''

''Ah, Frannie. Joe's wife. Now I remember,'' he said.

Frannie could feel Joe Smith's eyes on her face. When she looked at him, she saw that he was as rattled by his father's words as she was. Hearing her name upset him. Why should it? Unless…

''This isn't my wife, Dad,'' Joe corrected his father. To her he said, ''He gets confused easily.''

She was the one who was confused. Who were these men? She looked from father to son, trying to make sense of everything that had happened since they'd arrived. It was obvious that the older man's mental faculties were impaired. Frannie, however, wasn't convinced that he'd referred to her as Joe's wife because he wasn't thinking clearly.

"Whose children are these?" the older man demanded, aiming a finger in their direction. "You and Joe don't have children."

"Yes, they do. Us," Alex blurted.

"Alex, be quiet. Please," Frannie pleaded, wondering if things could get any eerier.

She looked at Joe Smith, trying to see in his eyes some kind of explanation. What she saw told her that this man couldn't be her ex-husband. His were the eyes of a stranger who looked just as uncertain as she was.

"I need you to stay with my father while I run out to the garage and get the generator going." She must have looked as if she was about to bolt and run, for he added, "Will you do that for me? Please. He's frightened." There was something in his voice she'd never heard in her husband's—a plea for understanding based on love for someone else.

"Very well, we'll stay, but only until it stops raining," she answered.

Without another word, Joe Smith disappeared into the darkness, his footsteps echoing on the wooden risers as he went up the stairs. Several more cracks of thunder split the air, prompting another chorus of shrieks from the kids.

"I don't like it down here," Emma said, sidling up to her mom to put a hand on her arm. "There are spiderwebs all over the place."

"The storm will soon pass, and then we'll be able to leave," Frannie said, squeezing her hand.

"I wish we'd never come. It's all Alex's fault," Emma reminded her.

"You should be thanking me. I found Dad."

Joe Smith's father directed the light onto Alex's face. "Am I your dad?"

"I think you're my grandpa," Alex replied.

"Alex!" Frannie reprimanded.

He didn't take the hint. "If he's that man's dad, that makes him our grandpa, right?"

"Grandpa? I'm not grandpa to anyone," the old man stated indignantly. "My grandbabies died."

Could Dennis have told his father his children were dead? The very thought made her shiver with disgust.

"What's your name?" Alex asked the old man.

"Name? You can call me what everyone else calls me. The Admiral," he answered.

Just then the bare bulbs dangling from the ceiling flickered to life. "We've got power," the old man said triumphantly.

Within minutes, footsteps on the stairs announced Joe's return. He looked at Frannie and asked, "Everything okay?"

She wanted to say no, it wasn't. How could it be? She was in a strange home during a severe thunderstorm with a man she might have once called her husband. She didn't understand how it was possible. This man was a stranger to her...or was he?

"Is it a tornado?" Alex asked as the storm continued to howl.

"Just a bad thunderstorm," Joe Smith answered.

"How do you know it's not a tornado?"

"There's no funnel cloud."

"How can you tell? It's dark."

It surprised Frannie that Joe Smith didn't get impatient with the endless questions Alex threw at him. It was not the reaction she would have expected from Dennis, who'd often complained to her how annoying it was to have a four-year-old ask ''why'' after every statement he made.

''What about the plane?'' The Admiral asked Joe questions, too.

''It'll be fine, Dad. It's not here, remember? I took it in to have some work done.''

''Winds that can break branches can twist wings,'' the Admiral said, looking at Frannie as he spoke.

She shivered, and Joe noticed. ''Are you cold?''

She shook her head. ''No, I'm okay.''

Only, she wasn't okay. She'd been dropped into somebody else's dream—at least, that's how it seemed. The whole situation made her feel powerless. And trapped. With two men who might or might not be her ex-husband and her ex-father-in-law.

But it wasn't a dream. The deafening thunder and her children's nervous chatter told her that. They remained in the basement while the winds howled, hail pelted the ground and lightning streaked the sky. There wasn't much for anyone to do but wait for the storm to end, the Admiral, Frannie and her kids huddled in a circle in the middle of the basement, Joe staring out the narrow pane of glass that was the only window.

As soon as the storm had passed, he announced, ''It should be safe to go up now.''

Alex and Emma shot out of their chairs and up the stairs. Luke scrambled out of Frannie's arms, wanting to follow them. Joe helped his father, who shrugged off his hand and determinedly climbed the stairs unassisted. Joe motioned for Frannie to go ahead of him.

She would have run up the stairs as fast as her children had, if it weren't for the Admiral's slow gait. Joe bumped against her as she paused to wait for his father to continue.

By the time they reached the main floor, the kids stood several paces back from the door. "It's still lightning," Alex announced.

"That's in the distance," Frannie told him, and motioned for him to open the door and step out onto the porch. As they did, she heard gasps.

"Look at all the trees that fell over!" Alex called out in amazement.

A forceful voice behind them said, "Don't step off the porch just yet."

Alex looked to his mother. "Can we?"

She looked at Joe, who said, "I want to make sure no power lines are down."

Frannie put her hands out and instructed her kids to come closer to her. "Wait right here for a few more minutes."

Joe headed out into the drizzle with a flashlight. While he was gone, Alex asked, "What are you going to do about him?"

Frannie knew that her son was referring to Joe Smith. "There's nothing to do, Alex."

"Aren't you going to call the police or something?"

"No. It's not that simple." *Life* was never simple when Dennis Harper was around.

"We can't just go home without telling somebody who he is," Alex argued.

"That's exactly what we're going to do. We're going to go home," Frannie stated firmly.

"But what if he runs away again?"

Frannie doubted that Joe Smith would take off in the middle of the night—not when he was responsible for his father. "I don't think that will happen."

"He owes us money," Alex said petulantly.

"I really don't want to be discussing this just now." Frannie's attention was diverted by Luke, who was splashing in the puddles on the deck. "Luke, where are your shoes?" she asked, looking around.

Emma's thoughts were on the man who looked like their father, too. "He acts as if he doesn't know us."

"Yeah, because he doesn't want to have to pay up," Alex said.

Once more Frannie called a halt to their conversation. "I'd like both of you to be quiet. He's going to be back soon, and we're going to leave. End of discussion," she said sternly.

Within minutes, Joe Smith returned. "I'm afraid I have bad news."

"Are the power lines down?" she asked.

"No, but the wind uprooted several trees and the road is blocked," he answered. "There's no way you're going to be able to get your car around them."

"Are you saying we can't get out?" Frannie hoped her face didn't show her panic.

"Unfortunately, the road's the only way out," he said soberly.

"He's probably lying," Alex said. "It wouldn't be the first time."

"You want to come take a look?" Joe challenged.

"I would," Frannie answered. She instructed Alex and Emma to stay on the porch with Luke, but they weren't about to be left behind.

"I'm coming, too," they said in unison.

"Watch your step," Joe called out as he aimed the flashlight beam toward the ground. "There are a lot of fallen branches."

By the time Frannie reached her car, she understood the reason for Joe Smith's sober expression. Right behind the station wagon was a huge oak tree that had been uprooted. Not only was it blocking the drive, but it had narrowly missed hitting her car.

"You're lucky you weren't parked back a few feet. Your car would have been crushed," he said, confirming her suspicions.

He directed the beam of light toward the road so they could see the twisted mass of fallen trees. "It's going to take a lot of work to get rid of that mess," he said grimly.

"How are we going to get home?" Emma asked in a tiny voice.

"You'll be able to drive home once the road is clear," Joe answered.

"And when will that be?" Frannie asked.

He shrugged. "There's no point in tackling it until the morning."

"Morning? What do we do till then?"

"You'll have to come inside," he stated, his tone indicating he wasn't happy with the plan.

Neither was Frannie. This wasn't just a bad dream. It was a nightmare. "If I come inside, it'll be to use your phone to call for help," she stated stiffly.

"And just who do you think you're going to call? Do you realize where you are?"

She did, which is why she shivered. "Someone must be able to come out and clear the road. The highway department..." Her voice trailed off.

"This isn't a public road. It's my drive. A *private* drive," he reminded her.

"Are you saying there's no one to call for help?" she asked on a note of disbelief.

She wasn't sure if his sigh was one of exasperation or reluctance. "I'll see what I can do. You might as well wait inside while I make the phone calls."

"We'll wait out here," Frannie told him, trying not to give any indication just how vulnerable she felt.

"You'll get eaten up by mosquitoes if you stay out here," Joe warned.

"We can sit in the car," Alex piped up.

Joe simply shook his head, then walked back to the house, leaving them alone in the dark. Within seconds, Frannie and her children were swatting at the bugs and hurrying to get inside the station wagon.

"I wish we could go home," Emma said, when the last of the doors had been slammed shut.

"We are going to go home. Just as soon as they get the trees cleared from the road." Frannie tried to keep her voice upbeat, even though she was every bit as tired and frustrated as her daughter.

"Yeah, and when will that be?" Alex asked sarcastically. "Next week?"

"It's your fault we're here," Emma reminded him. "We had to come home early from the arts festival just because of you, and now we're stuck in a car overnight because of you."

"We're not going to sleep in the car," Frannie interjected. "We're going to get out of here."

"When?" Alex demanded.

"As soon as Mr. Smith gets someone to help clear the drive," Frannie replied.

"Why don't you just call him 'Dad'? He *is* our father," Alex said.

"Do you think he really is our dad?" Emma asked her mother.

"I'm not sure," she answered honestly.

"Of course he is. *Look* at him," Alex ordered. "And remember, he's got the tattoo."

Just then, the subject of their conversation came walking toward the car. Frannie climbed out of the station wagon to hear what he had to say.

"The storm cut a pretty wide path. Trees are down all over the area. I couldn't find anyone to help with this mess." He waved the flashlight in the direction of the fallen trees. "You'll have to spend the night here."

"We can't." She folded her arms across her chest. "That's simply not an option."

"Unfortunately, it's your *only* option," he retorted.

"Don't say that," she said, although she knew it was the truth.

"The only decision you need to make is whether you want to spend the night in your car or come inside. I have extra beds." He sounded as if he was as tired as she felt.

Frannie wanted to tell him that she and her children would spend the night in the car, yet she knew it would be foolish. It wouldn't be wise to allow three kids in damp clothes to sleep in a station wagon that would provide little protection from the cool temperatures often found in the north woods. She really had no choice but to accept his hospitality.

"We'll come inside," she told him, then opened the car door. "Emma, grab Luke's bag, will you? We're going into Mr. Smith's house."

"We're not going to sleep here, are we?" Alex asked, as they followed Joe Smith back to the house.

"Just for tonight," Frannie replied.

"I don't want to sleep in the same house as him," Alex told his mother in a low voice that carried on the night air.

Frannie very much wanted to say, "I don't, either," but she managed to bite her tongue.

At the house Joe held the door open as they all filed back inside.

"What's going on?" the Admiral asked when he saw them.

"Fallen trees are blocking the drive. Frannie and her children are going to have to spend the night," Joe explained.

"Where are they going to sleep?" the elderly man wanted to know. "We only have three beds."

"Don't worry about it, Dad. We'll make it work."

The look Alex gave his mother told her he had his doubts.

Then Joe Smith said, "If you follow me, I'll show you where the guest bedroom is." Frannie followed him down the hallway, pulling Luke by the hand, the twins right behind them.

Joe Smith flipped on a light switch that illuminated a bedroom with a large four-poster bed carved out of pine. "Two can sleep in here and two in my room."

"Your room?" Frannie eyed him suspiciously.

"It's right next door. I'll sleep on the sofa."

"That's not necessary. The four of us can stay here," she told him, eyeing the double bed.

"There's no need to crowd four people in one bed."

He disappeared briefly, then returned carrying several white T-shirts that he tossed on the bed. "Here— You can sleep in these."

"I can sleep in my underwear. I do at home all the time," Alex announced with a bravado Frannie wished he'd put away.

"You're not supposed to, are you, Mom?" Emma looked up at Frannie, who really didn't want to be discussing sleeping apparel.

Apparently, neither did Joe, for he said, "If anyone's hungry, there's plenty to eat in the kitchen."

"No, I think we're fine," Frannie answered, although she was anything but fine. She was a basket of nerves. If it turned out that Joe Smith was Dennis Harper… She shook her head and refused to even consider that possibility. It was much less stressful to think of him as a stranger than as the man who used to be her husband.

"The bathroom's across the hall." He showed her where linens were kept and cautioned her that the water in the shower became hot very quickly.

She nodded, wishing he wouldn't look at her as if he understood her uneasiness. She wanted to dislike him, to feel nothing toward him, yet there was something in his eyes that told her he wasn't without compassion.

Then, he can't be Dennis Harper, a tiny voice in her head assured her.

"If the kids want to stay up for a while, there are games in the cupboard next to the aquarium. Normally the TV works, but the storm blew the satellite dish off the roof."

"It's all right. I'm sure they're tired," Frannie told him.

"I'm not tired," Alex protested.

"Me, neither," Emma seconded.

"Me, neither," Luke mimicked.

Frannie didn't comment, but waited for Joe Smith to leave the room. Then she pulled Luke onto the bed beside her and started to unlace his shoes.

"Can I get something to eat?" Alex asked. "He said we could, and I bet he's got a lot of food in that refrigerator. Did you see how fancy it was? It's got an ice dispenser on the door."

"Did you see all those cans of pop he had stacked in the basement?" Emma asked.

"He must have a lot of money. He's got a Lexus besides the SUV," Alex added.

Another reason why Frannie knew Joe Smith couldn't be Dennis Harper. Her ex-husband lacked sense when it came to money, and it was hard to imagine that he suddenly would have learned fiscal responsibility. He'd preferred to spend his money on entertainment, rather than investments and mortgages. Besides Frannie doubted he could ever be content to live on a lake in the middle of the woods.

"If he's got a lot of money, how come he's not giving us any?" Emma wanted to know.

"Because he's a deadbeat," Alex answered.

"Alex, please," Frannie pleaded. "Can we not talk about your father?"

"But he's why we're here."

She sighed. "Yes, but the man who owns this house is not your father." Frannie was surprised at how easily the words came. Instinctively she knew Joe Smith was not Dennis Harper.

"Oh, yeah? Then, why does he look just like him? And why does he have the same tattoo on his arm? And why is he left-handed? And why does he scratch his ear before he answers a question, just the way Dad used to?"

These were things Frannie had asked herself, but she'd rationalized them with one easy explanation: coincidence. It wasn't uncommon for men who'd been in the Navy to have that tattoo. And lots of men were left-handed. And some people scratched their ears before answering questions. Coincidence. That's all it was.

"But he doesn't smell the same. Dad always smelled like perfume," Emma said.

He did, thought Frannie. Dennis had always worn a liberal amount of cologne. Joe Smith smelled only of the outdoors. She wondered if he ever wore any men's fragrance. He looked as if the only things that mattered to him were clean clothes and a shave.

"Emma's right. He doesn't smell the same," Frannie said as she traded Luke's damp T-shirt for a dry one she found in his travel bag. "I'm telling you, Alex, this man is not your father."

"I think he is," he said, challenge in his voice. "And so does Emma." He turned to his sister and asked, "Don't you?"

She didn't look as certain as he did, but still she answered, "I guess."

"See?" Alex faced Frannie with his hands on his hips.

"We'll talk about this in the morning," she said, pulling back the covers on the bed. "Right now, everyone's tired."

"I'm not," Alex boasted. "He said we could play games in the living room if we wanted."

That was exactly what Frannie didn't want her kids to do. Yet there was no stopping Alex. While she put Luke to bed, he took Emma and went in search of the games. Frannie was forced to stay with her three-year-old until he fell asleep, before going to see what the twins were doing.

To her dismay, they had made themselves right at home. Emma was in the kitchen with Joe Smith, instructing him in the art of making grilled cheese sandwiches. Alex was seated at the counter next to the Admiral. Between them were two game boards.

"Look! The Admiral has Battleship," he said to his mother.

"Yes, and I'm going to sink your destroyer. I-7," the Admiral said with a twinkle in his eye.

"Hit and sunk," Alex responded.

Frannie asked Emma, "What are you doing?"

"I'm showing Joe how to make a grilled cheese sandwich. The Admiral's hungry," she answered. Around her waist was a dish towel, tied to look like an apron.

"I'm sure Mr. Smith knows how to make grilled cheese," Frannie said, meeting Joe Smith's eye.

"Not the good way," she answered. "He just toasts two pieces of bread and puts a piece of cheese between them when they're done. You don't get gooey cheese that way."

A shiver ran up and down Frannie's spine. That was exactly how Dennis had made his cheese sandwiches. Frannie stared at Joe Smith, looking for some sign that Alex was wrong—that he wasn't Dennis Harper.

"Emma tells me you taught her to cook," he said.

Before Frannie could respond, Emma said, "Alex knows how, too. We take turns cooking dinner for Mom when she works late. You should always know how to take care of yourself."

Joe's eyes met Frannie's. "Yes, you should. You have a smart mom."

She wasn't sure why she blushed. It wasn't delivered as a compliment, but as a statement of fact. She quickly looked away, not wanting him to read anything in her eyes.

"Okay, I need a plate!"

At Emma's demand, Joe swung open a cupboard door and pulled out a dark blue dish. He held it as Emma put the sandwich on it.

As he stood helping Emma, Frannie had a sense of déjà vu. This is how it was supposed to be—a father and daughter making sandwiches side by side.

What she was thinking must have shown on her face, for as he carried the plate to the counter and set it down, he looked at Frannie and said, "She's not my daughter."

Frannie felt as if she were on a seesaw. One minute she was on solid ground, feet planted and convinced that Joe Smith was not Dennis Harper; the next she was in the air, wondering if it *was* Dennis pulling a major scam.

Across the counter, the Admiral was laughing. Then he looked at Joe and said, "My grandson beat me."

Joe's eyes darkened. "Dad, Alex isn't your grand-son."

"But you said Frannie is his mother." The old man looked confused.

"Frannie *is* his mother, but I'm not his father," he explained.

Frannie knew that Joe hadn't missed the look in Alex's eyes. It said, *I don't believe you.* But Joe didn't try to convince Alex of anything. He simply said, "Dad, eat the sandwich Emma made for you. I need to check on something." Then he disappeared outdoors.

Seeing Frannie's puzzled look, the Admiral said, "It's the plane. He has to make sure it's locked up."

"He's got a plane?" Alex asked, his eyes wide.

"Oh, sure," the Admiral answered. "He's a pilot, you know."

Before Frannie could remind her son that his father didn't know how to fly, Alex said, "It's been a long time since you've seen him. Maybe he took lessons."

"Joe, you should sit up straight. Slouching makes a man look weak," the Admiral barked at Alex as if he were issuing a military command.

"I'm not Joe. I'm Alex."

The Admiral frowned and looked around. "Where's Joe?"

"He just stepped outside for a minute, remember?" Frannie answered.

He looked confused, then he gave Frannie a satisfied grin and said, "You're a good woman. I'm so glad you married my son."

Frannie shivered. It was true the Admiral wasn't thinking clearly, but it was also very unsettling to be the center of his confusion.

Worn out from the day's events, she put an arm around each of the twins and steered them toward the bedrooms, ignoring their protests. Not wanting to sleep in Joe Smith's bed, Frannie transferred a sleeping Luke from the guest bedroom into the master bedroom. When Alex questioned her reasons for the move, she simply said, "Don't ask questions, Alex. For once just do as you're told."

If she'd hoped that by looking into Joe Smith's bedroom she'd gain some insight into just who he was, she couldn't have been more wrong. Other than the necessary furniture—bed, dresser and night-stand—the room was devoid of personal items—no photographs on the dresser, no books on the night-stand. There were several prints on the wall, all of them seascapes. But it was the framed poster over his bed that made her mouth drop open. It was a copy of a lithograph done by the graphic artist Escher. Frannie had a poster of the same print hanging in her living room.

As she left the bedroom, she met Joe.

"Is everyone ready for bed?" he asked.

Frannie mumbled yes, and slipped into the room she was to share with Emma, annoyed at the memory his question had stirred. There was something about the way he'd said the word *bed* that had made her remember the last time she'd slept with her husband.

Dennis had come back into her life at a time when she'd thought their marriage was over. The separation papers had been filed and they'd not been together in three years. He'd shown up late one night while the kids slept. He'd said he was sorry for running out on her, begged for a second chance because he realized that she was the best thing in his life.

He'd made all sorts of promises, and like a fool she'd believed that he had changed and that this time he would keep them.

With the arrival of dawn had come the realization that the only chance he'd wanted was to have sex with her again. He didn't want the twins, he didn't want her and he certainly didn't want the baby that she later discovered they'd conceived that night. All Dennis Harper had ever wanted was a good time.

Now, four years later, she found herself stuck in the middle of the north woods with a man who looked enough like her ex-husband to make her wonder if she'd been fooled again.

One thing she knew was that she wasn't going to get any sleep until she got off this emotional seesaw. Being careful so as not to disturb her daughter, she climbed out of bed and went in search of Joe Smith.

CHAPTER FIVE

AS HE DID nearly every summer night, Joe went down to the dock where he sat on a bench, collecting his thoughts and reflecting on the events of the day. Only the occasional call of a loon and the slap of water against the wood pilings broke the silence.

He liked being near water. He always had. It was one of the reasons he'd followed his father's footsteps and gone into the Navy. Sitting on the edge of a freshwater lake, however, was not quite the same experience as being on the deck of a ship after sunset, when all he could see was darkness.

What was it his father had always said? "If you think you're such a big shot, go stand on the deck of a carrier in the middle of the Pacific. Then you'll see just how unimportant you really are."

Joe had no illusions as to his importance in the universe. At one time he'd been cocky enough to believe that because he'd graduated at the top of his class, had an admiral for a father and was trained for naval intelligence work, he wasn't simply another cog in the wheel of life. Now he knew differently.

Instead of flying military planes on intelligence missions, he transported fishermen to remote lakes in sparsely populated regions and delivered cargo to small midwestern towns. He had no military rank, but he did have his father and he would do whatever was necessary to see that he didn't lose him, too. If there was one thing that he had learned in the past two years it was that civilian life had an advantage he and his father needed. Anonymity. They could go about their lives without any intrusions.

It wasn't a bad life. The lake gave him a sense of tranquility, especially late at night with nothing but the sounds of nature for company.

Tonight, however, he found no serenity. He wasn't calmed by the loons or the water slapping against the dock. His thoughts were on the occupants of his house—or more importantly, one occupant. Frannie Harper.

She and her three kids had pushed their way into his home, disrupting his life and threatening his peace. They were intruders, and he didn't appreciate the fact that his father, in his confusion, welcomed them. For two years Joe had managed to keep the outside world right where he wanted it—far away from his home and his father. Now, thanks to one woman, what little peace of mind he'd acquired was in jeopardy.

Joe wanted to believe that come tomorrow he'd be able to convince Frannie that he wasn't Harper. When it came to her son, however, he wasn't as sure. The boy had mentioned going to the police. That was something Joe had to make sure didn't happen. What he didn't need was an investigation—bogus or not— to put him under the scrutiny of the law.

He shook his head, amazed by the irony of his situation. Ever since he'd arrived in Minnesota, he'd worried that despite all his efforts, someone from his father's past would find them. Having worked in naval intelligence, Joe knew what a man needed to do to drop out of sight. Creating new identities was relatively easy; it was keeping anyone from finding out they were new that was the difficult part. Despite all the precautions he'd taken not to arouse people's suspicions, he never stopped worrying that someday someone would find them.

Little did he know that his biggest threat would come from a kid mistaking him for his father. He could just imagine the headlines in the local paper: "Boy Looking For Deadbeat Dad Uncovers Fugitives."

Except that Joe and his father weren't really fugitives—at least, not in Joe's mind. They were more like victims, forced to flee injustice. Though he doubted that the local authorities would see things the same way.

"Mr. Smith?"

Joe jumped up at the sound of the woman's voice. He was surprised he hadn't heard Frannie Harper's approach, but when he turned he saw the reason why. She was barefoot.

"What is it?" He wished his voice didn't sound so gruff, but he resented her presence. And not just because of the threat she presented. Something about Frannie Harper stirred his blood—and it had nothing to do with her accusations about his identity. It had more to do with the way her skirt clung to her shapely legs and the bit of cleavage the loosely fitting top exposed.

"We need to clarify something," she stated.

"I hope that something isn't my identity, because as far as I'm concerned it's already clear who I am." He looked out across the water, intending to give her the impression that the subject bored him.

She stepped into his line of vision and forced him to look at her. "I'd like some answers."

"Am I not the one who should be asking you the questions?" he protested, rising.

As if suddenly realizing how close she was to him, she stepped back, stumbling near the edge of the dock. When his hands reached out to steady her, she shook free of them.

He hated that she found his touch repulsive, but what was even more disturbing was the heat that spread through him at the sight of the wind molding the flimsy fabric of her skirt and top to her body. Even in the darkness he could see the outline of her breasts.

Anger pushed its way to the front of his emotions. He didn't need a physical reaction to this woman. "You've been acting like you're the inconvenienced party in all of this mess, yet you're the one who came to my home with unfounded accusations. What I'd like to know is why me? Why my home?"

"Alex decided he wanted to find his father, so he made some posters. He put his picture on them and put them up all over Minnesota," she answered. "A woman called and said they'd seen someone in the area who looked like…the man on the poster."

"So you hunted me down."

"I didn't hunt anyone down," she retorted. "Alex was the one determined to find you. He bought a bus ticket to Grand Marais. As soon as I found out what he'd done, I got in my car and followed."

"So you showed this poster around town and someone told you where I lived?" It was rather unsettling to think that anyone in the area would have been eager to peg him as a deadbeat father.

"Alex showed it to a teenage girl who works at one of the diners. She thought you looked like…" Again she paused. "Well, she gave us the directions to this place."

Joe couldn't believe it. Never would he have thought his cover could be blown because of a couple of kids.

"I didn't want to bring Alex here," she continued, "but I was worried that if he didn't see for himself that you weren't his father, he'd just come back again. He's a very determined little boy."

"And now he's even more determined because he's convinced I *am* his father," Joe said soberly.

"Yes. You haven't exactly given him reason to think you're not."

He could tell by the suspicious tone in her voice that she was thinking similar thoughts. He knew she had a point. If he weren't using a false identity, it would have been much easier to give the boy the proof he needed. As it was, he needed to be careful about how much he revealed about himself.

He raked a hand across hair that was buzzed short on top. "We've been through this already. I told you I'm not his father. If you're his mother, you should know that."

"I should," she agreed.

But she wasn't sure. It was there in her voice and in the way she stared at him. Joe wanted to be angry at her, yet she looked so vulnerable, her arms wrapped around herself as if she needed to ward off the cold even though it was an unusually warm summer night.

"You called me Mr. Smith only a few minutes ago," he reminded her.

She cocked her head and asked, "Would there be any point in calling you Dennis?"

"Since it's not my name, no." To his relief, she didn't argue the point. "However, it would make things a lot easier if you believed me when I say I'm Joe Smith."

"Yes, well I've never been very good at believing strangers...or my ex-husband."

"Well, maybe this will convince you I'm telling you the truth." Catching her completely off guard, he pulled her close, his mouth claiming hers in a rough, aggressive kiss that should have been passionless. He wanted to punish her for putting his father's safety at risk, for accusing him of being someone he wasn't and for making him remember what it was like to want a woman.

What he didn't expect when he planted that kiss on her lips was that her mouth would be so soft and incredibly sweet tasting. Or that she'd whimper—not with anger but with pleasure—as he coaxed her lips into a response.

As if she suddenly realized what was happening, she pushed at his chest with her hands. He immediately let her go.

"Do you still think I'm your husband?"

"Ex-husband," she said quietly, then walked around him and sat down on the bench he'd vacated only a few minutes ago. She sighed as she rested her head in her hands. "I don't know what to think. I wish I could go to sleep and wake up and put this whole day behind me."

"What bothers you most? That your son thinks I'm his father or that you're not sure I'm not?"

She lifted her head to look up at him. "They both bug the hell out of me."

She stared across the lake at the outline of pine trees. "Either you're a good liar or fate has played a terrible trick on all of us."

He ignored the little voice in his head that said, *You've been lying about who you are for two years,* and told her, "It's fate playing a nasty trick. I'm not a liar."

She didn't look at him, but stared out at the lake. "I'd like to believe that."

"So why don't you? Because I happen to look like your ex-husband?"

"It's not just how you look," she answered. "It's a lot of things."

"You mean the tattoo. Lots of men who've been in the Navy have the very same tattoo in the very same place," he insisted.

"You like cheese sandwiches toasted, not fried. You use a straight-edge razor, not an electric shaver. The shower curtain hangs inside the tub, not out. You keep your garbage under the sink." She enumerated the points on her fingertips.

"And so do millions of other people," he argued.

"When is your birthday?"

"It's in November."

He pulled out his wallet, removed a plastic card and handed it to her. "Here's my license."

She frowned. "You don't have the same birthday."

"Because I'm not him," he said, taking the fake ID from her. "You're going to doubt the government?" he asked, waving the license in front of her.

"What was your mother's name?" Before he

could respond, she flapped her hands and said, ''No, don't answer that. You could easily make up a name.'' When he chuckled sarcastically, she looked at him. ''Well, it's true. You could make up all kinds of stuff. It's much more difficult to prove you *are* somebody than to prove you're not.''

''I shouldn't have to prove anything,'' he said. ''And maybe I'm the one who should be suspicious of you. You were married to this guy, you had three children with him, yet you tell me you can't recognize him.'' He didn't like putting her on the defensive, but if this issue didn't get resolved soon, his father's safety could be in jeopardy.

''Maybe if he had been a devoted husband and father who actually spent time with his family instead of sailing around the world, I wouldn't have so much trouble remembering what he looked like,'' she said, not bothering to hide her bitterness.

''Or maybe it's convenient to forget what he looked like,'' he suggested.

She jumped to her feet and confronted him. ''What's that supposed to mean?''

He shrugged. ''Come on, Ms. Harper. You expect me to believe that you can't look at me and not know if I'm your husband?''

''Ex-husband!'' she bellowed. ''For your information, Mr. Joe Smith—'' she punctuated his name with a grittiness ''—the reason I don't know is that I erased the man from my memory and if I could have erased him from Alex's memory, I would have done that, too.'' She stepped closer until her face was only inches from his. ''He's a deadbeat. A loser. Pond scum. And another thing,'' she continued. ''Just so you understand. I sure as hell don't need a man to take care of me or my kids. I can take care of them and myself just fine.'' Without giving him a chance to utter another word, she bolted for shore.

Joe watched her hurry away, thinking how foolish he'd been to make their encounter so confrontational. Instead of easing the tension, he'd widened the chasm of suspicion between them. Not a wise thing to do, considering that if she didn't believe he wasn't her ex-husband, one of the first stops she could make when she left tomorrow morning was the sheriff's office.

He had no choice but to go after her, to convince her that he wasn't this deadbeat Dennis Harper. He needed to make sure her son didn't do something foolish, like call the authorities.

He caught up with her as her bare feet hit the sandy shore. ''Frannie, wait!'' he begged, placing his left hand on her right arm.

''What are you going to do? Kiss me again so you can show me how unlike you and Dennis are?''

He let her go. ''If I kiss you again it won't be because I want to prove anything,'' he said, surprised by the emotions she managed to arouse in him. When it looked as if she might head toward the house again, he said, ''I'm sorry. I won't touch you. Just give me a few minutes. Please.''

Her whole body relaxed.

''I shouldn't have said that.'' His tone was apologetic, his hand still warm from where it had touched her flesh. ''This hasn't exactly been a good day for me, either. Four people I've never seen before in my life arrive at my home and accuse me of being their deadbeat father and ex-husband.'' He made sure he prefaced husband with *ex*. "Do you think we can go back to the part where you called me Mr. Smith?"

She looked as if she was going to say no, but then slowly she nodded. "It would give me great peace of mind if you were Joe Smith," she said, her voice weary.

"Then have some peace of mind," he said quietly. "You saw my driver's license."

The look she gave him told him she knew that it wouldn't be difficult to get a fake ID. "There are just so many eerie coincidences. Even your dad calls my son Joe and refers to me as your wife."

"Because he's not well. You've seen how easily confused he is about things."

She nodded. "Does he have Alzheimer's?"

He shook his head. "No. He suffered a head injury in an accident." He explained as briefly as possible what had led to his father's dementia, concluding with "One minute he's as sharp as a tack, the next he's confused."

"So you're saying that the only reason he says Alex looks like you when you were his age is because of his confusion?" She lifted one brow.

"Is that so hard to believe?"

"What about his attitude toward me? When I said my name was Frannie, he acted as if that's what it should be. He said I was your wife," she said. "Even you flinched when he said that."

"Yes, I did." He didn't want to have to tell her, but knew that if he was going to convince her to leave the next morning and not make any trouble for him, he had to be honest. "What you saw on my face at that moment was probably the same thing I saw on yours when you first saw me at the wood pile.'' He hesitated, then said, "My ex-wife's name is Frannie. Actually, it was Frances. The only person who called her Frannie was my dad.''

She stared at him in disbelief. "You're kidding me, right?''

"No. I know it's another crazy coincidence.''

She pushed all the hair away from her face, revealing exquisite bone structure. "This is too bizarre.''

"She was from Virginia Beach. We were married nine years before we divorced,'' he added, as if that would convince her that he was telling the truth.

"Do you have pictures of her?''

He shook his head. "We didn't exactly part on the best of terms.''

"Do you have any children?'' she asked.

"No.''

"Then, when your father said his grandbabies were…'' She didn't finish the sentence, but they both knew to what she referred.

"My wife had two miscarriages.'' What he didn't tell her was that during one pregnancy she'd carried twins. Even he had trouble comprehending that coincidence. "So you see, Frannie, there are logical explanations for the similarities you think you see in me and your ex-husband.''

She eyed him pensively, as if weighing the evidence he'd presented against what she knew to be true. Not for the first time Joe noticed what a lovely picture she made, standing there in the midnight-blue darkness. It was important that he convince her he wasn't her ex-husband—not only for her son's sake, but for his, as well. He didn't want her to look at him as if he repulsed her.

"Think back to when you first saw me, Frannie," he pleaded. "Sure, you were shocked to see someone who looked so much like your ex-husband, but didn't your instincts tell you right then and there that I wasn't him?"

It was a long time in coming, but finally she said, "Yes."

"Trust those instincts, Frannie."

"I do trust them."

"And?" He held his breath, waiting for her answer.

She straightened her back, smoothing her curls away from her face in a nervous gesture.

"I know you're not Dennis," she admitted, looking not at him but out at the water.

He felt as if a great weight had been lifted off his chest. "You're right. I'm not."

She looked at him then, her eyes holding his for several seconds before she said, "I'm sorry…for everything that's happened today."

Again, she looked frail and vulnerable. He had to fight the urge to take her into his arms and hold her close. "You only did what you thought was best for your children."

She rubbed her hands across her arms, as if she were cold. "Yes, well, it's done with now. I'm going to try to get some sleep so we can leave as soon as possible in the morning." She muttered a good-night and started back toward the house.

He would have liked to invite her to sit for a while on the dock so he could find out more about her, but he knew it was foolish to even think along such lines. The less he knew about Frannie Harper the better. The last thing he needed to do was compromise his and his father's future because of his infatuation with some woman.

WHEN FRANNIE WOKE the following morning, she was alone in the bed. She heard nothing but the buzzing of a chain saw in the distance.

She glanced at her watch and saw it was after eight. Normally she awoke every day at six. Yet it didn't surprise her that she'd slept in this morning. She'd been awake half the night, haunted by what had happened in the past twenty-four hours—especially what had happened in the hour before she'd gone to bed.

Any doubt she'd had that Joe Smith was Dennis had been erased with their encounter late last night. A warmth spread through her as she recalled the way he'd kissed her. She'd wanted to act outraged by his boldness, but the truth was that he had proved his point. The moment his mouth touched hers, she'd known she'd never shared such an intimacy with him before.

And never would again, she told herself. Today she'd leave this house and try to forget all about the crazy events of yesterday.

Yet could she forget? She still didn't understand how two men could look so much alike and not be related. If Arlene hadn't told Frannie that Dennis's twin brother had died as an infant, she would have suspected that Joe Smith could be his twin. She remembered her mother saying that every person had a double. Could that explain Joe Smith's incredible likeness to Dennis Harper?

One thing Frannie was sure of was that explaining to Alex that Joe wasn't his father would be difficult.

She couldn't very well say, "I've kissed him, Alex. It's not him."

After pulling on her clothes, she grabbed her purse and headed for the bathroom. A look in the mirror confirmed what she already knew. She'd had a restless night. Dark circles rimmed her eyes, and any number of wild creatures would have been happy to use her tangled hair for a home. She dug in her purse for a comb, then dragged it through the snarls, grimacing as she tugged. After washing her face and hands, she squeezed a dab of toothpaste onto her finger and did her best to scrub her teeth.

When she'd finished her grooming, she sighed at her reflection, wishing she could bestow a healthy dose of confidence on the uncertain woman staring back at her. She took a deep breath, then went to find her children. A quick peek in Joe Smith's room told her they weren't sleeping.

As she passed the living room, she saw Luke. He sat on the Admiral's lap, his thumb in his mouth, while the silver-haired man read to him from his favorite book, *Alexander and the Terrible, Horrible, No Good, Very Bad Day*. Frannie chuckled to herself, thinking how appropriate it was that Emma had brought it along.

As she stepped into the kitchen she saw Emma at a small wooden table in the breakfast nook eating a bowl of cereal. "Where's Alex?" she asked.

"He's outside with Dad watching the guys cut up the trees," Emma answered.

Frannie sighed. "He's not your father."

"Alex thinks he is."

"Well, Alex is wrong. You do believe me, don't you?"

To Frannie's relief, she nodded. "I think so. He doesn't talk like Dad."

"No, you're right. He doesn't." Frannie glanced out the kitchen window to see her son. "What guys are out there?"

Emma shrugged. "Some guys who came over in a truck. Luke wouldn't eat breakfast."

Frannie stepped back into the living room. "Luke, aren't you hungry?"

The three-year-old craned his neck to look at his mother. "I'm reading."

The Admiral turned, too, and smiled. "Good morning."

She returned the greeting and the smile. "Looks like it's going to be a nice day," she said, glancing to the windows where the morning sun pierced the panes of glass.

"It's going to be a beautiful day. Luke and I are going to go outside as soon as we've finished this wonderful story." He lifted the book. "Oh, and he needs to eat some breakfast, too, don't you, Luke."

The little boy nodded vigorously, then sank back against the old man's chest and waited for him to continue reading. Except for an uncle who occasionally stopped by, the three-year-old didn't have any male role models in his life. Frannie's parents had divorced when she and Lois were teens, her father moving halfway across the country and out of their lives. Her stepfather, Richard, was a wonderful grandfather, but working overseas meant he didn't get to spend much time with the children.

As Frannie glanced at the box of cereal on the table, Emma said, "Luke's not going to want to eat this stuff. It's got nuts and raisins in it."

"We can stop and get something to eat on the way home," Frannie responded.

The Admiral heard her and called out from the other room, "You shouldn't start out on a journey without a good breakfast. I could make Luke some pancakes."

That had her son forgetting all about the book and scrambling to get down off the Admiral's lap. "Mommy, I want pancakes."

"You can have some when we stop to eat at a restaurant on the way home," Frannie promised.

"But I want them now," he insisted.

"You can have a bowl of cereal." When she picked up the box, he howled.

"Nooooo!" He wrapped his chubby little arms across his chest. "I don't like that cereal. It's yucky. I want pancakes."

"And pancakes you shall get," the Admiral declared, heading for the kitchen. "I'll make them myself."

Unsure whether Joe wanted his father using the stove, Frannie said, "How about if we do them together? You know where everything is, so you can round up the ingredients and I can do the cooking part."

To her relief, the Admiral didn't protest. Slowly but systematically, he pulled out all the necessary items from the cupboards and the refrigerator, with no indication of any memory problems or cognitive disability. Encouraged, Frannie took the opportunity to ask him questions she hadn't asked Joe last night.

"This is such a beautiful spot, Admiral. Have you lived here very long?"

"Only since we left the Navy," he responded.

"Joe's like me. A true sailor. Loves the water... always has, and always will."

"Then you're in the right spot. There are a lot of lakes in this area," she said, measuring flour into a bowl.

He paused to look out at the lake. "It's not the same as living near the ocean."

Emma spoke up. "Lake Superior looks like an ocean to me."

The Admiral smiled. "Yes, it does at times, doesn't it. But once you've sailed the Pacific, nothing can compare." A faraway look came into his eyes.

"Were you originally from Minnesota?" Frannie asked. "Is that why you chose to come back?"

"I didn't choose to come here," he answered.

A forced retirement, Frannie concluded silently, thinking how difficult it must have been to adjust to a life so different from the one he'd known. "You're not unhappy here, are you?"

Again, there was that distant look in his eyes. "I should be in command. I would be if it weren't for Joe..."

Frannie suspected it was only natural that the Admiral would blame his son for his retirement. He probably wasn't even aware of his diminished mental capacity. Not knowing the circumstances under which he had left his military command, she wasn't sure of the appropriate response. She was relieved that Alex chose that moment to enter the house.

"We're going to be able to leave pretty soon. They're almost done clearing away the trees," he announced.

That had the Admiral bending to look out the

kitchen window. "Can't see from in here. I'd better go check," he said before slipping outside.

"What are you doing?" Alex asked his mother, even though Frannie thought it was rather obvious that she was cooking pancakes.

"I'm making your brother some breakfast. You want some, too?"

"No. I want to get out of here so we can go to the police," he answered.

Frannie flipped the pancakes. "We're not going to the police."

"Mom," he said in exasperation. "It's him!"

"No, it's not." She punctuated each word with a jab of the pancake turner in his direction. "I ought to know, Alex. I was married to your father."

He came to her side. "I can't believe he's got to you."

"What do you mean 'got to me'?" she demanded.

"He's telling you all sorts of lies and you're believing them!"

"They're not lies, Alex."

"Why don't we ask Gramma? She'll know," he challenged.

"That would be fine if she were home, but you know your grandmother's on vacation with her friends." Frannie didn't add that it was very unlikely they would hear from her, too.

She thought she might have pacified him for the time being, but he didn't look happy. He walked over to the phone and looked at it.

"What are you doing?" Frannie asked.

"Getting the phone number. In case Gramma wants to call and talk to them."

Frannie nodded, seeing no harm in his having Joe

Smith's phone number. She had no doubt that once she explained the situation to Arlene, her mother-in-law would confirm what Frannie already knew and Alex refused to believe.

It wasn't long before the Admiral returned. "You having a short stack, too?" he asked Alex, as Frannie set a plate of pancakes on the table.

She watched her son glance from the table to the griddle. There was no mistaking the desire in those brown eyes.

"I can make more," Frannie told him, which made him pull out a chair. While he and Luke ate, the chain saws continued to buzz in the background. About halfway through breakfast, Frannie noticed they stopped. She expected Joe Smith to walk through the door, but he didn't. Even after they'd finished eating and all the dishes had been put away, there was no sign of him.

"Are we going to leave?" Alex asked, after she sent Emma to gather their things together.

"As soon as I make sure the road's clear," Frannie answered. "You keep an eye on Luke, and I'll go outside and check."

Frannie slid her feet into sandals that were still damp from the drenching they'd had yesterday. As she stepped onto the porch, she was struck by how peaceful everything was this morning. The rain had left its fresh scent, enhancing the fragrance of the pines.

"Mr. Smith?" she called out tentatively as she rounded the corner of the garage. As she stepped onto the gravel road, she saw that all that remained of the fallen trees was a trail of sawdust. Frannie wondered what had happened to all the debris.

"Mr. Smith?" Again she called out his name, but there was no answer. She walked a bit farther down the road, craning her head to see if there were any more trees down from the storm.

"Looking for anything in particular?" The voice came from behind her and caused her to jump.

Annoyed that he'd sneaked up on her, she said, "Yes. You. Why didn't you answer me when I called out?"

"I didn't hear you. I'm sorry. I didn't mean to startle you." Today he wore a plain white T-shirt that emphasized the muscles in his arms. And he definitely had muscles in his arms. She forced her eyes to his face. It was familiar, yet it wasn't.

"What happened to the trees?" she asked. Dumb question. As if it mattered what had happened to them.

"One of my neighbors hauled them away. He works for a logging outfit," he answered.

She looked around her. "Does this mean we can leave?"

"Whenever you're ready," he answered.

Relief washed over her. "Good."

She glanced at him then. He was anxious for them to be gone...and why shouldn't he be? They'd barged in uninvited, created all sorts of tension. She knew that before she left, she owed him an apology.

"I know you're anxious to be rid of us, but before we go there is something I need to say," she said.

He shifted uneasily, his face becoming guarded. She didn't blame him. After the way she'd lashed out at him last night, he had every right to be cool and distant.

"I want to thank you for giving us shelter last night."

"You're welcome."

He continued to stare at her with those deep brown eyes, eyes that in the light of day she could see were so different from Dennis Harper's.

"And I also want to say I'm sorry I didn't believe you when you said you were Joe Smith. I should have. I knew the minute you opened your mouth that you weren't my ex-husband, and I should have listened to my intuition. Because of Alex and how difficult this has been for him, I let some feelings cloud my thinking."

He nodded, his face revealing nothing of what he was thinking. "Apology accepted."

"I think the only reason I had any real doubts was the fact that emotionally I was drained. Having Alex run off the way he did and not knowing what had happened…" She shivered at the thought.

His face softened. "I don't think there's any need to rehash things this morning. You came here looking for someone, you didn't find him, the storm delayed your leaving, and I offered you a place to stay." It was obvious that he wanted to put it all behind him, too. "I do have a favor to ask you, though."

"Sure. What is it?"

"You've seen the way my father is. What he doesn't need is to have some child protection worker come out here asking questions."

"Of course not. I wouldn't do such a thing. I told you I know you're not Dennis Harper."

"It wasn't you I was thinking would contact the authorities."

"You think Alex will?"

"You yourself said he was determined," he reminded her.

She sighed. "He is. I guess I can't blame him. He was only four when his father left. And you do look like him."

"What are you going to tell him?" he asked.

"The truth."

"That I'm simply a man who looks like his father?"

She nodded. "I think he'll understand," she answered, although she wasn't as confident as she led him to believe. Feeling rather awkward standing there next to him wearing yesterday's clothes, she thought it would be better to say as little as possible and get back on the road. "Well, it's a long drive back to Minneapolis. I'd better go inside and get the kids."

He didn't stop her, and Frannie felt a bit disappointed. She would have liked to talk to Joe Smith a while longer, to get to know him a little better. Then she chastised herself. And for what purpose? He was a stranger who looked like her ex-husband. That was all she needed to know.

A short while later when she returned with her children, she found him looking under the hood of the old station wagon. Puzzled, she asked, "What are you doing?"

"Checking your oil," he said as he straightened, wiping his hands on a cloth rag. "You shouldn't start out on a long trip without checking to make sure it's not low."

"And is it?"

"Down a quart." He went into the garage and

returned carrying a plastic funnel and a small bottle. He unscrewed the cap, then poured its contents into the engine. When he was finished, he snapped the hood back in place. "Done."

She stared at him, wondering how she ever could have ever mistaken him for Dennis. She must have been gawking at him, for he asked, "Something wrong?"

She shook her head. "No, I was just thinking how very different you are from my ex-husband. Thank you for checking my oil."

"No problem." He gave her another half smile, and she felt her heart give a funny little kick.

"Mom, are we going or aren't we?" Alex called out.

"Get in the car," she ordered her kids. They climbed in.

Then she turned to Joe and said, "You're a good man, Joe Smith. Nothing at all like Dennis Harper." Before he could say anything, she climbed into the car.

As she drove away, all she saw in the rearview mirror was a strong, muscular figure standing in the drive.

CHAPTER SIX

ALEX WAS QUIET as they began the long journey home. Frannie knew she needed to talk to him about everything that had happened, yet she thought it would be better to wait until he was back in his own room where they could speak privately. When he didn't mention the subject of his father once, she hoped it meant Alex had accepted that Joe Smith wasn't Dennis.

She was wrong. As soon as he stepped inside the house, he went straight for the telephone.

"What are you doing?" she asked him.

"Calling Auntie Lois."

"She's not coming home until Tuesday," Frannie said.

"I'll leave a message," he retorted, and continued dialing.

Frannie listened as he said, "This is Alex. I found my dad. Call me."

As soon as he'd hung up the phone, she said gently, "Joe Smith is not your father."

"That's what you think."

"It's what I know," she stated firmly. She went over to him and gently placed her arms on his. "Listen to me. He's not your father. He showed me his driver's license."

"It could be a fake."

"It's not a fake, Alex. You have to believe me about this. I don't want you making trouble for Mr. Smith. His father's not well—you saw that. They don't need the hassle of strangers coming to their door and investigating their identities. Do you know how upsetting that would be for the Admiral? He's confused enough as it is."

Alex thought about what she had said, his teeth tugging on his lower lip. She took advantage of his hesitation to press home her point. "Think about it, Alex. You saw how the smallest of things can upset the Admiral. Can you imagine what it would be like for him if the police were to show up at his door?"

He still didn't speak, but continued chewing on his lip.

"All I'm asking is that you please wait until we've talked to your grandmother."

"Why? She wasn't there. She didn't see him."

"She'll know whether your grandfather was an Admiral." It was the only argument Frannie could use; it was clear Alex wasn't going to listen to her deny that Joe Smith was her ex-husband.

Again he picked up the phone. "Then I'm going to call Gramma." He dialed and waited. Frannie knew there'd been no answer when he returned the receiver to its cradle, a look of disappointment on his face. "She's not home yet."

Frannie gave him a hug—or at least as much of one as he would allow. "I know this has been difficult for you."

"I'm all right," he said, wiggling away from her and then disappearing into his room. When Luke would have run after him, Frannie stopped him.

"You come with me. You need a bath," she said, scooping him up in her arms.

"I wanna go with Alex," he whined, but she paid no attention. After everything that had happened this weekend, Frannie understood her older son needed to be alone. She only wished it were as easy for her to go to her room and slam the door on the rest of the world.

But time didn't stop because a mother needed a few minutes to catch her breath. It just kept ticking away, filled with responsibilities.

"I'm hungry," Emma said. "What's for dinner?"

Tick, tick, tick.

"YOU'RE BACK. Was it him?" Josh asked Alex the following morning.

"It sure looked like him, but my mom doesn't think it is." He slid his backpack from his shoulders and set in on Josh's bed. He unzipped the bag and pulled out two socks.

"What are those for?"

"You'll see." He slid a sock over each of his hands, then dug into the backpack and pulled out a metal object.

"What is that?"

"It's a paperweight." He set it down next to Josh's computer. "See. It's a ship."

Josh peered at it from several different angles. "Cool. Is it his?"

"Yup. I found it in his room."

"You took it?" When Alex nodded, he asked, "Why?"

"To get his fingerprints so I can prove he is my dad," he stated matter-of-factly.

"And how are you going to do that? You don't know any cops," Josh reminded him.

"No, but my aunt does." When Josh would have touched the paperweight, he said, "Don't! You'll contaminate it."

Josh chuckled. "Contaminate what? Fingerprints only work if the guy's got a record. Your dad's never been arrested, has he?"

Alex frowned. He didn't think so—at least, he'd never heard his aunt say he was a criminal, just a deadbeat. Maybe Josh was right. Maybe they didn't fingerprint bad fathers.

"Doesn't matter," he said with more confidence than he was feeling. "My aunt will know what to do. She's really good at locating deadbeats."

"You should have gotten a piece of his hair. Then you could have done DNA testing," Josh told him.

Alex hadn't thought about that. Not that getting a strand of hair would have been as easy as slipping the paperweight in his backpack. Then he realized that he could have taken the hairbrush that had been on the vanity in the bathroom. Why hadn't he thought of that? With the white socks covering his hands, he picked up the paperweight and returned it to his backpack.

"So what was he like?" Josh asked.

He shrugged. "He was just a guy."

"Was he creepy?"

"Uh-uh. He was actually kinda nice. So was my grandpa. He lives with my dad. It's the first time I've ever seen him."

"You never met your grandpa before?"

Alex shook his head. "He likes to tell jokes. He made me laugh."

"How come he doesn't make your deadbeat dad pay up, then?"

"I think it's because he's got Oldtimers' disease or something. He gets confused a lot."

"So what are you going to do now?"

"I'm not sure. I'm working on a plan." He took the socks off his hands, stuck them in a side compartment of his backpack, zipped it up and then heaved the pack on his shoulder.

"You leaving already?" Josh asked.

"Yeah. I told my mom I'd be right back. And I need to talk to my aunt Lois and call my gramma."

"Don't forget to ask about the DNA," Josh said, as Alex walked toward the door.

"Don't worry. I'll get this guy yet," he said, then headed home.

"IT'S BEEN FOUR DAYS and she's still not home," Alex said as he put the phone down. "How long a vacation is Gramma taking?"

Frannie knew that he'd tried calling his grandmother every day since their return from Grand Marais and had had no luck in reaching her. "You heard her say she has the entire summer off and she was going to make the most of it by visiting her friends." Frannie understood his frustration. She, too, had wanted to talk to Arlene about Joe Smith.

"How come she doesn't call us and tell us where she is?"

Good question, Frannie said to herself. She easily could have said, "Because your grandmother just does *what* she wants *when* she wants without regard to others." But that would have been an answer uttered out of frustration. It was true that Arlene was a free spirit, but she did care about her grandchildren.

Instead, Frannie said, "Because when people go on vacation they aren't supposed to have to check in with their family. It's their time to have fun. She sent us a postcard from California."

And another one came that very afternoon. Frannie read it to the children. "Hello family! Going up the west coast to see my friend Marcy in Seattle. Might even take a trip to Victoria. Don't worry about me. I'm fine. Miss you all. Home in a few weeks. Love, Gramma."

"Didn't she give a phone number for Marcy?" Alex asked, when Frannie had finished reading the postcard to them.

Frannie almost laughed out loud. "No, there's no number."

His shoulders sagged. "How am I gonna talk to her if we don't even know where she is?"

"She says she'll be home in a few weeks." Frannie tried to sound optimistic.

He groaned. "By then he could be gone."

Frannie didn't need to ask Alex to whom he referred. She didn't think for a moment that Joe Smith was going to disappear, yet she doubted she could convince Alex of that.

Lois arrived in the middle of the discussion and asked, "Why the long faces?"

"Alex is missing his grandmother," Frannie answered, not sure she wanted to discuss the subject of Joe Smith with her sister.

Lois tousled Alex's hair affectionately. "Hey, won't an auntie do?"

He just looked at his aunt and said, "Nothing's going right," then headed for his room.

Lois looked to her sister for an explanation. "This isn't about that guy that looks like Dennis, is it?"

Frannie nodded reluctantly. "Alex just won't admit he's wrong about him."

"I know. He called me the other day and wanted to know about fingerprints."

"Fingerprints? What did he do? Take something from the Smiths' home?"

She lifted her brows. "He didn't say. When I told him that it wouldn't do much good to fingerprint this Smith guy since his father's prints aren't on file, he started asking me about DNA."

"Oh, good grief." Frannie sank down onto the sofa. "No one can say he isn't tenacious. You didn't tell him how to get a DNA sample, did you?"

Lois patted her shoulder. "No, I told him it would make more sense to get someone who knows both Dennis and his father to confirm that Joe Smith and his dad aren't them."

"That would be Arlene."

"Exactly."

She threw up her hands in frustration. "Arlene, who's impossible to reach."

Just then Emma burst through the front door, out of breath. She'd been playing outside with a friend, but having seen her aunt's car had obviously come running.

"Hi, Auntie Lois! Are you going to have dinner with us?"

"That's exactly why I'm here. How about if we all go out for pizza tonight?" She looked to Frannie for approval. "My treat, of course."

"I thought you had a date tonight," Frannie said, one brow raised in curiosity.

"Plans changed."

"You don't look too upset over it."

"I'm not. I found out he goes through women as fast as day-traders dump stocks."

"What are day-traders?" Emma asked.

"People who play the stock market," Lois answered. "So what do you think?" She addressed Frannie and the kids. "You up for some pizza?"

It didn't take any arm-twisting to convince Alex that he should join them. The subject of pizza seemed to make everyone but Frannie forget about grandparents, dads, potential boyfriends and just about everything else. As they all piled into Lois's car, no one said another word about Joe Smith.

But Frannie was having a hard time forgetting about the man. It had been that way ever since she'd returned to Minneapolis. And it wasn't because of his uncanny resemblance to her ex-husband.

No, Joe kept popping into her mind because of the way he'd kissed her. It had been a long time since any man had made her go weak with a single kiss. She didn't like the feeling. Nor did she like the delicious little tremor that traveled through her every time she remembered the way his lips had felt on hers. She wanted to forget that kiss. To forget Joe.

Only, she found that difficult to do, especially when Lois asked questions she wasn't able to answer. Like why hadn't Joe shown Alex photographs of him with his mother? Or a high school yearbook or a college diploma or any number of legal documents that quickly would have put to rest any mistaken identity?

Frannie knew that there was a bit of mystery about Joe. He'd said very little about himself except that he flew planes and took care of his ailing father. It was probably all she would ever know about the man. *And it is all you need to know,* a tiny voice whispered inside her head.

That didn't stop her from thinking about him, or from wishing she could unravel the mystery.

EVER SINCE Frannie Harper and her children had gone, Joe had been restless. He wanted to attribute his uneasiness to the fact that their intrusion into his quiet and orderly world had forced him to look over his shoulder again.

The truth was that meeting Frannie hadn't simply started him watching for the authorities. It had reminded him of what was missing in his life. A woman. Children. Maybe that's why he was having trouble forgetting her.

Or rather, forgetting how sweet she'd tasted when he'd kissed her. He wished he could forget that night. If there was one rule he'd made for himself, it was to never kiss an unwilling woman. With Frannie he'd broken that rule. It was a good thing she'd gone back to Minneapolis the next day.

For the first few days after her departure, Joe had kept an eye on his driveway, hoping there wouldn't be more unexpected visitors. Even though Frannie had assured him that she wouldn't go to the authorities, he wasn't sure that a sheriff wouldn't come calling. By the end of the week, however, he began to think that his worry had been unfounded. He wanted to believe that the young mother had been

able to convince her son that there was no need to
contact the police.

Then on Friday there was a letter in his mailbox
with no return address. The postmark indicated it had
been mailed from Minneapolis. Joe tensed as he slid
his finger beneath the flap and ripped open the envelope. Inside was a folded piece of lined notebook
paper. As he pulled it out, a photograph fell to the
ground. Joe picked it up and saw that it was a snapshot of Frannie and her three kids. Joe knew where
in Minneapolis it had been taken, recognizing the
sculpture behind them—a giant metal spoon supporting a cherry.

Seeing the picture of Frannie did funny things to
Joe's insides. She wore another long skirt and a
loosely fitting blouse that covered her from shoulders
to ankles, but he knew that beneath all that cotton
were curves that could make a man's heart race. All
four of the Harpers looked happy, smiling with impish grins as they posed for the camera. Joe wondered
what kind of man would desert such a beautiful family.

He turned his attention to the letter. *Dear Dad,* it
began, and Joe grimaced. So the kid hadn't given up
hope that Joe was his father.

This is a picture of us last summer at the
skulpcher garden in Minneapolis. It's where we
went for our vacation because we didn't have
any money to go on a real one. If you paid your
bills we could maybe go to a cabin at a lake or
to Wisconsin Dells.

Joe shook his head. It angered him to think there
were men like this Dennis Harper. Joe had only spent

a few hours with Alex, Emma and Luke, yet he could
see they were good kids, kids who deserved to have
a father in their lives. He continued to read.

Mom still has to make payments for the oper-
ation Luke had when he was a baby. Until she
got her job at the newspaper, we didn't have
any insurance.

Newspaper? Was Frannie Harper a reporter? He
raked a hand over his head, wishing he'd asked her
what she did for a living. It could be she worked in
a newspaper office doing clerical work. Or in human
resources. Or in production. He didn't want to think
that she was an investigative journalist with a nose
trained to look for stories that people chose to keep
hidden. Because that meant she may have sniffed a
story when she'd spent the night in his home.

Uneasiness had Joe setting the letter aside and
reaching for his laptop. He needed to find out just
who Frannie Harper was. Sitting at the kitchen table,
he accessed the Internet, and in only a few minutes
had learned she was a photojournalist who worked
for a small weekly paper in the metropolitan area of
Minneapolis and St. Paul. Several of her photographs
were posted on the paper's Web site. He enlarged
each of them to get a better look at her work, im-
pressed by the emotion she'd captured with her camera.

As he put away his laptop, he wondered if he
should contact Frannie to find out what—if any—
investigating she'd done on him. He knew that if he
did, he risked raising her suspicions.

He picked up Alex's letter. As he continued to read the boy's words, Joe realized that whether he wanted it or not, he'd been dragged into the lives of the Harpers.

How come you don't want us? I bet Grandpa would feel better if you would let us be your kids. He likes us. He told me so. Mom says I can't do anything about who you are until I talk to Gramma. I don't know when she is going to be home again. Until I talk to her I am going to keep writing to you and reminding you of your obligashuns. Alex.

Joe wished he could forget about Alex and his mother—rip up this letter and pretend they'd never been stranded at his home. Pretend they hadn't mistaken him for another man. Pretend they didn't exist.

He knew he couldn't. And not just because he worried that Frannie Harper might use her connections at the paper to investigate his background. Another emotion kept him from ignoring the letter. In less than twenty-four hours, Frannie and Alex Harper had managed to make him care about them.

He could understand why he'd been drawn to Frannie. She was a lovely woman and he was a man who'd been alone far too long. But Alex? What was it about the boy that made him feel as if they'd established some connection?

Maybe it was because Alex reminded Joe of something he'd lost—the opportunity to be a parent. If it weren't for the fact that his wife had suffered two miscarriages, Joe would have been the father of three children very close in age to Alex, Emma and Luke.

He knew it was possible that Alex's plea for a father rubbed a sore spot that had never truly healed—the place in his heart that still grieved over the loss of three children.

Dennis Harper hadn't lost his children. He'd tossed them aside, not wanting to be a part of their lives. Anger at the stranger festered inside Joe. It wasn't fair that Alex had such a deadbeat for a dad. Nor was it fair that Joe, who'd wanted children, had had his opportunity to be a father stolen from him. He knew it wasn't likely that he'd ever know the love of a son like Alex, not when he was forced to live as a fugitive. If only...

"Joe?"

His father's voice reminded him that this was not the time for sentiment. He couldn't allow emotions to rule his head. All that mattered was keeping his father safe. He didn't have time to worry about a ten-year-old boy who had the misfortune of having a rotten dad. Or his mother. He needed to forget both of them.

But he found that difficult to do when each new day brought another letter. Joe thought about not reading them, but within minutes of finding one in the mailbox he'd ripped it open. With every word he read he found it more difficult to remain indifferent to Alex's pleas. Nor could he forget about Frannie Harper. He hated to think of her children being without a father. Or of her having to bear her burdens alone.

He stared at the stack of letters, debating whether he should follow his instincts—those that told him something needed to be done. He went back to his laptop. Within minutes he had her phone number and address on the screen.

All he had to do was call her. Tell her about the letters. Ask her what he could do to help remedy the situation.

How come you don't want us? Alex's words echoed in his head.

Joe knew he had to put an end to the letter writing—not just for Alex's sake, but for his own. He would call Frannie tomorrow.

IT HAD BEEN A HECTIC DAY for Frannie. First Luke had fallen off the bed and hit his head on his metal dump truck, necessitating a trip to the ER for stitches. Next Emma had received the news that her very best friend Ashley was moving to Pennsylvania and had needed a shoulder to cry on. Then Alex had gotten into a fight with one of the neighbor boys, coming home with a bloody lip and a bruised ego, which Frannie had discovered was far more difficult to mend than the cut on his face.

By dinnertime she was tired, she had a headache and she wondered how she would get through the remainder of the day. Then Ashley invited Emma to sleep over, and Lois called to say she had an extra ticket to the Twins game and would take Alex. That left Frannie alone with Luke, who was content to sit next to her, watch an animated video and eat popcorn.

It was all Frannie could handle that particular evening. By the time the video had ended, she was tempted to crawl into bed herself, but knew she needed to let Alex in when he came home. As she tucked in Luke, she noticed something dark and small near his pillow.

"What's this?" she asked, reaching for the metal object.

"A ship," he answered. He grabbed it from her hands and pushed it across his pillow, making a humming sound.

"I can see it's a ship, Luke. Where did you get it?"

He looked over his shoulder and giggled.

"Luke, did you take that from Alex?" Again she reached for it. "Let Mommy see."

One thing she knew about her younger son was that he liked to make a game out of everything. Tonight was no exception. He hid the ship under his pillow, then shoved both his hands behind his back and said, "Guess where it is, Mommy!"

Frannie played along. "Behind your back?"

He pulled both hands out and said, "Nope!" Then he pulled the ship from under the pillow. "See?"

Frannie discovered the ship was actually a paperweight with the U.S. Navy insignia on the bottom. Her heart sank.

"Show Mommy where you found it, Luke," she instructed the three-year-old.

He hesitated, a guilty look on his face, so she said, "It's okay. I won't be angry."

He tumbled out of bed and went over to where Alex's backpack rested on the floor. With his finger he pointed to the open zipper, smiling slyly. "In there."

"Okay. Come back to bed now," Frannie ordered.

He came running across the room and into her

arms. After a bedtime story and a good-night kiss, Frannie left with the paperweight in her hand.

A TALK WITH ALEX confirmed Frannie's suspicions. The paperweight belonged to Joe Smith. She told Alex that they would call him tomorrow evening as soon as she got home from her assignment.

When she arrived home, however, she discovered that Joe had already called and left a message for her. Her heart banged against her chest at the sound of his voice.

"Frannie, it's Joe Smith. We need to talk."

Alex, too, heard the message. "It's Dad. I knew he'd call."

Frannie sighed. "He didn't say, 'It's your father.' Maybe he called because he noticed his paperweight was missing. I'll find out," she said ominously as she picked up the phone.

Alex was about to make a beeline for his bedroom when she hooked an arm around him and said, "You stay right here. You're going to apologize for taking it."

Frannie's heart beat erratically as she punched in the numbers. The phone rang several times before Joe answered.

She took a deep breath and said, "Hi. It's Frannie Harper. Am I calling at a bad time?"

"No. Not at all. Thank you for returning my call."

"Yes, well, it's funny you called because I was planning to call you today myself."

"You were?" He sounded surprised.

"Yes." She tried to still her fluttering nerves. "I found out last night that we have something of yours. A small paperweight in the shape of a ship."

"So that's what happened to it."

"You missed it?"

"I noticed it wasn't on the desk, but I thought my father had moved it and couldn't remember what he'd done with it," he answered.

"Alex brought it home with him. He's not a thief—" she was quick to point out "—he wanted to get something with your fingerprints on it." There was dead silence on the other end, making Frannie very nervous. "He thought he could prove you're his father," she added quietly.

"Are you saying he went to the authorities and checked my fingerprints?"

Frannie wasn't surprised that he sounded upset. "No. My sister told him it wouldn't do any good. Dennis isn't a criminal."

"Thank goodness for that," he said on a sigh.

"I'm sorry, Joe, for yet another inconvenience," she added. "I'm sure that paperweight must have sentimental value."

"Actually, it's my father's."

She chuckled nervously. "Then, chances are it wouldn't even have had your prints on it. I don't think Alex realized that. I'm going to give the phone to him because he wants to talk to you, too," she said, then passed the receiver to her son.

Alex looked as if he were being given a dose of poison to swallow, but Frannie refused the plea for mercy in his eyes and forced him to take the phone.

To her relief, he sounded remorseful, apologizing to Joe in a way that made her think she had done something right as a parent after all. That sentiment was quickly forgotten, however, when before ending the conversation he challenged Joe to a DNA test.

Frannie grabbed the phone from her son. "Joe, I'm sorry. Alex had no right to ask that. I certainly don't think it's appropriate or necessary in this situation."

Alex stomped off to his room, which suited Frannie. It was difficult enough talking to Joe without her stubborn son trying to persuade her to say things better left unsaid.

To her surprise, Joe didn't find Alex's suggestion outrageous. "If we did a DNA test he would know once and for all that I'm not his father," he said. "There's something you should know, Frannie."

Her heart skipped a beat. "What's that?"

There was a short pause, then he said, "Alex has been writing to me every day. He's sending pictures, lecturing me on how bad a parent I've been."

"I'm sorry. I didn't realize—" She broke off, embarrassed. "I've told him you're not Dennis, but he simply refuses to believe me."

"Has he been able to talk to his grandmother?"

"He wrote to you about her?"

"He's told me quite a few things about your family."

That made Frannie wonder exactly what Alex had said in his letters. She briefly explained the reason they hadn't been able to reach her mother-in-law. "Unfortunately, she is the one person who could convince Alex you're not his father."

"Which means until he hears from her he'll continue to foster the false hope that he's my son. I'm sure you don't want that any more than I do."

"No, I don't," she agreed.

"Then, a paternity test may be the logical resolution to all of this. At least that way there would be no second-guessing on anyone's part."

"You're willing to take one?"

"Yes. We both know what the results will be."

"Yes, but the inconvenience…"

"Is worth the peace of mind," he finished for her. "It needs to be done, Frannie. He's telling me things a boy shares with his father."

And it bothered him, as it would any man with a conscience, she thought. Joe was a man who cared about people. She'd seen that for herself.

"What do you think?" He waited for her answer.

"I think it's kind of you to offer to do such a thing. I'll ask my sister what's the best way to handle this. She's a lawyer."

"There's no need to get anyone else involved. I've already checked with a couple of labs here in the Duluth area. There's also a company that will send someone to your house to get the sample from Alex. We wouldn't even have to meet to get this done."

She wondered if that was what he preferred. "Can I think about this and get back to you?"

"Yes, but I'd like to take care of it as soon as possible. The longer Alex thinks of me as his father, the greater the disappointment is going to be when he learns the truth."

She knew he was right. "All right. You can go ahead and schedule the appointment in Duluth."

BECAUSE JOE HAD REQUESTED that no one else be involved in the testing, Frannie hadn't asked her sister's advice. She had, however, planned to tell Lois about the DNA test—but Alex beat her to it.

"We're going to Duluth tomorrow to get a DNA test," he announced to his aunt the minute she'd walked in the front door.

"You're doing what?" Lois gave her sister a glare that demanded answers.

"Alex asked Joe Smith if he'd take a DNA test, and he agreed," Frannie explained.

"This way he won't be able to hide from us," Alex added. "DNA doesn't lie. You said so." He looked at his aunt.

"No, it doesn't," Lois agreed.

"So you approve?" Frannie cast a sideways glance at her sister.

"Sure, but what puzzles me is why you're going to Duluth to have it done. I could have arranged for it to be done right here in Minneapolis. You wouldn't have had to even see this Smith guy."

"I appreciate the offer, but as it turns out, I have an assignment in Duluth, and since it involves staying overnight at a hotel, I thought it would be an opportunity for me to take the kids away for a couple of days." She didn't tell her sister that she'd specifically requested the assignment, or that Joe had offered to pay for the DNA test.

"They're going to have to take blood out of my arm," Alex boasted.

"You'll probably faint," Emma warned him.

"Will not. You're the one who cries at the doctor, not me."

Frannie managed to change the topic of conversation, not wanting to talk about Joe with her sister. She should have known, however, that Lois wouldn't let it rest until she was satisfied with the answers she'd been given.

"Okay, so you're going to Duluth on an assignment. That doesn't mean you have to do the DNA testing there," she said as she stood next to her car.

"I know that," Frannie replied. "But this isn't only about the DNA test."

"Since when?"

"Since Alex took the paperweight. I thought it would be a good idea for him to return it in person. It could be valuable, and I didn't think I should return it through the mail."

She could feel her sister's eyes on her, studying her.

"Send it by courier."

Frannie shoved her hands to her waist. "What's wrong with us going to Duluth to take the test?"

"Nothing. I just wish you had let me handle it."

"Why? It's not that big a deal."

"You meet a guy who's a dead ringer for your ex-husband and you don't want me to be concerned?"

"He's *not* Dennis."

"You said he looks just like him. If you hadn't told me Dennis's twin brother had died, I'd think this guy could be his long lost brother. You want me to run a check on him?"

Frannie threw up her hands. "Please don't. It's embarrassing enough that Alex has been writing letters to him telling him all sorts of personal things about our family. I don't need him to find out my sister's checking up on him, too."

"If he's got nothing to hide, it shouldn't matter."

"Spoken like an attorney," Frannie stated dryly. She leaned against the open car door, a plea in her eyes. "I would appreciate it if you would try to look at this from Joe Smith's perspective."

"You seem to be awfully concerned about just that," Lois said, her eyes narrowing. "Frannie, I hate to even have to ask this, but you're not attracted to this guy because he looks like Dennis, are you?''

"No!" Her denial came immediately because it was the truth. What she didn't add was that she *was* attracted to Joe Smith—but for reasons she couldn't explain to Lois. She knew it was better not to even try. "Do you think you could stop cross-examining me like I'm some hostile witness?''

Lois reached for her sister's hand. "I'm sorry. I'm just doing what a big sister is supposed to do. I'm also your lawyer. I'm supposed to watch out for you.''

"I know. And I appreciate your concern, but there's no need for you to worry about any of this.''

Just then Emma stuck her head out the front door. "Mom, telephone's for you!" she called out. "I think it's your work.''

"I gotta go,'' Frannie said, giving Lois a quick hug.

"All right. Call me when you get back, all right?''

Frannie nodded, relieved to have the conversation end. As much as she loved her sister, she didn't need to answer questions about emotions she didn't understand. Nor could she explain that when she pictured Joe Smith, she didn't see a man who looked like her husband. She saw someone very different. A man with strong convictions. A man of commitment. A man she wished she had met under different circumstances.

CHAPTER SEVEN

JOE ARRIVED at the clinic early. Instead of going inside, he parked his SUV and rolled down his windows, content to listen to a Santana CD and gaze at the scenery below. Because the clinic sat atop a steep hill, he had a bird's-eye view of the harbor. On such a warm summer day traffic was heavier than usual, as recreational boaters spending the afternoon on the water vied for the right-of-way with tour boats and freighters loaded with ore.

Since he'd moved to Grand Marais, Joe had come to Duluth often with his father, who never seemed to tire of watching the ships sail in and out of the harbor. Joe knew his father loved being in the port city, as it was the closest he could get to the life he had once known as a career naval officer.

Today, however, Joe had asked Letty to stay with his dad. He doubted the Admiral would understand why he was meeting Frannie, nor did there seem to be any point in telling him. It would only add more uncertainty and confusion to his already unstable world.

Like Frannie, Joe wanted the paternity issue settled as quickly as possible, which was why he had agreed to meet her at the Duluth clinic. He had read Alex's letters and knew that with each passing day, the boy's belief that Joe was his father only grew stronger.

Joe knew that dispelling that notion would be much less complicated if he could only reveal his true identity. If he weren't using an assumed name, he could have produced indisputable proof that he wasn't Dennis Harper. Hidden in a safety deposit box were legal documents that stated he had been born Joseph Hawthorn. Joe wished he could tell Frannie his real name, but not knowing what she'd do with the information meant that was a risk he couldn't take.

Thinking of her, he glanced toward the street, looking for the dark green station wagon to pull into the parking lot. Today would more than likely be the last time he'd see her. Once she had the results of the DNA testing, there would be no reason for them to have any further communication.

It was for the best, but that didn't keep him from wishing he could see her again. Her independent attitude intrigued him, as did the way she hovered over her kids, ready to do battle with anyone or anything that threatened them. He also liked how her eyes darkened with emotion when she was angry and the enticing movement of her hips when she walked.

He closed his eyes and tried not to think about her. A man in his position had no business thinking such thoughts about any woman, yet Frannie Harper had left an impression on him that was hard to ignore. He wanted to know what it would be like to get to know her...all of her. If they had met under different circumstances, at another time in his life...

He sighed as he opened his eyes and forced his attention back to the clinic. Convincing Alex Harper that he wasn't the boy's father was the hurdle he needed to leap so that he could get back to taking care of his father. If he were smart, he would regard Frannie Harper as Alex's mother and nothing else.

Only she didn't look much like the mother of a ten-year-old when she climbed out of the station wagon a few minutes later. She wore a pair of blue shorts with a white top that emphasized her youthful figure. Joe wasn't sure of her age, but figured she couldn't have been past thirty. As she bent over to unstrap Luke from his car seat, Joe caught a peek of flesh that normally was hidden by her shorts. He quickly looked away, but it was too late. His body had reacted.

He pulled his keys from the ignition and climbed out of the SUV, just as Frannie and her three kids walked past.

She smiled at him and said, "Hello. Have you been waiting long?"

"Not long," he answered. "You had a good trip?"

"Yes. What about you?"

"It was fine." He felt ridiculous making small talk. He had the crazy urge to tell her that she looked good. Really good. A narrow copper-colored metal band held her blond curls away from her face, emphasizing the exquisite bone structure. "We should go inside."

"Yes, but before we do, Alex has something for you." She put her hand on her older son's shoulder, urging him to step forward.

Joe saw that the boy had the missing paperweight in his hands and a contrite look on his face.

"I'm sorry I took this," Alex said, handing it to him. "I hope you're not mad."

"No, I'm not mad," Joe reassured him. "Thank you for returning it."

Alex didn't say another word, but simply eyed him suspiciously.

"He never should have taken it and he's been punished," Frannie added, which caused Alex to look at Joe with even more distrust.

"I know Alex didn't intend to do anything wrong," Joe said. "He was simply trying to find an answer to a question. Isn't that right, Alex?"

Some of the suspicion slid from the ten-year-old's face as he nodded.

Then Joe said, "We should go inside so we can get a step closer to finding that answer for Alex. I'll put this—" he held up the paperweight "—in the car and be right in."

Frannie nodded and ushered her kids into the clinic, while he went back to his SUV. By the time he entered the reception area, she had already started to fill out the necessary forms. The woman at the front desk gave Joe an identical clipboard with instructions for completing the paperwork.

He could feel two sets of eyes on him—Alex's and Emma's. Frannie, however, didn't look up as he took a seat across from her. Over the top of the clipboard, Joe could see her long slender legs crossed at the knees, distracting him from the papers that needed his attention.

She finished ahead of him, and subsequently Alex's name was the first one called to have his blood drawn. Frannie went with him, carrying Luke in her arms and leaving Emma to wait in the reception area.

She sat quietly, looking away whenever Joe glanced in her direction. When he had finished filling out the papers, he gave the clipboard back to the receptionist. As Joe went to sit back down he saw that Emma had moved to the vacant chair next to his. He reached for a magazine on the table. Flipping through the pages, he could feel the young girl's eyes on him. He wondered if she wanted to talk to him. Did she, too, think he was her father?

"Would you like a magazine?" Joe asked, motioning to where several periodicals lay scattered across the table next to his chair.

"No thank you," she said politely.

She wore her blond hair the same way her mother did—pushed straight back from her forehead, except that her headband was a wide strip of leather, not metal. Joe noticed she had the same delicate bone structure as Frannie and the same small rounded nose, yet her eyes were brown.

"Do you think they use a big needle to take your blood?" she asked Joe.

"I hope not. I don't like needles, and especially not big ones."

"Me, neither," she said with a shy smile.

Curious, he asked, "Emma, you don't think I'm your father, do you?"

"Not anymore," she admitted. "You kinda look like him, but I can't really remember him. He's all fuzzy in my head."

Joe felt himself softening toward the girl. "It's been a long time since you've seen him, hasn't it?"

She nodded, her lips closed tightly.

"You must miss him."

"Mom says you can't miss something you never had."

"Does she?" Joe asked rhetorically, wondering what other things Frannie had told her children to help them cope.

"He's not a very nice man so we're probably better off without him," she stated pragmatically.

That was one statement he wasn't about to contest.

"It's too bad you're not our dad," she said on a sigh. "The Admiral would make a nice grandpa."

It was said with such innocence, Joe couldn't help but be touched by the sincerity. "Thank you. That's a very nice thing to say about my father. I know he'd appreciate hearing that."

"Are you going to tell him?"

"Do you want me to?"

Again she smiled shyly. "I guess it's okay."

"For somebody like my father, it's probably the nicest thing anyone could say to him."

"Really?"

"Really."

She didn't comment, but sat quietly for a brief time before announcing, "We're going to Canal Park when we leave here."

"That sounds like fun. There's a lot to do there."

"We couldn't stop the last time we were here because my mom was kinda crabby because of...well, you know," she said with a lift of her brows.

"Yes, I do," he commiserated.

"My friend Ashley told me when she was in Duluth with her mom and dad there was a carnival here, but I didn't see one. Do you know if they have a carnival going on?"

"No, I'm sorry I don't."

"It probably doesn't matter because we're going to stay overnight at a motel with a pool so we can go swimming. I'd rather go swimming than go on rides," she said.

"You're staying overnight in Duluth?"

"Uh-huh. My mom asked her boss if she could take some pictures for the paper and he said yes, so we get to stay overnight." She leaned closer, as if to share a secret. "It's gonna be free because she's working on a story."

Curious, he was about to ask Emma if she knew what pictures her mother would be taking, when a nurse called his name. Not wanting Frannie to leave before he was finished, Joe said to Emma, "Would you tell your mother that I'd like to talk to her before you go?"

"Sure."

"You won't forget, will you?"

"Uh-uh, I won't," she promised.

To Joe's relief, Frannie was sitting in the reception room when he returned. When she saw him, she rose.

"Emma said you wanted to speak to me about something?"

He glanced behind her to where the twins sat watching their every move. "They told you the results would be mailed in a week?"

She nodded. "We'll each get a notarized, legal document. Everything seems fairly straightforward, don't you think?"

He nodded. "Yes. It's just a matter of waiting for the results—Emma said you're staying overnight in Duluth."

"Yes. They wanted to see the sights."

"Want some company?"

"You want to come with us?" It was obvious from the look on her face that she didn't understand why he'd even make such an offer. Neither did he. There was no reason for them to have any further contact, yet he was reluctant to say goodbye to her.

"I thought it might be helpful."

"Helpful?" She looked puzzled.

You don't want to be doing this, a little voice warned him. *Leave now. You've provided the blood sample for the paternity test. You've done all you need to do.*

He didn't listen to the voice. "For Alex. If he spent some time with me he might realize that I'm not his father." It wasn't exactly a lie, but it wasn't the true reason, either.

They spoke in voices that were barely above a whisper, which had the two little people behind them craning their necks to hear. Frannie glanced at the kids, turned back to him and asked, "You said the letters were—" she shifted from one leg to the other "—I guess what I'm trying to say is, wouldn't that only make things more awkward than they already are?"

"Not for me. What about for you?"

It had been a while since he'd looked into a woman's eyes and asked a silent question. By the way she lowered her gaze, he knew that she'd understood this wasn't simply about Alex.

"If circumstances were different, I might have taken you up on your offer." She gave him an apologetic smile.

"You would."

"Yes, I would." This time she held his gaze, and

he could see in her eyes the same message that had been in his. She was interested. Plain and simple.

She glanced again at her children, then back at him. "They're not sure about you," she said in an even lower voice.

"What about you, Frannie? Are you sure about me?"

Again she held his eyes. "Yes."

The receptionist chose that moment to call Joe over to the desk, where she asked him to sign one more form. When he was done, he asked, "Is that everything? We can go?"

Getting an affirmative response, Joe turned and saw that Frannie had gathered her children around her and was getting ready to leave. She extended her hand to him. "Thank you for doing this. I appreciate you coming here today."

"You're welcome," he said, taking her hand in his. It was warm and soft, making him wish he could touch more of her. Seeing the direction his thoughts were taking, he quickly released it.

"I hope everything works out for you."

"Thank you." He held the door for them as they filed out, Emma and Luke each calling out "Bye" as they ducked under his arm. Alex went silently past him.

Joe wondered if the boy had finally accepted that he wasn't his father. Not that it should have mattered to Joe. The trouble was that in a very short time a bond had been established between him and this single mom and her children. He hadn't wanted it to be there, but nevertheless, it was.

As he drove back to Grand Marais, he couldn't stop thinking about them. What were they doing at

Canal Park? Was Alex still sullen or had swimming in the indoor pool lifted his spirits?

One thing Joe knew for certain. They were no longer any concern of his. That should have given him some peace of mind.

It didn't.

By the time he arrived home he was feeling even more restless than he had when he'd left Duluth. Letty noticed, attributing his mood to overwork. She offered to stay and make dinner for the two men.

"That's very kind of you, Letty, but I don't want to put you out," he told her.

"It's no trouble. I enjoy cooking, and to tell you the truth, I really don't feel much like going home to an empty house tonight."

"You have no plans for this evening?"

"Oh, heavens, no. I told you. Anytime you need me to sit with your father, all you have to do is ask. Would you like me to stay the night?"

It was an offer too great to resist. "Actually, I'd like to go back to Duluth if you're sure it wouldn't be an inconvenience for you."

"Of course it's no inconvenience. You go to the city." She gave him a gentle shove. "Heavens, there's more for a young man to do in Duluth than there is up here in the woods, right?" She gave him a wink.

Joe smiled. "Thanks, Letty. You're a peach. I think I'll pack a bag in case it gets too late to drive back tonight."

FRANNIE SPENT MOST of the afternoon at Canal Park feeding the seagulls and watching the ships sail under the aerial lift bridge. Within walking distance from their hotel, the park had much to offer tourists, including a paved walkway skirting the shore of Lake Superior and a marine museum.

After eating burgers at a fast-food restaurant, the four of them went back to the hotel. Emma and Alex never tired of swimming, but Luke, already exhausted from being outside most of the afternoon, fell asleep shortly after they returned. Not even the lure of the kiddie pool and its splashing fountain could keep him awake.

With a poolside suite, Frannie could sit on the patio right outside their room, keep an eye on the sleeping Luke, yet still watch the twins as they swam in the pool. She sat with a towel wrapped around her waist, her one-piece suit still wet from her brief venture into the water with Luke.

"Mom, watch!" Alex called out, climbing out of the pool to run and jump back in, creating a huge splash. "I didn't hold my nose that time," he boasted when his head surfaced.

"Good for you," she called out, waving her approval.

Both kids called to her often as they played in the water. That's why when she heard Alex call out again, "Mom, look!" she expected to see him trying some daring stunt.

He wasn't. He was pointing toward the courtyard leading into the pool area. Frannie leaned forward to see what had captured his attention. What she saw was Joe Smith walking across the cobblestone floor.

Dressed in a pair of dark slacks and a light blue shirt, he looked out of place among the swimsuit-clad bodies lounging around the pool. Out of place, but definitely not uncomfortable. He walked with a quiet confidence that was very different from Dennis's cocky swagger.

She wondered why he was here. It was obvious he was looking for someone by the way his eyes surveyed the area. When his gaze settled on her, she realized she was that someone.

"Joe, hi!" she said, feeling extremely self-conscious at her lack of clothing.

Alex had climbed out of the pool and come over to the patio, water dripping from his wet suit. "What are you doing here?" he demanded of Joe.

"Alex, remember your manners," Frannie reprimanded gently.

Joe looked at Alex. "I have to take care of some business."

"What kind of business?" Alex stood with his arms crossed over his chest and his wet head held high, looking very much like a king defending his throne.

"Alex!" Frannie glared at her son, wishing he would go back into the pool. "I said remember your manners."

"Come on, Alex! We need you to make the teams even," Emma called out, as several kids lined up on opposite ends of the pool to play water volleyball. Frannie could see that Emma didn't find Joe's return as interesting as Alex did.

Joe nodded toward the pool. "Looks like they're waiting for you."

Alex glanced over his shoulder to the kids in the water. "I'll be right there," he called out to them, then he turned to Joe and asked, "Are you here to confess?"

"No, Alex. I have nothing to confess."

From the look on her son's face, Frannie could see he didn't believe Joe.

Then Joe said, "Think about it, Alex. Would I have taken the blood test if I knew it would turn out positive?"

Alex frowned. "Until I see it with my own two eyes, I'm not going to believe it," he said. "You might be able to fool Mom, but you can't fool me." Then he ran and jumped back into the pool.

Joe turned to Frannie. "I guess you were right. It doesn't matter what I say."

She shook her head. "He needs the proof."

"What about you, Frannie?" Joe asked, his eyes fixed on hers.

"You already know the answer to that one," she told him. "I'm surprised you're here."

"So am I," he admitted, looking out over the enclosed area. "I shouldn't be. I try to live an uncomplicated life."

"Then, why did you come?"

He turned back to her. "Because I couldn't stay away."

Her heart reacted immediately to his words, beating erratically. "You mean because of all this stuff with Alex," she said weakly.

"No, I mean because of you." The look in his eyes meant she could no longer pretend he was simply here because she was Alex's mother. "I got all the way back to Grand Marais and I said to myself, 'What am I doing here when I'd rather be someplace else?'"

"I don't know what to say, Joe."

He hooked a patio chair with his foot and pulled it toward him. Then he sat down, straddling it so that his arms rested across the back, and faced her. "Frannie, I'm thirty-three years old. I don't know what your experience has been, but mine is that there are very few times in life when you meet someone and feel a strong connection. I felt that when I met you."

"It would be hard not to after what my son has put you through," she reminded him.

"If that were the case, I'd be annoyed with you, not attracted to you."

He had admitted it. He was attracted to her. Not that she hadn't recognized the silent messages his body language had conveyed.

"Joe, the way we met…" She tried to explain, but didn't quite know what to say.

"Was pretty unusual. I know," he finished.

"It isn't just that."

"Am I wasting my time being here?"

This was her chance to put a stop to any thoughts he might have that something could develop between the two of them. She thought about saying yes, but every instinct she had persuaded her not to be practical. "No."

"Good. I didn't want to think that I was getting so rusty at this that I didn't recognize the signs." He gave her a crooked smile that sent a wave of heat through her body. Excitement made her feel all tingly, as if she were a teenager flirting with the cutest boy in school.

She wasn't a teenager. She was a single mom and she couldn't quite ignore reason. "Joe, I'm really glad you're here but…" She struggled to find the words to tell him it wasn't going to work between them.

"My being here complicates things. We've already established that." He glanced toward the pool. "I know Alex has a weird mix of feelings toward me, but that will all be resolved in a week."

Which meant he intended to start something with her. She was both excited and nervous. "Joe, I have three kids."

"I can count. So what? Are you saying men aren't interested in you because you have kids?"

"Yes, and if you were a single mom you'd know what I'm talking about."

"I'm not afraid of your kids, Frannie."

"You have every right to be after everything that's happened. Most men would—" he cut her off.

"I'm not most men."

No, he definitely wasn't. There weren't many single men who would have had the patience Joe had shown Alex.

"Okay, we've determined your kids aren't a problem," he said. "What about your ex?"

"What about him?"

"Does it bother you that I look like him?"

He watched her steadily as he waited for her answer, and Frannie wondered how she ever could have mistaken him for Dennis. Maybe at first when she'd seen him she'd thought about her ex-husband, but now she only saw a very attractive, intriguing man.

"You don't look like him. I mean you do on the outside, but you're so different from him on the inside that you don't remind me of him at all," she admitted candidly.

"Different in a good way, I hope," he said with another half smile.

"Yes. In a good way," she replied, her answering

smile equally flirtatious. "I really am glad you decided to come back, Joe."

"I am, too." He glanced through the patio door into the hotel suite. "So where's Luke?"

"Asleep."

"How long before the other two are?" He glanced toward the pool. "The way they're jumping around out there, I can't imagine they'll be up very late. The pool closes at ten and the hotel restaurant is open until eleven. We could get something to eat or have a drink in the bar."

She shook her head. "I can't leave them alone in the hotel room."

"I could arrange for room service out here on the patio."

"You don't know how my kids can prolong going to bed," she warned. "It could be late before they've settled down."

"I don't mind waiting. The question is, do you?" He fixed her with another of his penetrating stares, which sent tiny shivers of expectation up and down her arms.

"A glass of wine might be a nice way to end the day, but no dinner," she finally said.

"Not even a few appetizers?"

"Maybe a few," she agreed.

He got up from the chair. "You take care of your kids, and I'll take care of the food and wine. Will ten o'clock be okay for you?"

"Maybe we should make it ten-thirty," Frannie suggested, hoping she could get Alex to sleep before Joe returned. What she didn't need was for her son to be the third party at her date.

Date. Was that what this was? Joe Smith was attracted to her—there was no mistaking that. To her surprise it wasn't scary, but exciting. For the first time in years there was a good-looking man expressing an interest in her—not as a photographer, not as a mother, but as a woman.

"Ten-thirty it is," he told her, giving her a wink that told Frannie it definitely would be a date.

THE FIRST THING Joe did after leaving Frannie was to check into his own suite at the hotel. Then he called Letty to let her know that he'd decided to spend the night in Duluth. Next he called room service and ordered a bottle of wine, two glasses, several appetizers and an assortment of chocolate truffles.

As he waited for time to pass, he sat in the barrel-shaped chair in his room and listed all the reasons why he shouldn't meet Frannie. At the top was the simple fact that he couldn't be completely honest with her. Not a good way to start a relationship, yet under the circumstances he had no choice but to keep his identity a secret.

For the past two years he'd avoided getting involved with any woman. Now he found himself taking risks he had no business taking because of his attraction to Frannie.

Although, it didn't have to be risky if he didn't see her again after tonight. Tomorrow he'd go back to Grand Marais and she'd return to Minneapolis. The lab tests would prove that he was not Alex's father, and thus they'd have no reason to see each other again.

They had no reason to see each other now, he reminded himself. So what was he doing here in Duluth? He thought about ringing her room and telling her something had come up so he wouldn't be able to see her. But as the clock ticked closer to ten-thirty, he knew he wouldn't. He wanted to be with her, to catch a whiff of that floral scent she wore, to see that smile that could make him forget about everything but being with her, to hear the husky voice that reminded him of moonlight on the beach.

When he crossed the swimming pool courtyard and saw her waiting for him on the patio outside her room, he knew he'd made the right decision. The only light came from the pool, which shone like an emerald in the darkened atrium. As he drew closer to her, he saw she wore a long denim skirt and a pink knit top that had a tiny zipper instead of buttons down the front.

"You were right," she said. "The kids went right to sleep."

"You look lovely," he told her, wishing he could think of a more original greeting, but it had been a long time since he'd had to come up with one. And then there was that zipper on her shirt. It was lowered just far enough to reveal a tempting valley between her breasts.

When a knock at the door announced the arrival of room service, she excused herself. Seconds later, Joe watched as the waiter pushed a cart into the room and then out onto the patio. He draped a white linen tablecloth over the wrought-iron table, then transferred from the cart to the table two place settings of

china and flatware, the food, the wine and two can-
dles that he lit before leaving.

"Such elegance," Frannie said, fingering the linen
napkin. "I'm not used to this. Normally the kids and
I stay in places where you're lucky to get plastic cups
and a clean towel."

He liked the fact that she didn't seem embarrassed
by such a statement. He pulled a chair out for her
and said, "I've seen my share of those places, too."

"I'm sure as a pilot you've done more traveling
than I have," she said, before taking a sip of the wine
the waiter had poured.

He realized he needed to be careful how much he
told her about himself, and decided it would be better
to change the subject. "Then, you don't do much
traveling for business?"

"No, with the kids, I haven't been able to accept
work out of town, at least not until now. We're only
staying in this nice hotel because I'm working."

He smiled. "I know. Emma told me."

"Then, you know I'm a photojournalist?"

"It was in one of the letters Alex sent."

She shook her head. "Should I feel embarrassed
over what he told you?"

He swirled the wine in his glass. "Not at all. You
have good kids, Frannie."

"Good kids who talk too much," she said with a
chuckle.

He put a spoonful of calamari on his plate. "I find
what they have to say interesting." He looked at her
across the candlelight and said, "I find you interesting. Tell me about your work."

"As my kids said, I take pictures that tell stories."

''What's the story you want to tell tomorrow?''

''It's a personal interest piece, so I'll try to capture the story of a man's life. That's the challenging part. Anyone can take a picture, but to capture emotion is another thing.''

''Were you always interested in photography?''

She took a sip of wine, then said, ''Actually, I wasn't. I more or less stumbled into the field. After my divorce, I went to work for a newspaper as an office clerk, which meant I did an assortment of jobs—mostly those that no one else wanted to do.''

''One day a photographer needed an extra pair of hands. I supplied them. Before long, he was showing me how to work in the darkroom, and the rest is, as they say, history. I was lucky. Not many people get on-the-job training in photography.''

''So you didn't go to college?''

''Not for photography. After high school my girl-friend and I went to Florida. We were going to be marine biologists.''

She chuckled, and he asked, ''And what's so funny about that?''

''I liked the thought of living in Florida and being around the ocean more than I liked science. I only lasted one semester at college. I met Dennis, dropped out of school and got married.'' She shook her head in regret. ''Not the smartest move I ever made.''

''Were you a teenager when you married?''

She nodded. ''I was almost twenty.'' She sighed wistfully. ''It seems like a lifetime ago. If I knew then what I know now…''

''Hindsight's twenty-twenty and all that,'' he said with a knowing grin. ''And be honest. Aren't you glad you're doing the work you're doing now rather than cutting open some diseased sea creature?''

She smiled. ''Yes. Take this assignment I have tomorrow.'' She went on to tell him about the man she was to photograph.

Joe liked listening to her talk about her work. She was passionate as she explained the business and how it was changing, her eyes sparkling as she described the challenges of working under deadline yet still capturing images with meaning.

''You find your work emotionally and intellectually stimulating. That's good. Not everyone does,'' he said, refilling her glass with wine.

''I do like it. And I've been rambling on about it. I'm sorry.''

''Don't apologize,'' he said covering her hand with his. ''I'm interested.''

''Tell me what it's like to be a pilot.''

He shrugged, not wanting to talk about himself. ''The hours are good,'' he said with a grin. ''And the scenery can be breathtaking at times. I work for a small flight service that provides both cargo and passenger service. Mainly they fly fishermen to lakes where there's no other access.''

''You're not from Minnesota originally, are you?''

''No, my family's from out east, but being the son of a military man I don't really call one place home. When I was growing up we moved often. I've lived on quite a few naval bases.''

''So how did you end up on the North Shore?'' she asked.

''It's scenic, it's quiet, plenty of fishing...seemed

like a good place for my dad,'' he answered cautiously.

"He told me he didn't choose to retire here,'' she said.

"When did he tell you that?'' he asked, wondering if there was anything else his father might have said to Frannie.

"That morning after the storm. I think he misses the military.''

Joe nodded. "It's been a difficult adjustment for him.''

"What about for you?''

He shrugged. "Personally, I prefer civilian life. And this is a beautiful part of the country.''

Realizing it was necessary to steer the conversation away from himself, he changed the subject again. By the time the last of the wine had been poured, they'd covered a wide range of topics from favorite movies and books to current events and politics. He knew they would have gone on talking, but Luke staggered into the parlor. Joe saw him out of the corner of his eye.

"Someone's up,'' he said, gesturing toward the glass patio door.

Frannie slid the door open, and Joe heard Luke say, "I gots to go potty, Mommy.''

"Come on,'' she said, scooping him up into her arms and carrying him to the bathroom. A few· minutes later, when he'd been tucked back in bed, Frannie returned.

She didn't sit back down, but remained standing. "I had no idea it was so late!''

Joe knew it was his cue to leave. Reluctantly, he rose. "I enjoyed tonight, Frannie."

"Me, too. I'm just sorry it has to end."

"I'd like to see you again."

"Joe..." Her voice had an apologetic tone to it that he didn't like.

There was only one way to convince her she shouldn't end this. He pulled her into his arms and kissed her. She seemed startled at first, her lips firm and unyielding as he pressed against them. Then, as he slowly coaxed a response from her, her body relaxed, her arms sliding across his shoulders. She pulled him closer, her lips parting to receive his tongue. As the kiss deepened, she moved against him, letting him know she wanted him as much as he wanted her.

When the kiss finally ended, they were both breathing heavily. "Guess what happened the night of the storm wasn't my imagination, was it."

She simply shook her head.

"You felt what I did, didn't you?"

She nodded.

"Good. I want to see you again," he said, his forehead gently pressing against hers, his breath warm against her cheek.

"But you live in Grand Marais and I live in Minneapolis."

"Aren't you going to be in Duluth tomorrow?" he asked next to her ear, nibbling along her neck with his lips.

"Yes, but so are my kids."

"Just because I like kissing you doesn't mean I

can't be happy simply being with you,'' he said huskily.

To his surprise, she pulled his head back to hers, leaving him in no doubt that she, too, liked kissing him.

''I'd better go,'' he said when it had ended, then placed one more butterfly kiss on her mouth before starting across the courtyard.

''What about tomorrow?'' she called after him.

''I'll be in touch,'' he answered, then went back to his room before his hormones got him into any more trouble.

CHAPTER EIGHT

JOE WAS HANDSOME, intelligent and romantic. What more could a woman ask for? He stood before Frannie with a dozen red roses in one hand, a box of chocolates in the other and a look in his eye that sent shivers of pleasure through her.

"I want you."

The words flowed around her, intoxicating her like a fine wine. She'd forgotten how powerful physical attraction could be.

"Who's that?" she asked, noticing the older woman behind him.

"A licensed child care provider. She's going to stay with the kids so we can spend the entire day together without any interruptions."

Excitement bubbled up inside her. "You did all this for me?"

He nodded. "I want you."

For Frannie they were three heart-stopping, breath-taking words.

"Say that again," she murmured.

"I want you!"

"Again," she begged.

"I want food!"

Food? With a jerk Frannie opened her eyes and saw Luke leaning over her. It had been a dream. She wasn't with Joe, but on the pull-out sofa with a three-year-old in her face. She sighed.

Last night had been no dream. She felt a tingle of pleasure at the memory. She and Joe had shared a bottle of wine, eaten calamari and crab cakes and talked into the wee hours of the morning. He may not have said the words ''I want you,'' but his kisses had conveyed that message very well.

''Mommy, get up. I'm hungry.'' Luke interrupted her thoughts for a second time.

She glanced at the clock. It was barely past six and her head ached. ''It's too early to get up. Let Mommy rest a bit longer,'' she pleaded, grimacing at the thought of how little sleep she'd had. What had she been thinking to allow Joe to stay until almost three in the morning?

She knew the answer to that question without any great soul-searching. Last night he'd made her remember what it was like to be a woman, and she'd liked that feeling. So much so that she hadn't wanted him to leave even though she knew it was crazy to be entertaining thoughts of asking him to stay.

''But Mommy, I'm hungry,'' Luke whined.

''All right,'' she mumbled, throwing the covers aside and getting out of bed. As she staggered across the room, she grimaced in pain, unsure whether the headache was from a lack of sleep or from having had more than one glass of wine.

Whatever the cause, she needed aspirin. She found some in her purse, quickly swallowed them with a glass of water, then dug through the bag of food she'd brought along for the kids until she found the box of cereal and a small bowl.

Using the remote control, she turned on the TV,

set Luke beside her on the bed, poured the cereal into the bowl and handed it to him. "Watch TV and eat your Cheerios while Mommy rests, okay?"

She knew she couldn't go back to sleep, but she needed to lie down and close her eyes or else the throbbing in her head would never go away. She couldn't afford to miss her appointment with Howard Peterson—not after she'd been given the hotel suite at the newspaper's expense.

To her relief, Luke was content to watch cartoons and munch on his cereal. However, she'd just lowered her head to the pillow when he said, "Mommy, I can't hear the TV."

Without lifting her head, she groped for the remote, bringing it close so she didn't have to lift her head to see the buttons. "We have to keep it low so we don't wake up Emma and Alex," she told him as she increased the volume slightly.

Hearing his "okay," she closed her eyes, willing the pain reliever to take effect so that the top of her head didn't feel as if it might follow the shuttle into orbit. Oh, why had she allowed Joe to refill her wineglass?

Because she liked wine. Besides she hadn't had all *that* much to drink. Certainly not enough to warrant such a throbbing headache. She'd shared the company of an attractive man who'd made her feel special. It had been one of the nicest evenings she'd had in a very long time and worth the headache she was suffering from this morning.

She allowed her thoughts to drift back to their conversation. There'd been none of the usual posturing men and women often did when getting to know one another. It had been easy—so easy that Frannie had felt as if she'd been talking to a good friend.

Only, this morning it wasn't the talking that stood out in her mind. It was the way she'd reacted to his kisses. She supposed it was only natural. Since Luke was born there'd been very little kissing in her life. And none that could even come close to being as passionate as last night's.

When Joe had kissed her at the lake, it had been to prove something. Last night he'd taken her in his arms for completely different reasons. There had been no mistaking the hunger those kisses had stirred. It was an intoxicating thought, and one that stayed with her as she drifted in and out of sleep.

The next time Frannie opened her eyes, Emma was next to Luke and was channel surfing with the remote. Frannie forced herself to her elbows and asked, "What time is it?"

"Seven-fifteen," Emma answered. "Were you dreaming? You had a funny smile on your face."

Frannie hoped her face wasn't as red as it felt. "Actually, I had a headache, which is why I fell back to sleep. Is Alex up?"

"Uh-uh. Do we really get breakfast free?"

"Yes, it's included with the room." Frannie sat up. "We should probably get going. My appointment's at ten. Watch Luke while I shower, okay?"

"Sure."

By the time she'd showered and dressed, Alex, too, was lying on the pull-out sofa, watching TV. As soon as he saw his mom he asked, "Can we go swimming this morning?"

"I told you I have work to do," she reminded him.

"Not till ten." He went over to the patio door and

pulled back the heavy drape. There in plain sight was the table still set with linen and the dirty dishes. "Where'd that come from?" He shot his mother an accusing glance.

"I had room service after you went to bed last night," she replied, trying to make it sound as if it were no big deal. "Emma, find Luke's shoes, will you? Everyone needs to get dressed so we can go eat. I have to be at Howard Peterson's by ten." She walked over and pulled the curtain shut again.

But Alex's curiosity had been aroused. He once more pushed it aside and opened the patio door.

Emma shrieked, "You can't go out to the pool in your pajamas!"

He didn't go out to the pool. He stepped onto the patio and examined the dishes on the table, then he stood in the open doorway, his hands on his hips. "How come there are two glasses?"

Frannie could have kicked herself for not getting rid of the evidence. All she would have had to do was gather the dishes onto the room service tray and set them outside the door. Someone would have picked them up. Now Alex was snooping around like a detective examining the scene of a crime.

"Room service always sends two of everything," Frannie lied, ignoring the guilt that pounded her conscience like the waves pounded the rocky shores of Lake Superior. She stepped around him and began gathering the dishes onto the serving tray. "Go get dressed so we can have breakfast."

He picked up the empty wine bottle. "You drank a whole bottle of wine?"

"Alex, did you hear me?" Her voice became stern. "I said go get dressed."

She gave him one of her looks that warned him he'd better drop the subject and do as he was told or risk her wrath. To her relief, the look still worked, and he stepped back inside the suite, mumbling something to Emma as he passed her.

Frannie didn't ask her daughter what he'd said, but took the tray with the incriminating dishes and set it outside the door. As Emma helped her tidy the room and put their things back in the suitcase, Frannie could see that her daughter was as curious as Alex was about what had happened after they'd gone to bed.

After all the lies that Dennis had told the children, Frannie had sworn always to be honest with them, even if the truth meant answering difficult questions. She didn't want to break that vow, but today she didn't need the distraction a discussion involving Joe would create. Later she would tell them he'd been there last night, but not now.

By the time they headed for the dining room where breakfast was being served, she'd had enough curious looks from both Emma and Alex to send her on a mammoth guilt trip. Frannie could only hope that Joe wouldn't be at breakfast. What she didn't want to have to deal with over oatmeal and muffins was her growing attraction to the man, as well as Alex's increasingly suspicious feelings regarding him.

While the kids headed for the serving line, she made a quick survey of the room. About half the tables were taken, and to Frannie's dismay, Joe was at one of them. He sat alone at a large round table, a newspaper in front of him, a cup of coffee next to his hand.

It didn't take long for Alex to see him, too. "What's he doing here?" he asked his mother.

"Probably having breakfast like everyone else," Frannie answered. Just then, Joe looked up. His smile made her breath catch in her throat.

"Why's he coming over here?" Alex asked as Joe set the newspaper aside and started across the dining room.

"I don't think he's eaten yet. There aren't any dishes on his table," Emma guessed.

Luke had spotted the scrambled eggs and was making it known that he wanted some. Frannie reached for a tray, welcoming the diversion.

"Maybe he wants to eat with us. It's not very much fun to be by yourself," Emma said as Joe approached them.

"He's not going to eat with us, is he?" Alex looked at Frannie.

"I don't know," Frannie answered, putting some scrambled eggs onto Luke's plate.

"Mom, don't let him!" Alex begged her.

She sighed. "Please don't do this, Alex. The man has been very patient and understanding of everyone's feelings, especially yours. Just be quiet and behave yourself."

He looked as if he wanted to sulk, but Emma remarked, "Oh, look! Chocolate chip pancakes. And they even have whipped cream! Hurry, Alex. There aren't very many left."

Alex grabbed a tray and headed toward his sister. Relieved, Frannie added a small cup of applesauce and a muffin to Luke's tray, just as Joe's voice sounded over her shoulder.

"Good morning."

"Hi. I'm getting Luke his breakfast," she said, stating the obvious.

"I can see that," he said with a heart-stopping grin. "Did you sleep well?"

"Fine, thank you," she muttered. "And you?"

"Very well." The look in his eyes told her he was remembering what had happened between them last night. It was as if they shared a secret, and Frannie, to her embarrassment, blushed.

"Mom, where should we sit?" Emma relieved the tension, looking at her mother with a full tray in her hands.

"Why don't you join me? There's plenty of room," Joe suggested. "And it's right next to the beverage bar."

Before Frannie had a chance to respond, Alex said, "It's better to be up front 'cause then we can go back for more food if we want."

It wasn't because of Alex that Frannie hesitated. She'd realized that she'd never eaten a meal with her children and a man other than Dennis. She'd never made it to that point in any relationship, and a little voice in her head told her she shouldn't be at that stage with Joe.

However, the truth was, seeing Joe made her feel good. But if he was going to be scared away by her children, she figured she might as well make the discovery now, rather than later.

"Near the beverage counter is good. Thank you, Joe," she said, motioning for Emma and Alex to follow her as she carried Luke's tray to the table that held Joe's coffee cup and newspaper. She ignored the clicking of her older son's tongue.

As soon as the three kids had beverages, flatware

and napkins, Frannie went back to the serving line to get her own tray. Joe was right behind her.

"I lied earlier," he said close to her ear.

"About what?" she asked, aware of his nearness.

"Sleeping well. I tossed and turned because I couldn't stop thinking about you, Frannie." The words were like a soft caress.

"We had a nice time last night," she said, willing her hand not to shake as she reached for half a grapefruit. She'd forgotten how to flirt with a man, and she felt very inexperienced and nervous.

"It was better than nice," he said, spooning up some eggs.

Determined to be poised, she looked him straight in the eye and said, "Yes, it was."

"I'd like to spend today with you."

"Unfortunately, I have work to do," she reminded him, turning her attention back to the food.

"What about the kids?"

"They're coming with me."

"I could come along and keep them entertained for you," he offered.

"As much as I'd like to say yes, I'm not sure that's such a good idea." She glanced over her shoulder—as she expected, Alex watched them with an eagle eye.

He noticed. "Because of Alex?"

"Because I'd be distracted," she said with a slow grin.

"I'll take that as a compliment."

"It was meant as one," she said, finally warming to flirtation.

"Good, because last night was…" He paused, his gaze not allowing her to look away. "I know this is going to sound crazy, but even though we haven't spent very much time together, I feel as if I've known you a long time. Everything seems easy…and right.''

"I know what you mean. I feel that way, too," she admitted. "In a short time we've discovered a lot about one another, haven't we."

"I want to get to know more." There was more than desire in his voice. There was promise. And hope.

"That will be a little simpler once we get the lab results," she said as she reached the end of the serving line. She paused to wait for him.

"And Alex accepts I'm not his father."

"Yes." They started toward the table, ending any further conversation.

It was with more than a little trepidation that Frannie sat down with Luke on one side and Alex on the other. She wanted to think that in public her children would be on their best behavior, but she also knew that Alex was already cranky, and when it came to Luke, she never knew when her son would do something outrageous.

To her relief, there was no food thrown, no bathroom words uttered for shock effect, no bickering over imagined offenses. It helped that Alex chose to be quiet, that Emma was fascinated by everything Joe said and that Luke actually ate with a spoon instead of his fingers.

The only difficult moment came after Luke asked for more chocolate milk. Joe went to get it, and returned with a full glass. Before Frannie could reach over and help Luke, he had grabbed the glass and it tipped over onto the table, shooting a stream of dark brown liquid in Joe's direction. Luke howled, and

Joe's eyes widened as chocolate milk pooled in his lap.

"Oh my gosh, I'm sorry," Frannie exclaimed, reaching over to right the tipped glass. "Emma, go get extra napkins," she ordered, trying to mop up as best she could with the one she had.

Joe shoved his chair back to get away from the milk still trickling over the edge of the table. Frannie tried to calm Luke and at the same time not be appalled by the size of the wet spot on Joe's trousers.

"Joe, I'm so sorry," she repeated, having to talk louder than normal to be heard over Luke's wailing. "This is my fault. I should have told you to only fill the glass halfway."

He waved away her apology. "Don't worry about it. I'll be fine," he said, taking the stack of napkins Emma held out to him. While he blotted his trousers, Frannie managed to get Luke to stop crying by holding him on her lap.

When she tried to get Luke to return to his own chair, he refused, keeping his head tucked close to her chest, his lower lip pushed out in a pout. He continued to stare at Joe. So did Emma and Alex, who watched him attempt to clean up his trousers.

"You look like you wet your pants," Alex said with obvious amusement.

"Alex!" Frannie chastised him, mortified.

"You know what, Alex? I think you're right," Joe said as he continued to wipe at the milk. "What I need is one of those towels the football players have dangling from their waistbands. That would cover it, don't you think?" he said with a wink.

"You could carry a jacket and then no one would

see it,'' Emma suggested. ''If you want, I can let you use mine.''

Joe bestowed a grateful smile on her. ''That's all right, Emma. It's not a big deal.'' As if to prove his point, he got up and went over to the beverage counter to get Luke another glass of chocolate milk. This one he only filled halfway.

Frannie tried to get Luke off her lap and back into his own chair, but again he refused to budge. When Joe returned, he set the glass in front of Frannie.

''There you go, Luke. This one's a little easier to handle.'' Then he tousled the boy's hair affectionately.

''Thank you, Joe,'' Frannie said. Then she reached for the glass and held it up for Luke, who placed his fingers next to hers and took a long swallow.

''Now I know you're not my dad,'' Emma remarked, as Joe sat back down. ''He always yelled at us if we got anything on his pants. Remember, Alex? He never wanted us to sit on his lap because he was worried we'd get dirt on him. Sometimes he even spanked us if he had on his good pants.''

Alex didn't say a word, but continued to eat his pancakes, his eyes downcast. Joe, on the other hand, looked at Frannie, his eyes filled with empathy.

''Emma, finish eating,'' she instructed, not wanting the topic of conversation to be her ex-husband. ''We're going to have to leave pretty soon so I won't be late for my appointment.''

Alex finally lifted his head. ''How long is it going to take?'' It was evident he wasn't enthusiastic about having to go with his mother.

''Not long,'' Frannie answered. ''Mr. Peterson said there's a park right across the street from his

house where you, Emma and Luke can play.'' She
avoided Joe's eyes because she didn't want him asking again if she wanted his help.

Not that she needed to worry about it. He said
nothing about his plans for the rest of the day and
appeared to be content to say goodbye to all of them
as they left the cafeteria. She wondered if the chocolate milk fiasco had caused him to have a change
of heart.

When she returned to her room she discovered she
was wrong. She'd just walked in the door when he
phoned.

''Hi. I know you're getting ready to leave for your
appointment, but I needed to call and tell you one
more thing.''

Just hearing his voice was enough to make her feel
short of breath. ''And what's that?'' she asked, trying
not to let him know the effect it had on her.

''That I would never hurt any of your children,
Frannie.''

She had to swallow back the lump of emotion that
threatened to block her throat. ''I know that,'' she
said, because she believed it to be true. Her instincts
told her that he was a good man and that she had
nothing to fear from him.

''And I also want to tell you that I want to see
you again.''

''That's two things,'' she told him, smiling to herself.

''I could add quite a few more, but I guess I'd
better let you get to work. You just need to answer
one question. Will I see you again?''

Frannie knew this was her opportunity to tell him
she was worried about how fast everything was hap-

pening. She could easily put an end to their relationship before it went any further. If she said no, she'd never hear from him again. He was that kind of man.

Saying no would be the sensible thing to do. After all, he was a single man taking care of his father in Grand Marais, and she was a single mom taking care of three kids in Minneapolis. She knew better than to expect anything to develop between them.

"Frannie, are you still there?"

"Yes."

"Will I see you again?"

"It's not going to be easy. Grand Marais is a long way from Minneapolis.

"Let me worry about that, okay?"

"Okay. What about next week…after we get the lab results."

"Great. We'll celebrate."

"Celebrate?"

"That I'm not Alex's father. I'm not a deadbeat, Frannie."

"I know." And as she hung up the phone, she knew that what he said was true.

FRANNIE DECIDED not to mention her evening with Joe to her sister. She knew she would have to tell Lois *when* and *if* something developed. Right now, Frannie didn't want to talk about feelings that were so new and unfamiliar. She should have realized, however, that her children regarded her life as an open book to be shared with the world.

"All right, out with it," Lois commanded the following evening when she stopped by on her way home from work and plopped herself down next to Frannie on the back stoop.

"Out with what?" Frannie asked, keeping an eye on Luke who was making tunnels and roads in the sandbox.

"Alex told me about the wine."

"The wine?" Frannie feigned ignorance.

"At the hotel in Duluth. You're either becoming a lush or you had someone to help you drink it. Which was it?"

Frannie knew she'd been caught. "When did Alex tell you that?"

"That's not important," Lois said with a wave of her hand. "Two glasses, two dirty plates...sounds to me like you had a guest. Now, let me guess. You picked up a strange man in the bar?" She held up her hand before Frannie could deny anything and said, "No, wait! I bet you met a guy while you were swimming with the kids at the pool."

"Since you already know the answer, why don't you just come out and tell *me* what happened?" Frannie asked dryly.

"All right. What is going on with you and this Joe Smith?"

"Nothing is *going on*," she replied. "We had some wine and we talked, that's all." She wondered if her nose grew with that statement.

"Alex said you had breakfast with him, too."

Frannie sighed impatiently. "For Pete's sake. We ran into him in the cafeteria. It wasn't arranged."

"So he stayed over in Duluth because you were there?" She could feel her sister scrutinizing every facial gesture she made.

"Will you stop? I feel as if I'm in the witness box."

"I'm not interrogating you, I'm just curious, that's

all. You're my little sister, and I wouldn't be a good big sister if I didn't look out for you.''

"You think I can't take care of myself when it comes to men? Lois, I'm thirty years old.''

"Yes, and most of the teenagers I see are more worldly about men than you are.''

"Gee, thanks.'' Again sarcasm was her only defense.

"It's true. You've had one lousy boyfriend your entire life, and he turned out to be one lousy husband. You're a babe in the woods when it comes to men.''

"Believe me, I learned everything I need to know about men when I divorced Dennis,'' she assured her.

"That's what has me concerned. Are you sure you're not attracted to this Joe Smith because he looks like Dennis?''

"We've been through this before. Joe doesn't look like Dennis. I mean he does, but he doesn't.'' Frannie realized how strange that must sound to her sister. "Haven't you ever noticed how people's appearances change once you get to know them? When you first see Joe you can't help but notice he looks like Dennis, but then once you talk to him and discover what kind of guy he is, you realize he's nothing at all like Dennis.''

Her sister didn't look convinced, and Frannie added, "You'll see what I'm talking about when you meet him.''

Her sister's brows lifted. "I'm going to get to meet him?''

"If things work out, yeah,'' she said, although the thought of her sister meeting Joe did make her a bit nervous.

"Then, you're definitely interested in this guy?"

She knew there was no point lying. "I like him. He's different from most men."

"Different how?"

She shrugged. "I don't know, he just is. Look, if you don't mind, I'd really rather not talk about this. I mean, something could develop between us, then again maybe it won't."

"What about Alex's feelings?"

"That's what has me being cautious. Alex's attitude makes it very awkward for all of us. I'll be relieved to get the DNA test results so I can show him that he's wrong about Joe being his father."

"Please don't get upset with me for asking this, but are you one hundred percent sure he's not Dennis?"

Frannie chuckled. "Of course. You think I wouldn't know if I were kissing my ex-husband?"

Lois gasped. "You said talked! Now you say you kissed?"

"Just shush. Here comes Emma." Frannie was grateful that her daughter came bouncing into the backyard. She'd said far too much already. Sooner or later she'd tell Lois just how fast she'd fallen for the man. But not yet.

FRANNIE WAS WITH HER EDITOR going over the shots she'd taken in Duluth when one of her co-workers stuck her head inside the office and said, "There's someone out front to see you."

"Can you ask who it is?"

"I already did. Says his name is Joe Smith."

Joe was here? Frannie was almost giddy at the thought.

What she was feeling must have shown on her face, for her boss said, "You want to finish this after lunch?"

"You don't mind?" Frannie asked, then on feet that felt more like wings, went down to the lobby to find Joe.

He stood in the reception area, examining framed copies of the newspaper that hung on the wall, his hands in the pockets of his khaki pants. To Frannie, he had never looked more attractive, and her heart did a little flip-flop.

"Hi, Joe."

He turned, and her heart rolled right over in her chest as he gave her the most tantalizing smile. It said, "I'm happy to see you," and had her grinning right back at him.

"I couldn't wait a week," he said, looking at her as if she were the most beautiful sight he'd ever seen. Apparently it didn't matter to him that she wore an old pair of jeans and a faded tunic top. "I thought I'd take you to lunch—that is, if you're free."

"You drove all the way down here to take me to lunch?" If he wanted to sweep her off her feet, he'd accomplished his goal.

"Actually, I flew. There are advantages to having your own plane."

She chuckled. "I guess there are."

"So what do you say? Will you have lunch with me?"

"Yes, I'd love to," she said, seeing no point in playing any games. She wanted to be with him and would have done whatever was necessary to arrange her schedule to fit his. She looked down at her clothes and said, "I'm not exactly dressed for any-place fancy, though."

"That's good because I hadn't planned on going to anyplace fancy," he told her with another grin.

The place he had planned to take her was a park within walking distance of the newspaper's head-quarters, one with bike paths and hiking trails that followed a stretch of the Mississippi. It was a popular place during the lunch hour, as workers often es-caped from their offices to walk along one of the paved paths or sit on one of the benches to soak up the summer sun.

Joe managed to find a quiet, secluded spot near the water's edge, far away from the inline skaters and joggers. He spread a blue-and-green plaid blanket on the ground, where they ate sandwiches he'd bought at a deli and drank iced tea from cans. Even though Joe made no attempt to kiss her, it was the most romantic lunch Frannie had ever had.

Neither wanted their time together to end. As he walked her back to her office, he offered to check into a hotel and stay the night so that they could have dinner. Frannie was tempted to say yes, knowing that if he had a hotel room there was a good chance they'd share more than kisses.

She also knew that until the business with Alex had been settled, she couldn't take that step. So once again they agreed to wait until after the test results came before making any more plans.

The rest of the afternoon she found it difficult to concentrate on work, wondering just when she'd see him again.

Normally time flew by, but the rest of the week seemed endless to Frannie, who eagerly picked up the mail hoping to find the test results. It didn't help that every day Alex asked, "Has it come yet?" adding to her own anxiety.

Except for the daily enquiry, Alex had been unusually quiet. Frannie suspected that he was finally beginning to accept that Joe wasn't his father. She regarded the entire situation as a no-win deal for her son. As much as he professed to hate his father, she'd seen the look of hope that came into his eyes whenever the mail carrier came down the street.

But the test results didn't come by regular mail. Nor did they come within a week. They came on the eighth day, early in the morning by special delivery. Alex, who normally would have been home, had already left to spend the day at Valleyfair Amusement Park with his little league team.

Frannie knew before she opened the envelope what the contents would say. It didn't take DNA to confirm what she already knew. Joe Smith was not Dennis Harper.

That's why when she tore open the seal and read the notarized document inside, she gasped. According to the very official-looking legal report, the conclusion drawn by the DNA test was that Joe Smith was the biological father of Alex Harper.

FRANNIE'S MOUTH went dry, her heart raced in her chest. She stood staring at the paper, her hands trembling so much that the print on the document blurred. *Joe Smith was Dennis Harper.* It had to be a mistake, but then she read the letter that said paternity could be determined to a ninety-nine percent accuracy.

Feeling sick, she clutched her stomach. Images flashed in her mind. Being in his arms, kissing him, touching him, him touching her. Lies! All lies! How could she have been such a fool!

I feel as if we've known each other a long time. His words echoed in her head. They *had* known each other a long time! He was Dennis Harper, only instead of simply being a lousy husband and father, he was now pretending to be another man. He'd played yet another game with her and she'd been foolish enough to fall into the trap.

She shuddered at the thought of how she'd fantasized about making love with him. That certainly would have made his little game worthwhile. Disgust consumed her, distorting all rational thinking.

She grabbed her head with her hands, trying to think of what she should do. None of it made any sense.

She reached for the phone and dialed her sister's office number. "Hi, it's Frannie. Can I speak to Lois?"

"I'm sorry but she's in court all day. I don't expect her back until late this afternoon," the receptionist told her. "Shall I have her call you?"

"Yes...er no, it's all right. I'll catch up with her later," Frannie said, slamming down the receiver. *In court all day.* It could be hours before she spoke to her sister.

Frannie was beside herself. She needed to do something and to do it now. She couldn't let the man get away with this!

Again she reached for the phone. This time she dialed her neighbor. "Lisa, it's Frannie. Is there any chance the kids could stay with you today? I wouldn't ask you if it wasn't really important."

"MISTAKE, IT HAS TO BE a mistake." Frannie wasn't sure how many times she repeated those words to herself as she drove to Grand Marais. Probably about the same number of times she told herself "DNA doesn't lie."

This trip to Grand Marais was nearly as torturous on her emotions as the last one had been. While searching for Alex she'd been overwhelmed with worry, fearing for his safety, panicked by the unknown.

This time she was filled with anger. It was a powerful emotion. She could think of nothing but confronting Dennis face to face.

If she could find him.

Maybe he'd agreed they wouldn't see each other again until after the test results came because he knew he'd be gone. Maybe he had already moved his father far away from the small Minnesota town. It wouldn't surprise her. He never stayed in one place long.

The thought that she could be on a wild-goose chase caused her heart to pound in her throat. Was she making this trip for nothing?

At the next exit she stopped at a pay phone and dialed Joe Smith's number. It rang and rang and rang. Her heart rate increased. Had he already made his escape? Was she behaving irrationally, coming all this way without considering the consequences?

Of course she was. When it came to Dennis, there had never been any rational behavior. Instead of thinking clearly, she acted quickly. It had always been that way. It was the reason she'd married him. It was the reason she was in her car and driving to

Grand Marais instead of waiting for Lois to help her sort through the mess.

If she were rational, she'd turn back. Only, she couldn't. She needed to know why he'd lied. What he thought he'd accomplish by pretending to be another man. How he could be so cruel to his own children. How he could break her heart.

As she pulled into the long drive leading to his home, she no longer mumbled to herself but talked out loud as if she had an audience. "If he's not here, I go straight to the police," she stated firmly.

But he was there—at least, both of his cars were. She parked behind them and climbed out. Up to the door she marched.

With her fist she pounded on the screen door. "I know you're in there," she called out, but there was no response. Boldly, she stepped inside. The kitchen, the living room and the breakfast nook were all vacant. A peek into each bedroom revealed nothing.

Then she saw them. The suitcases. They were next to the rear door. So he *was* getting ready to make his escape!

Where was he? she asked herself when it became evident that the house was empty. On her way back outside she caught a glimpse of something in the water. It was a man.

"I've got you now and you're not going to get away with it," she warned, as she headed toward the beach.

CHAPTER NINE

WHEN WEATHER PERMITTED, Joe liked to begin each day with a swim. Before the sun had even risen this morning he'd taken his father to the hospital where the Admiral would undergo a series of neurological tests for the next few days. After spending the morning with his dad, Joe had come home feeling tense and in need of exercise. A look at the cool, sparkling water had him grabbing a towel and heading straight for the lake. One by one he shed his clothing, dropping each piece in a pile on the shore.

When he'd first moved to Minnesota, he'd been reluctant to swim in the nude, even though the real estate agent had assured him that Nature's Hideaway was truly what the name implied. Joe's retreat provided the ultimate in privacy on a lake with no public access. Still, Joe had needed to experience the isolation for himself before he'd trusted the agent's word.

Except for a farmhouse belonging to an elderly woman on the opposite side of the lake, there was nothing but trees along the shoreline. No people, no boats—just ducks, loons and an occasional beaver disturbing the water. Nature was Joe's only company when he swam.

But today nature seemed to take on the shape of a woman. He glanced toward the shore and squinted, convinced he must be seeing things. Then a woman with blond hair stepped onto the dock, and he knew he wasn't.

It wasn't just any woman. It was Frannie. Joe swam closer to the dock, stopping in water chest-deep so as to keep most of his body hidden.

"Frannie, what are you doing here?"

"Get out of the water." There was no warmth in her voice, no smile on her face.

"Frannie, I can't get out with you standing there."

"I spoiled your getaway, did I?" she drawled sarcastically.

Getaway? Did she realize that he wasn't wearing any swim trunks? "All right you caught me," he said giving her a big grin. "Now, if you'll just go wait for me in the house, I'll be with you shortly."

"You think I'm leaving you alone for five minutes? I saw the suitcases."

He wondered what she was talking about. "You think I'm going somewhere?"

"Not if I have anything to say about it. Now get out of the water." She barked at him as if he were a child who'd disobeyed her instructions.

"I can't get out."

"Why not?" she asked impatiently.

"Because the only thing keeping you from seeing all of me *is* the water," he told her.

"You're naked?"

He expected she might be shocked, but he didn't think she'd be disgusted. Could this be the same woman who had trembled with desire when he'd held her in his arms?

"There's no point in wearing swim trunks when

you have an entire lake to yourself,'' he justified, not that it made a difference in her demeanor.

"Get out of the water,'' she ordered again.

"Frannie, didn't you hear me? I said I'm not wearing swim trunks.''

She put her hand on her waist. "So what? I've already seen what you have, and believe me it's of little consequence.''

She'd seen what he had? "You're not making any sense.''

"And what kind of sense would you like me to make, *Dennis?*''

Dennis? She thought he was her ex-husband? "We already settled that I'm not Dennis.''

"No, you lied and told me you weren't. And I was stupid enough to believe you—again.'' She shook her head. "I can't believe what a fool I've been! You're despicable! How could you be so low as to lie not only to me, but to your children? Especially to Alex. Don't you know what this is doing to him?'' Her voice rose to the edge of hysteria. "Now get out of that damn water, and for once in your life tell the truth!''

He waded toward her, keeping a cautious distance as he approached the dock. He suspected that given the chance, she might just kick him. Eyes that only a few days ago had been full of affection, now were filled with loathing.

"Frannie, I'm not your ex-husband,'' he stated in no uncertain terms.

She reached into a straw purse that was big enough to hold a litter of puppies and pulled out a manila envelope. "Then, why does this say you are?'' she asked, waving the envelope in the air.

"What is that?"

"The lab report. It says you're Alex's father."

"Then, it's wrong."

"DNA doesn't lie. You saw the statistical information. They can determine a probability of paternity ninety-nine percent—or greater," she reminded him.

"Then, an error was made. We fell in the one percent," he told her. "You can't possibly believe I'm Dennis—not after everything that's happened between us."

"Oh, yes I can, because it's just the kind of cruel, sick joke you'd pull. Well, it's the last one you're ever going to play on me or my kids. Stay in the damn water. I'm sure the authorities will love to see this." She spun around and headed for the shore.

Joe quickly climbed out of the water and onto the dock. "For God's sake, Frannie. How many times do I have to tell you I'm not him!" he said in frustration as he went after her. When he caught up with her he reached for the manila envelope in her hand. "Give me that paper."

She snatched it back, saying, "You're all wet. And…" She paused, her eyes slowly roving over his naked body. Her face, which had been red with anger, lost its color.

Without saying a word, he bent to retrieve the beach towel he'd left lying on the shore next to his clothes. He wrapped it around his waist, knotting it on the side.

He extended his hand. "Can I see the report?"

She gave it to him, and he pulled out the document inside. "This can't be right. Tell me you don't think this is accurate." He stared into her eyes, imploring her to have faith in him, but all he saw there was confusion.

"Frannie, you've got to believe me. I'm not Dennis," he repeated.

"You..." she began, but stopped. "You...you don't have a scar down there."

"A scar down where?" he asked.

Slowly, a finger unfurled from her fist to point at his groin. "The scar where you had your appendix removed."

"I haven't had my appendix removed," he said quietly.

"Then..." Her eyes widened.

"I told you. I'm not Dennis Harper."

"But the lab..."

"Is wrong. If you want a closer look at my abdomen, feel free, but I can tell you right now, there's no scar. I haven't had my appendix out. You want me to produce medical records to prove it?"

She shook her head, rubbing two fingers across her forehead. "I don't understand how your DNA could match Alex's..."

"They made a mistake," he finished for her. "Frannie, you see I have no scar."

Her eyes flew to his groin, then back to his face. Meeting his gaze, she blushed and looked away. He placed a finger on her chin, lifting it so that she was forced to look at him.

"Mistakes happen—even in the best labs."

She nodded, then took a step back.

"Let's go up to the house. I'll call the lab to find out what went wrong," he said, stooping to pick up his clothes. Neither one spoke, as they made their way up the hill.

When they reached the house, she said, "I'll wait here," motioning to the island counter in the kitchen. He nodded and was about to go change, when she asked, "Why are there suitcases next to the back door?"

He realized now what she'd meant by his getaway. She'd thought he was doing a vanishing act. "My father went into the hospital this morning for some tests. I told him he didn't need to bring much, but he packed nearly all his clothes. I haven't unpacked them and put them away."

She nodded in understanding.

"Did you think I was running out on you, Frannie?"

She pushed her hair back from her forehead and said, "It wouldn't be the first time a man's done that to me."

He moved closer to her, wishing he could erase the vulnerability exposed on her face. "That exhusband of yours had a way of running out on you, did he."

"His own mother doesn't even know where he is," she said bitterly.

Again anger for the unknown man surged in Joe. He'd known Dennis Harper could still affect Frannie emotionally, but today Joe had seen just how deeply the wounds the other man had inflicted were.

"I'm sorry he hurt you, Frannie."

She shrugged. "I survived and I like the person I am now much better than the woman I was back then."

"You're a very special woman. He doesn't deserve you."

She smiled then, a small yet poignant smile. "I won't argue that one."

He didn't want to talk about her ex. He wanted to talk about the two of them. "I'll go get dressed and then I'll call the lab, all right?"

She touched his cheek with her fingers. "All right."

WHILE JOE was getting changed, Frannie again looked at the papers inside the manila envelope. According to the lab, Joe's genetic markers matched Alex's, yet Frannie knew he couldn't be Alex's father. She'd only made love with one man in her lifetime. That man was Dennis. Dennis, who had a scar across his abdomen that no amount of time would ever erase.

Yet the lab claimed that DNA testing was the most conclusive and widely accepted method to test for true biological relationships. Confused and needing answers, she didn't wait for Joe to return, but called the lab herself. She was talking to the communication coordinator, making notes on the back of the manila envelope, when Joe walked into the kitchen.

He rested a hip against the counter, facing her as she finished her call. As soon as she'd hung up the receiver, he said, "You talked to the lab?"

She nodded. "They stand by their claim that the test results are accurate."

"Then, we'll repeat the test with another lab."

"We can do that," she said, her eyes on the notes she'd scribbled on the back of the envelope.

"We *have* to do that." He went to the refrigerator and pulled open the door. "Do you want something to drink? I'm having a beer, but I have soda."

"No, thanks. I'm fine."

He popped the top of a beer can, took a long sip, then looked her straight in the eye and said, "As much as I wish I could say I had the pleasure of being part of Alex's conception, we both know that isn't true."

"Yes." His provocative words sent a tiny shiver through her.

"So you agree that we should redo the test?"

She sighed. "It's a lot of money, Joe."

"Don't worry about the expense. I'll pay whatever is necessary to get this mess cleared up," he said.

She shook her head. "I can't let you do that. You already paid once. Besides, we might get the same results."

He frowned. "Frannie, you just agreed I'm not Alex's father."

"I know, but there is another reason why you could have turned up as a genetic match," she said, toying with the flap on the envelope. She'd written several phrases down while talking with the representative from the lab. She slid her thumb over the words *identical twins,* unsure how to broach the subject.

He stared at her. "What other reason could there be? You read the brochure they gave us. Everyone has different genetic markers."

She took a deep breath and said, "Everyone except identical twins."

He had been about to take a swallow of beer, but paused with the can in midair. "You think I'm your ex-husband's twin?"

From the look on his face she could see just how

ridiculous a possibility he thought it was. "It would explain the DNA results," she said quietly.

He chuckled without humor. "Well, you can forget that explanation. It's simply not possible. I know who I am."

"Joe, there has to be a reason why your genetic markers matched Alex's."

"Yes, the lab made an error," he insisted, his voice rising.

"But you look enough like Dennis to be his twin."

"Well, I'm not," he denied vigorously. "Frannie, you're way off base with that idea. I'm not adopted."

"I didn't say you were."

"You just implied it by suggesting something absurd," he argued. "My dad has pictures of my mother when she was pregnant with me. I'm not adopted. They wouldn't have kept something like that from me."

"Joe, I'm sorry," she apologized, unhappy with the distress she was causing him. "Would you just let me explain?"

"Explain what?" he asked a bit impatiently.

She searched for the right words. "It's as confusing to me as it is to you, but I think you should know that Dennis did have a twin brother."

"Then, doesn't that disprove your theory?"

"No. His brother died from SIDS when he was only two months old."

He gave her another puzzled look. "I'm not following you."

She knew that he was going to think that her next suggestion was even more absurd than the last.

"Maybe the baby boy that his parents brought

home from the hospital and who died two months later was not Dennis's twin.''

"You can't possibly believe there was a mix-up at the hospital and my parents were given somebody else's baby?'' He pushed away from the counter and shook his head. "Frannie, if you think that, you've been watching too many movies. I was born in a military hospital. My father was an officer in the Navy. It couldn't have happened.''

"How can you be so sure? You and I both know that there are documented cases where babies were switched at birth.''

"But it didn't happen to me,'' he said adamantly. "My mother would have known if it had. You don't think she would have realized that the baby in her arms belonged to someone else?''

"Joe, what happened to your mother? I know she died when you were a child, but you never speak about her.''

"She died from injuries she sustained in a car accident. I was only eleven.''

"I'm sorry. It must have been very painful for you.''

He nodded. "She was a good person.'' He looked Frannie squarely in the eye and said with conviction, "She *was* my mother, Frannie. If she hadn't given birth to me, she would have told me. I know she did.''

Frannie wasn't going to argue that point. "Where was your dad stationed when you were born?''

"In Guam.''

"Joe, Dennis was born in a military hospital in Guam.''

He kept shaking his head. "That doesn't prove anything, Frannie."

"No, but it does mean you can't ignore the possibility."

"It's not a possibility," he declared firmly. He ran his hands over his face, then said, "Look. I know you're only trying to find answers to a puzzling situation, but hasn't what's happened between you and me so far shown you that speculating can be a waste of time? Look at the erroneous conclusions that have already been drawn since the day we met. I think we owe it to everyone involved to make sure that an accurate test has been performed before we do any more guessing."

Frannie wasn't convinced that hadn't already been done. There were too many similarities for her not to believe Dennis and Joe were identical twins.

"I'm sorry," she apologized. "I know this is difficult for you. The last thing I want to do is make this any more complicated than it already is, but, Joe, what happens if the next test results are the same?"

"We'll cross that bridge if we get there," he replied. "For now, the only assumption I can make is that someone made an error at the lab. Now, can we change the subject?"

Frannie wanted to put her arms around him, to shower him with comfort that would take away all the doubts her questions must have put in his head. As much as he wanted to deny it, she knew he hadn't taken what she'd said lightly. It was there in the lines on his face and in the uncertainty in his eyes.

She knew it was easier for him to doubt the accuracy of the paternity test than it was to consider the possibility that the identity he'd had for thirty-three years was false. No one, not even Joe, could predict the changes such a discovery would bring.

Frannie thought of the Admiral. For a man in his condition to suddenly discover that his only son had been switched at birth could be devastating. On the other hand, Arlene could learn that the son she thought had died as an infant was still alive.

Maybe Joe was right. It was better not to discuss the subject until the second DNA test had been done.

"All right. No more talk about the results. But first I have to say one more thing," she said. "I need to apologize for the way I screamed at you down there on the dock."

The cloudiness left his eyes, replaced by a slight twinkle. "I'm just glad I never had my appendix out. When you were standing down there on that dock, I was thinking how lucky I was not to have left the oars in sight. The way those arms of yours were flailing, I'm not sure you wouldn't have clunked me over the head if one had been handy."

She grinned sheepishly. "I did wonder if I should grab a shovel from the shed on my way to the beach," she quipped. "I'm sorry I went off like that, but I got the report this morning and I was seeing red."

"There's no need to apologize, Frannie. In the short time I've known you I've discovered that you'd do anything to protect your children. That's a quality most men would admire in a woman. I know I do," he said, stepping closer to her.

Again, his words made her feel special. "I won't let Dennis hurt them anymore. That's why when I got that lab report, all I could think was that he'd fooled me yet again. I thought you'd sweet-talked me and filled my head with all sorts of lies."

He moved so that he was close enough to reach up and run the back of his fingers across her cheek. "It wasn't sweet-talking, Frannie. I meant everything I said."

She saw no reason for pretense. "I'm glad, because I liked what I heard."

He dropped his hands, shoving them into his pockets. "Do you know how many times I've thought about you these past few days and wanted to call?"

"Why didn't you?"

"Because this paternity stuff was hanging between us. And it's still there, isn't it." His gaze pinned hers as he waited for her answer.

"It doesn't have to be," she said, although she had to admit that she had the same apprehension he did—that somehow this mess would keep them apart. "What happened today—it isn't going to keep us apart, is it?"

He held her gaze. "I want to be with you, Frannie, but there isn't just this paternity stuff hanging between us. I'm all my father has and he needs a lot of care."

He was telling her the future didn't look bright for them. She swallowed back the lump of disappointment that threatened to affect her voice. "I admire the way you take care of your father. Actually, it's because of him that I was even attracted to you."

"How so?"

"That night of the storm when we first met...you looked like Dennis, yet you treated your dad with patience and understanding. The love you had for him—it's what made me realize that there was no way you could be my ex-husband.'' She smiled. ''I guess you could say you turned from a frog into a prince.''

''I'm no prince,'' he said soberly, moving away from her. He went to stare out the window, deliberately putting distance between them physically and emotionally.

''That's probably good, because as you saw today on the dock, I definitely don't behave like a princess,'' she said, wishing she didn't feel as if he'd just shut her out of his life.

He gave her one of those half smiles that made her heart do a funny little flip. ''Are you saying I've seen you at your worst?''

''Close to it,'' she admitted. ''Pretty scary stuff, huh?''

''I'm not a man who frightens easily.''

She took his hand in hers. ''Three kids would be enough to frighten most men away,'' she said.

He sighed. ''Why do you keep bringing up the subject of your kids? Do I honestly seem like the type of guy who'd avoid getting involved with a woman because she has children?''

She decided to be bold. ''Are we getting involved?''

He pulled her to him until their faces were only inches apart. ''We shouldn't be.''

''Because you have to take care of your father.'' She hoped that was the reason.

''This isn't a time in my life when I should be thinking about getting involved with anyone,'' he confirmed. ''Frannie, my life isn't as simple as it looks. Things have happened that—''

She quieted him with a finger on his lips. ''I've

made mistakes, too, Joe. We both have pasts we can't change.''

''There's a lot you don't know about me,'' he began, only to have her quiet him a second time.

''I know that you're a good man.'' She laid her palms against his chest, loving the strength she felt there.

''It's no wonder I can't stop thinking about you,'' he said, bringing her even closer so that she arched her body against his.

''You think about me a lot?'' she prodded shamelessly.

He chuckled. ''Ever since you and your kids landed on my doorstep I've had trouble thinking about anything else.''

She licked her lips. ''You make that sound as if it's a bad thing.''

''Bad? Uh-uh. More like frustrating. As much as I'd like to be with you, I know I can't.''

''You want to be with me?'' she asked provocatively.

''You need to ask?'' he said, moments before covering her lips with his. With a soft sigh, she pressed against him, matching his passion with her own in a kiss that left both of them short of breath.

''The problem is, there are obstacles to overcome,'' he said, pulling her fingertips to his mouth.

''Like distance.''

''And time.''

''Kids.''

''I told you they're not a problem,'' he said, giving her a quick peck on her mouth.

''Can we overcome the obstacles?''

''When you're in my arms, I feel like we could

do anything," he said in a seductive whisper. "I'm willing to try. What about you?"

For an answer, she kissed him long and hard. "I don't know where this is leading, but I do know one thing. I don't want to look back and regret that we didn't find out."

"It's going to lead to something good, Frannie," he said huskily.

She wanted to believe him. "I hope so."

"It will." He lowered his head and was about to kiss her again, when the phone stopped him. He released her to answer it.

To give him privacy, she stepped into the living room and stared out the windows at the lake. It looked cool and refreshing—exactly what she needed to cool her warm flesh. She smiled to herself as she remembered how hot and bothered Joe's kisses made her feel.

"That was my dad," Joe told her as he came into the living room.

"Is everything okay?"

He nodded. "He's just a little lonely. I promised I'd go see him."

She glanced at her watch. "And I promised my neighbor I wouldn't be late. I really need to be going. What about the paternity test?"

"I'll make the arrangements," Joe told her as he walked her to her car. "We can use one of the services that comes right to your home if you like."

She nodded. "That would be easiest. I'll tell Alex it needs to be redone, but not the reason why." When they'd reached her car, she said, "I know you don't want to hear this, Joe, but it might be a good idea to look up your birth records."

He frowned. "Until we get the results of the second test, there doesn't seem to be any point, does there?"

She could see that no matter what she said, he was determined to believe the lab had made an error. As she drove away she couldn't help but be filled with a sense of foreboding. She only hoped that no matter what the outcome of the next test, their relationship would survive.

AS SOON AS FRANNIE had gone, Joe knew he had to do two things: call the DNA lab and then go visit his dad. The phone call netted him nothing more than he'd learned from Frannie. The lab stood by its results, which left Joe wondering if something that had sounded so far-fetched could actually be possible. Did he have a twin brother?

He didn't want to believe it could be true, but he remembered the night at the lake when Frannie had asked him his birth date. She'd remarked that he was born the same year as Dennis and even on the same day, but a different month. When creating his new identity, Joe had used the same day and year of his birth, but had changed the month.

He told himself it was only another disturbing coincidence. As he drove to the hospital, he tried to recall if there had ever been any discussion between his mom and dad about the day he was born. Nothing came to mind.

He could remember what his mother had said to him on his first day of school, how she had looked when she baked cookies, the way she had clapped her hands at his accomplishments, yet he couldn't remember her ever talking about the day he was born.

That's why one of the first questions he asked his father when he arrived at the hospital was "Dad, you were there when I was born, right?"

The Admiral was finishing his dinner, relishing the chocolate pudding on his tray. "Actually, I wasn't. I was on duty. On a carrier somewhere in the Pacific."

"So Mom was alone?"

"Oh, no. Your aunt Mary stayed with her until I returned."

"Was Aunt Mary with her at the hospital?"

He ran the spoon around the edge of the cup to get every last bit of pudding. "I just said she was. Why all the questions?"

He shrugged. "Just curious. I know I was born at the naval hospital."

"Yes, and it's a good thing you were. Your mother wanted to have one of those—" His spoon fluttered in midair as he struggled to find the correct word. "Those—" he sighed in frustration at his inability to articulate. "The women who help with the babies..." He looked at Joe for assistance.

"You mean a midwife?"

"Yes. She wanted a midwife to come to the house, but I put my foot down," he said with authority.

Joe knew there were few times in his parents' marriage that his father hadn't put his foot down to get his way.

"I said when you're in a foreign country, you use the medical facilities provided by Uncle Sam," his father continued. "And it's a good thing she did."

"Why is that?"

He stared at him blankly. "Why is what?"

"Why was it a good thing Mom went to the hospital? Were there complications during delivery?"

"What are you talking about?"

"The day I was born. You said it was a good thing Mom went to the hospital. Did something go wrong?"

He set his spoon down and looked over the tray. "How come there isn't any Jell-O?"

"Dad, did Mom need special care at the hospital?"

"Why are you asking me that? You were there. I didn't want them to remove the machines," he said, his eyes becoming glassy at the memory, and Joe realized that he had confused Joe's birth with his mother's death. "I shouldn't have let them do it, Joe."

He reached across to touch his father's hand. "You made all the right decisions, Dad."

He looked around the room. "I hate hospitals." He sniffed. "It's the smell. You have to get me out of here, Joe." He turned woeful eyes on his son. "You're not going to leave me here, are you?"

"You have to stay until you're done with the tests," Joe reminded him. "Hospitals can be happy places," he said, wanting to turn the conversation back to his birth. "Like when babies are born. I'm sure Mom was happy to be in the hospital when I was born."

"Oh, she was excited about having you, all right. Had your name picked out before she even knew she was pregnant."

"Did she talk about being in the hospital? About

how many other babies there were the day I was born?''

He smiled. ''That was quite a night I missed. Your mother said they were coming faster than they could handle them. And then, of course, the power went out.''

''The hospital lost power?''

''Yes, because of the storm. It's a good thing Mary was with her. Your mother always panicked whenever there was bad weather.''

''Do you know if any twins were born at that hospital while I was there?''

He didn't answer, but simply stared at Joe with a blank look on his face.

''Dad, did you hear my question?''

A nurse poked her head in the door to ask how his father was doing, and the Admiral said, ''I'd be a whole lot better if you'd get me some Jell-O.''

She did as he requested, returning with a small cup of green gelatin. As soon as she'd gone, his father said, ''Conscientious, that one is.''

''That's good,'' Joe remarked.

''Yes, the Navy could use more like her.'' Once again, the Admiral looked confused. ''Now, what did I do with it?'' he asked, his eyes frantically roving over the tray.

''What are you looking for, Dad?''

''The…'' He made a prying motion with his hand.

Joe reached for the spoon on his tray and handed it to him. ''Here's your spoon.''

He smiled at him. ''You're a good son, Joe. It's too bad your mother's not here to see how handsome you've become. She always said you were going to be a looker.'' He pulled the foil top from the cup and dipped his spoon into the Jell-O.

''Do you think I look like her?'' He couldn't resist asking.

His father glanced briefly in his direction, his attention on dessert. ''Not one bit. You're a Hawthorn. You look like me,'' he bellowed, which made Joe grimace.

''Dad, we're Smiths now, remember?'' he said in a low voice, wondering if any of the hospital staff had heard his dad's declaration.

He brushed aside his comment with a flap of his spoon. ''Yes, I remember, but I don't like it, Joe.''

''I don't either, but it's important that you don't slip up and give the wrong name to anyone here at the hospital,'' he cautioned.

''Oh, for Pete's sake. I won't,'' he grumbled irritably.

''I know you won't,'' Joe said, giving his father's arm a pat, wishing that he didn't have to worry the older man with such a concern. It was difficult enough for his father to adjust to the loss of his memory. He didn't need the added stress of losing the name he'd been so proud to bear. Unfortunately, they'd had no choice but to use assumed identities.

''You still seeing that Harper woman?'' his father asked.

''I like her,'' Joe admitted.

His father shook his head in reprobation. ''And you're worried about me slipping up. She doesn't know about us, does she?''

''Of course not.''

''How much longer do you think you can carry on with her without her getting suspicious?''

''I'm not exactly carrying on with her, Dad.''

''When we moved here we made an agreement,'' he reminded Joe.

''I know. No women,'' he said with a crooked smile. He'd thought with his father's diminishing mental capabilities, that that promise had been forgotten, but it never ceased to amaze Joe how sharp his father could be at times.

''I know you made sacrifices to move here.''

''So did you. We made a choice, Dad. I don't have any regrets.''

His father eyed him curiously. ''You better be careful with that woman.''

''I will.''

They talked a bit about baseball, the weather and what Joe's flight schedule was for the upcoming week. When it was time for him to leave, his father said, ''It doesn't matter, you know.''

''What doesn't matter, Dad?''

''What name you use. You're still a Hawthorn. It's in your blood,'' he stated with an authority Joe knew better than to question.

If there was one thing Joe was certain about as he left the hospital, it was that he wasn't adopted. But just because he wasn't adopted didn't mean that he couldn't be Dennis Harper's twin. If there had been a bad storm and the power had gone out even briefly…

He shook his head, trying to dismiss such speculation. It was all way too bizarre. Surely government red tape was thick enough to prevent such a mistake. Weren't babies tagged with plastic ID bands as soon as they were born? If nothing else, his mother would certainly have noticed if they'd given her the wrong baby.

No matter how hard he tried not to think about it, the possibility haunted him the rest of the evening. He wanted answers, yet he knew that finding them could spell tragedy for him and his father. If Frannie or anyone were to go digging into his past, it could mean an end to the new life he'd created.

Joe had to hope that the second DNA test proved that he wasn't related to Alex Harper, because he wasn't prepared to sacrifice a man he'd known and loved all his life for one he'd never met.

JOE HAD TROUBLE falling asleep that night. Unable to stop thinking about the results of the DNA test, he got out of bed and went on the Internet.

First he read everything he could find about using DNA testing to determine paternity. Then he looked for information about identical twins and searched for case histories of babies that had been switched at birth. His father had always preached that knowledge was power, but tonight knowledge only made him feel helpless.

Instead of returning to bed, he opened a closet door and pulled a photo album from the shelf. It had belonged to his mother and contained pictures of his aunts and uncles, cousins and grandparents.

Joe studied each of the pictures, looking for his likeness in any of his relatives' faces. Other than the fact that they all had brown hair, he couldn't see any distinguishing features that would identify him as a Hawthorn or a Delaney, his mother's side of the family. Most of his cousins were older, which was prob-

ably why he had never noticed how little he resem-
bled them.

But it was his mother's and father's pictures that
he examined most closely. Did any child ever look
at his parent and see himself? He tried to remember
an occasion when someone had commented on how
much he looked like his mother, and came to the
conclusion there hadn't been any.

When he'd entered the Navy he'd often heard such
comments as "If you aren't a chip off the old
block," and "Boy, I can sure tell you are your father's son," but no one had ever said he *looked* like
his father. He glanced into the mirror, turning his
head at different angles to try to see his father's face.

You're still a Hawthorn. It's in your blood. His
father's words echoed in his head. Were they true?
Did Hawthorn blood run through his veins?

It was a question he wasn't sure he wanted answered. From everything he'd learned about Dennis
Harper, Joe knew he wasn't the kind of man anyone
would choose for a brother. He was a deadbeat
who'd run out on his wife and kids. What could Joe
possibly have in common with such a man?

Frustrated, Joe gave up looking for answers. There
was one absolute in his life. He loved his father and
would do whatever was necessary to protect his
physical and emotional health.

For as far back as he could remember, his father
had been there for him. Although most of his friends
had regarded the Admiral as a tough disciplinarian,
Joe knew that behind the rigid military persona was
a compassionate man who'd been both a mentor and
a teacher to his only son. He was the one person Joe

had turned to when he was troubled, the one he went to for advice.

But today Joe hadn't been able to tell his father what was troubling him. To do so would have caused the elderly man pain, and if there was one thing Joe couldn't do, it was to seek comfort at the expense of his father's peace of mind.

As Joe eased his weary body back into bed, he may not have resolved the issue of his biological identity, but he did know that no matter what the genetic markers found on his chromosomes revealed, he would always be Joe and Kathleen Hawthorn's son. No piece of paper would ever change that.

Now he just needed to find a way to keep anyone else from trying to prove the contrary.

CHAPTER TEN

"THIS IS IT—3411," the cab driver said as he pulled up to the curb in front of a small brick house surrounded by a chain-link fence. "You said you want me to pick you up in an hour, right?"

"Yeah, that's fine." Joe pulled several bills from his pocket and handed them to the driver.

One hour. It was enough time for him to say goodbye to Frannie, but he knew that no matter how much time there was, he would never be able to tell her the real reason he was ending their relationship.

He couldn't say that lies and love didn't make a winning combination. Nor that as long as he lived in the shadow of the past, there could be no future for them.

As he climbed out of the cab, he tried not to think about what might have been between him and Frannie, but instead focused on his father's situation. He unlatched the gate and started up the walk, stepping around the toy dump truck blocking his route. Next to it was a small red plastic pail filled with sand and a shovel. Joe could imagine Luke transferring sand from the bucket to the dump truck, although it appeared that most of the sand had landed on the sidewalk.

Luke wasn't the only one who'd been playing in the yard. Someone had taken colored chalk and drawn pictures on the sidewalk. Since most of the drawings were in pastel colors, he assumed it was Emma.

Like the house, the yard was small but neat. The grass was cut short, the flower beds edged with stone, the hedge running beside the fence recently trimmed. One half of the yard was shaded by a large oak tree, a rope swing dangling from a thick, gnarled branch. Daisies and marigolds bloomed next to the house.

Joe climbed the steps to the doormat that said Welcome to Our Home, and was about to lift his hand to knock on the wooden screen door when he saw Frannie. Barefoot and wearing shorts and a knit shirt, she was gathering the Legos scattered across the floor. As if sensing someone watching her, she straightened and turned.

"You're here!" It was obvious from her tone of voice that she was very pleased to see him. "I was just thinking about you."

He wanted to toss some flirtatious comment at her, but knew he couldn't. "I flew in this morning. I'm on a job."

"How did you get here from the airport?" she asked, glancing outside to the street and seeing no car.

"I took a cab," he said, wishing his heart wouldn't pump so fast at the sight of her. "Is this a bad time?"

"No, not at all," she said, opening the door in a welcoming gesture. "I just put Luke down for a nap. I was about to have a glass of iced tea. Would you like one?"

"Sure."

Joe followed her into the living room, where she

said, "Sit down. The sofa's a bit worn, but it's comfortable."

What caught Joe's eye as he entered the room wasn't the furniture, but the framed print on the wall. It was Escher's *Three Worlds,* a lithograph of a woodland pond.

"You like Escher," he remarked, feeling as if he and Frannie shared more than a physical attraction for one another.

"I saw the one in your room," she said, her eyes telling him that she, too, felt that connection.

Joe pulled his eyes away from hers, needing to distance himself emotionally. He'd come here to break up with her, not bond with her. He glanced at the photographs on the opposite wall and said, "Are these yours?"

"Some are."

"Like this one?" He indicated a picture of her three children running through a meadow, their arms reaching skyward in total abandonment.

"Yes, that one's mine. Some are from my mother's collection." She pointed to an oval frame with a photo of a very sober-looking couple. "Those are my great-grandparents."

Joe listened as she rattled off the names of several of her ancestors. Then he said, "You're not in any of the pictures."

"Yes, I am. Right there." She pointed to a photograph of a man, a woman, two girls and a boy standing in front of a lake. Each of the kids held a stringer of fish. "I was nine and had just been fishing with my sister and my cousin."

"That's your mom and dad?"

"No, my aunt and uncle. We were at a resort in Wisconsin. It was my first time in a boat."

"So where are your parents?" he asked, his eyes roving over the photographs.

"This is my mother and my stepfather," she said, pointing to a picture of a fair-haired woman and a lumberjack of a man sitting on a wooden glider. "That's my sister Lois," she added, putting a finger on a blond woman hugging Emma in front of a waterfall. "I shot that at Minnehaha Falls."

"Your sister looks like you," he noted.

"I look like her," she corrected him with an impish grin. "She's older. The guy playing in the snow with the kids there—that's my cousin Jeffrey. He lives in Denver. I shot that when he was here last winter."

He studied it closely. "Yeah, I can see the family resemblance."

"Look at this one. It's one of my favorites." She pointed to a small snapshot of two little girls sharing a tire swing.

"You and your sister?"

She nodded. "We used to love to swing on that big old tire in the backyard," she mused aloud. "Life was so simple back then."

"Were they happy times?"

"Yes...at least, they were until my mom and dad divorced," she answered.

"You don't have your father's picture up here?"

She shook her head. "I haven't seen him since I was seven."

Joe's eyes were drawn to a photo of a woman with big red hair and lots of jewelry. She sat playing cards with Emma and Alex. "Who's this?"

''That's Arlene Harper.''

''Dennis's mother.''

''Uh-huh. She was teaching them how to play poker the day I took that one. They used lima beans for money.''

Joe hadn't noticed the tiny piles of beans in front of the twins, because his attention had been drawn to the woman's face. It didn't look at all familiar. If she were his birth mother, wouldn't he feel something when he looked at her picture? He looked at the brown eyes, the pert nose and the rounded chin. Absently his fingers rubbed his own jaw.

Noticing Frannie's eyes on him, he swept his gaze over the photographs and asked, ''So these are all family photos?''

She nodded. ''It seems appropriate since this is our family room. I try to keep the kids' pictures recent. Alex is getting to an age where he's becoming a bit sensitive about having baby pictures on display.''

''Where is Alex?''

''He and Emma went to the movies with my sister.''

''So we're alone?''

''Except for Luke,'' she reminded him.

She looked so alluring in her little top and shorts, he had to fight the temptation to pull her into his arms and kiss her senseless. He shoved his hands into his pockets and tried to focus on the reason he'd come.

''I'm glad we're alone because we need to talk,'' he said.

''All right. Just let me get the tea,'' she said, then disappeared into the kitchen.

While she was gone, he looked around the room

she'd called their family room. Against one wall was a bookcase crammed with books—children's on the lower shelves and adult's on the upper ones. In the corner was a small cabinet that housed a portable TV. Floor pillows were stacked next to the sofa and a box of toys rested beneath the coffee table. Next to the side chair was a child-size rocker, a tattered blanket draped over its seat.

"Do you take lemon and sugar?" Frannie asked as she returned carrying a tray with a pitcher of iced tea and two tall glasses.

"No, thanks."

"Me, neither." She gave him a beguiling smile, then sat down on the sofa, setting the tray on the coffee table in front of her. As she poured the tea into the glasses she said, "I'm really glad you're here, Joe. How long can you stay?"

He sat down on the chair across from her. "Not long. I only came by because there's something I have to tell you."

The sparkle in her eye disappeared. "By the look on your face I can see it's not something pleasant." She handed him a glass.

"Everything that's happened...the paternity testing..." He was unsure exactly how to say what he knew he had to say.

She didn't help him out. she just sat waiting for him to continue.

"I guess there's no easy way to do this, Frannie, except to say that it would be better if we just let this whole thing drop."

Apprehension narrowed her eyes. "By this whole thing, you mean the DNA testing?"

"I've decided there's no point in having the test

done a second time." He was glad to have the iced tea, for suddenly his throat was dry. He took a long swallow.

"But I've already made the arrangements for someone to come here and draw the sample from Alex."

"Can't you cancel it?"

"But why? Do you think the first results were accurate?"

He took another drink of the tea, then set his glass down on the coffee table. "It doesn't matter whether they were or not."

"Of course it matters," she countered.

"No, Frannie, it doesn't to me. Whether or not the lab made a mistake isn't going to change the fact that I'm *not* Alex's father. If you recall, that *is* the reason we did the test in the first place."

"Well, yes, but the results have significance beyond paternity, Joe."

"Not for me they don't." As soon as he'd uttered the words he realized how harsh they must have sounded to her.

She stiffened. "What are you trying to tell me? That you don't want to know if you might have more family?"

She made it sound as if he was a first-class jerk if he didn't. He raked a hand over the back of his neck. "It's not that simple, Frannie. I'm worried that whatever the results are, I'm not prepared to deal with them at this point in my life. You've met my father. You know how he reacts to the tiniest of changes. It's a can of worms best left unopened."

"So you're backing away from this because of your concern for your father?" She stared at him, her eyes probing into his as if she were peering into his soul.

He looked away, afraid she would see more than he wanted to reveal. He reached for the half-empty glass, focusing on its contents. "You've seen how fragile my father's mental health is. If he were to suspect that I was searching for information that would prove I'm not his son..." He shook his head. "I don't want to even imagine what it could do to him."

"He doesn't need to know, Joe. Records can be searched, investigations can be made and results can be determined without involving him."

"But *I* would know and I wouldn't want to try to keep that from him." He looked at her. "Can't you see? It's easier not knowing."

"Are you sure it'll be easier, Joe?"

He wasn't, but he couldn't tell her that. He needed to convince her that leaving the past alone was the only way he would have peace of mind when it came to his father.

"Frannie, for thirty-three years he's been my dad. Don't you see? It doesn't matter what any DNA test shows. I have my father. How much longer I'll have him, I'm not sure, which is why I need to do whatever I can to make sure nothing hurts him."

She leaned forward, her arms resting on her knees. "Joe, I can imagine how unsettling this must be for you. I'm sure it's left you with a lot of questions. Maybe you think it's better not to learn the answers to those questions, but are you going to be able to forget that there's a possibility you could have more family?"

"Believe me, Frannie, I won't forget. It's just that

now is not the time for me to be searching for those answers.''

''Will there be a right time?''

''I believe there will, but right now my father's health has to come first.''

She nodded, although he could see she had her doubts.

''So what are you going to do, Joe? Pretend that the DNA test never happened?''

''No, only that it gave us inconclusive results.''

''Is that what you think?''

''It's what I have to believe.'' With his eyes, he pleaded for understanding. ''For my dad's sake.''

''And what about Alex? What do I tell him? He thinks the first test didn't work.''

''Then you tell him we decided it wasn't necessary to redo the test because you saw that I don't have a scar that his father has.''

He could see she wasn't happy with his answer. ''You could be his uncle.''

''I can't be his uncle now, Frannie.'' He lowered his voice in resignation.

''What do you want to be to him, Joe?''

He knew what he needed to say to answer that question, yet her expression made him wish those necessary words wouldn't destroy her hopes for the future. But he was sure they would. ''I think it would be better if I wasn't in his life.''

The look on her face made him feel as if he should be competing for the World's Biggest Dirtbag title.

She jumped to her feet and stood before him. ''Good grief! When you said you wanted to drop everything, you weren't just talking about the testing, were you,'' she asked rhetorically. ''You were talking about us, too.''

This was the moment he'd been waiting for. ''I'm sorry, Frannie. If circumstances were different I—''

''If they were different, what?'' she interrupted in anger. ''You wouldn't be saying goodbye to me? You are saying goodbye, aren't you.'' She stood, her eyes flashing with accusation.

He stood so that she wasn't towering over him. ''I don't want to, but we need to be realistic. It's not going to work out between us.''

She bit down on her lower lip before saying, ''I think it could.''

Joe shook his head. He wanted to find a way to remain a part of her life, but the truth was if he continued to see her, he put his father's life in jeopardy. He'd created a wall of lies that prevented him from searching for answers that were hidden in the past. As his father had reminded him, they had to accept the sacrifices that came with such actions.

''I wish I could agree with you, Frannie, but I can't,'' he said in somber resignation.

''So what does that mean? That once you leave here I won't see you again?'' When he didn't look at her, she tugged on his shirtsleeves. ''Tell me, Joe. Are you going to walk out that door and never come back?''

''I'm sorry.'' The words sounded inadequate even to his own ears.

She let go of him, wrapping her arms around her midsection as if warding off a chill. When she spoke he could hear how close to tears she was.

''Don't apologize, Joe. It's not like you made me

any promises. You made it clear from the start that you didn't give our relationship much of a chance.''

''Only because of my father's situation, not because of my feelings for you.''

''So you have feelings for me?''

There was such doubt in those beautiful eyes that it took every bit of his willpower not to show her just how much she meant to him.

''I wouldn't be here if I didn't care about you,'' he said, his voice softening. ''I could have called and said all of this over the phone.''

His words were of little comfort to her. ''Gee, thanks. I feel honored to have gotten the 'in person' dumping rather than the 'over the phone' one,'' she said with heavy sarcasm. She faced him with her hands on her hips, her eyes dark with emotion. ''You just go ahead and leave, because you know what? My kids deserve better than you. They deserve a man who doesn't run away at the first sign of trouble, a man who wants to be a part of their lives, a man who stays.'' The last part came out on a sob. She tried to stifle the tears but they trickled down her cheek. She turned so he wouldn't see them, but it was too late.

He grabbed her by the arm and swung her around to face him. ''Frannie, I wish I could be that man. I *want* to be that man, but I feel trapped. If I choose you, I may lose my father. If I choose my father, I lose you.''

''I don't want to lose you, Joe,'' she cried.

He stared into those beautiful eyes brimming with tears, and his heart ached. She was the ray of hope in the dark storm that had been his life for the past two years. How could he give up the one thing that had given him promise for the future?

The answer was, he couldn't. He pulled her into his arms and kissed her, a long passionate kiss that told her more than any words could ever say. Her lips parted under the deepening urgency of his mouth as desire flared between them.

He wanted her, more than he'd ever imagined it possible to want a woman, and from the way her body softened into his, he knew that she wanted him, too. He moved his hands up her arms until they reached her shoulders, pushing the fabric away until her creamy smooth flesh was exposed to his touch.

She moaned in surrender as he eased her down onto the sofa, his body on top of hers. Her hands found their way inside his shirt, slowly moving toward his waist. Joe trembled as they touched each other with an intimacy they'd never shared before. He stopped thinking about right and wrong, shoulds and should nots, reacting to sensations that pulsed through his body as she pressed against him. He needed her as much as he needed air to breathe, and the magic he felt in her arms convinced him he could find an answer to any problems they faced.

She was the woman he loved, and he couldn't let her go. Not now, not ever. Desire had them in its grasp, and it was only the sound of a woman's voice that stopped them from finishing what they'd started.

"Frannie, are you there?"

Suddenly hands that had been pulling Joe closer pushed him away, eyes that had only seconds ago been darkened with passion widened in panic. Frannie looked past him toward the door and gasped.

"We have to get up," she whispered to Joe, then wiggled out from underneath him, nearly shoving him off the sofa in the process.

"I'm sorry. I came right in…the screen door was open…I had no idea," the other woman, an older redhead, stammered. "I can leave."

"No!" Frannie stopped her, straightening her shirt as she scrambled to her feet. "It's all right."

"No, I think I will leave," the woman said. "I just remembered I was going to stop at the store to pick up some of that chocolate-mint ice cream the—" She never finished her sentence because she finally stole a look at Joe. "Oh!" She turned to Frannie for an explanation.

Before Frannie could begin an introduction, Joe was sure he knew who the redhead was. But even as Frannie confirmed his suspicions, he didn't know what to feel.

"Arlene, I'd like you to meet Joe Smith. Joe, this is Arlene Harper, my children's grandmother."

Arlene appeared to not know whether she wanted to shake his outstretched hand. She hesitated briefly, then put her hand in his. "It's nice to meet you, Arlene," he said.

"You look like—" She stopped suddenly, turning to Frannie. "You don't need me to tell you who he looks like, do you."

Frannie shook her head. "Alex found him through the posters." She chuckled nervously. "The trouble is, Alex can't see the differences."

"You mean he thinks he's…" Arlene's voice trailed off apprehensively. She studied Joe for several moments, then said, "He does look like Dennis, but I wasn't fooled."

"That's good to hear," Joe remarked dryly.

Arlene straightened her back and lifted her chin.

"A mother knows her own son. You're slimmer than my Dennis…and, well, you're not him."

"No, I'm not," Joe said quietly, wondering if he was, however, this woman's son. Nothing about her looked familiar. She was a stranger, yet strangely, there was something about her voice that he found soothing. Physically, he didn't see any resemblance between them, although he supposed the red hair could have come out of a bottle.

There was an uneasy silence that Frannie broke by asking, "So how was your trip?"

"It was wonderful. Ted and I saw so many beautiful places," Arlene said.

Frannie raised an eyebrow. "Ted?"

"That would be me," a voice called out.

Frannie looked toward the door, and Joe realized that Arlene hadn't come alone. A short, slightly balding man emerged from the entry.

He extended his hand first to Frannie, then to Joe, murmuring, "It's nice to meet you." Frannie went through the motions, looking even more uncomfortable than she had when she'd first noticed Arlene.

"I thought you were traveling with Georgia."

Joe detected a hint of irritation in Frannie's usually calm voice.

"I was part of the time, but then I met Ted." She looked affectionately at the balding man. "Or I guess I should say, we met again."

Frannie frowned. "Again?"

"We used to date in high school," Arlene explained, casting warm glances at Ted.

"You met at the reunion?" Frannie asked.

Ted answered for Arlene. "Actually, I didn't go

to the class reunion. We literally bumped into each other at a restaurant in Boise.''

"You've been in Boise?" Frannie looked at her ex-mother-in-law.

"Georgia wanted to go visit some friends," Arlene explained.

"Lucky for me," Ted declared, wrapping his arm around Arlene's waist and pulling her tight. "After all these years, who would have thought I'd find her again."

"I've been trying to reach you for weeks, leaving you messages," Frannie told her.

"I would have called, but we were having so much fun," Arlene told her, fluttering her eyelashes at Ted.

The longer Joe was in Arlene's presence, the more uncomfortable he became. As hard as he tried to focus on the conversation, he couldn't stop thinking about the test results and the possibility that this jovial woman could be his biological mother. It was obvious from her behavior that she was unaware of the paternity test, which only added to his uneasiness. He didn't think Arlene would be chatting the way she was if she'd seen the lab report.

When Frannie announced she'd make some coffee, Joe knew he had to leave. "I'm going to have to get going, Frannie," he announced.

"No! You can't leave!" Frannie pleaded. "Please stay."

Arlene seconded the request, placing her hand on Joe's. "If you leave, I'm going to feel as if I chased you away. I didn't mean to walk in on you and Frannie like that," she said apologetically, looking up at him with eyes that were as brown as his. She patted his arm, saying, "You just have to stay. We stopped at the cutest little bakery on our way here and bought some brownies. Ted and I'll get them from the car, while you and Frannie make the coffee,'' she said, grabbing Ted by the arm and leading him toward the door.

As soon as they'd slipped out, Frannie said, "I'm sorry. I had no idea she was coming."

He lifted one brow. "I believe you. But I do need to leave, Frannie."

"Why?"

"Isn't it obvious? I don't know what to say to her." He nodded toward the door.

"What do you want to say to her?"

That was the problem. He didn't know what he wanted to say to her, but he didn't admit that to Frannie. "She doesn't know about the paternity test, does she." It was more a statement than a question.

She shook her head.

Joe rubbed his jaw. "I shouldn't have come here today."

"But you did come, Joe, and now Arlene has seen you."

"Are you going to tell her about the paternity report?"

"I won't if you don't want me to, but that doesn't mean someone else won't."

He frowned. "You said Alex doesn't know the results."

"No, but my sister does."

"The attorney?" Joe groaned.

She took him by the hand. "Come into the kitchen with me. I need to start the coffee."

He pulled his hand away. "I don't want any coffee, Frannie. I shouldn't be here," he repeated.

"But you are here, and Arlene Harper is going to be back in this house in a few minutes. Joe, I don't want to be in a position where I'm forced to lie."

"Not even to protect my father?"

She didn't answer his question, saying instead, "You said you didn't want to open a can of worms, but isn't it already open?"

"And what do you suggest? That we say to this poor woman something like 'Hey, you know the son you thought was dead...well, he might be alive. And guess what, this might be him?'" He spread his hands in the air.

"I wouldn't just blurt it out. You think I don't know what a shock it's going to be for Arlene to hear something like that?"

"She's already rattled by my appearance. I know she said she could tell right away that I wasn't Dennis, but she's not as comfortable with it as she wants you to believe. And once she's with me, she'll start noticing the similarities you saw that first time we met, and then she'll start putting two and two together..."

"And get four, which is what she should get." She had lowered her voice to a whisper, keeping one eye on the door as she spoke. "I understand your need to protect your father, but doesn't Arlene have a right to know if she has another son?"

"That's a pretty big 'if,' Frannie."

"Is it?"

He glanced over her shoulder, worried that Arlene Harper was in fact overhearing their conversation. "I'm not denying that the possibility exists. All I'm saying is that to get to the truth could cause a lot of pain for my dad."

"You strike me as the kind of man who puts truth at the top of his list of what's important in life."

Again she was looking at him as if she could see into his soul.

"Frannie, you don't know what you're asking me to do."

The sound of voices alerted them that Arlene and Ted were about to return. Frannie methodically went to work setting up the coffeemaker, while Joe stood silently watching her.

"Here they are," Arlene announced, carrying a paper sack as if it were a carton of eggs. "The best brownies in Minnesota was what the sign said." She set the package on Frannie's table, then looked at Joe and said, "You like chocolate?"

"I'm afraid I'm not going to be able to stay for coffee." He glanced at his watch, then said to Frannie, "I asked the cab driver to pick me up at three. Maybe I should wait outside."

"Oh, please. Don't leave on my account," Arlene insisted. "Frannie, tell him he doesn't have to go."

"I think you should stay a while, Joe," Frannie said. "I can give you a ride to the airport later if you like. What time do you have to be back?"

He didn't answer, but said, "Could I talk to you before I go?"

She hesitated, and Arlene gave her a gentle shove, "Go on outside where it's nice and private. I'll finish this for you."

THEY STOOD near the single-car garage next to the alley. Frannie stared at Joe, wondering what he wanted to say, hoping that it had something to do with what had happened between them on the sofa before Arlene had walked in.

"About what was going on before your mother-in-law arrived...it doesn't change anything," he said.

That wasn't the something she wanted to hear. His words were like a scratch on a sunburn, reminding her that he had intended to break up with her.

"I guess there's no point in me asking you to stay to dinner, then." She tried to keep the bitterness from her voice, but was unsuccessful.

He didn't answer, but looked everywhere except at her. "Frannie, don't make this any harder than it is."

"I don't want to, Joe, but it hurts so bad to think about you leaving." There were few times in her life when she had swallowed her pride, but this was one of them. "We have something good between us. You must know that."

He stole a glance at her. "I do know that and I want to stay, but..."

The fact he was having this conversation told her he still had doubts about his decision. She made the most of his hesitation, saying, "Remember that night at the lake? You told me to follow my instincts, because they were right. What about your instincts, Joe? What are they telling you to do?"

He didn't answer right away, but kicked at a stone buried in the dirt. "This particular can of worms may be like nothing you've ever seen," he warned.

She put her hand on his arm. "I'm not afraid of what will come out."

He looked at her then and said, "Maybe you should be."

He looked so tormented that she wanted to kiss

away the worry lines on his face, yet she kept him at arm's length. He'd put up an impenetrable wall that she didn't dare try to breach.

"I'm willing to take my chances, Joe, if you are."

Just then a horn sounded. Arlene stuck her head out the back door and said, "There's a taxi out front."

Joe gave Arlene one brief look and said, "That's for me. Thanks."

"You're going to leave?" There was a note of panic in Frannie's raised voice.

"I'm sorry."

She could see by the expression on his face that nothing she could say was going to make him change his mind. "I'm sorry, too."

The taxi horn sounded again. He gazed at her intently and said, "It's important to me that the results of the DNA test stay confidential, Frannie."

"I know," she said, then watched him start toward the gate.

"Is this goodbye?" she asked. When he paused, she added, "Because if this is goodbye I want my last kiss."

"I can't kiss you, Frannie, because if I do, I won't leave."

And with those words he was gone.

JOE GLANCED AT HIS WATCH. It was only eight o'clock. Instead of sitting by himself in a hotel room, he should have been with Frannie. His body warmed at the thought of her. It was almost as if he could still taste her on his lips.

He shook his head, trying to rid himself of such thoughts. He couldn't. He'd thought about nothing else since he'd left her place. She'd been on his mind while he'd eaten the prime rib special in the hotel's dining room. She'd been there when he'd gone for a walk after dinner. And she was the reason he could stare at a shopping channel and listen to a movie star rave about the benefits of moisturizing cream.

He thought about calling a cab and going back to her house. He thought about it, but he didn't do it. He couldn't. Not as long as Arlene Harper was there.

Because she was one woman he didn't want to think about. He still couldn't believe she'd turned up on Frannie's doorstep the way she had. Frannie had said she was a little unpredictable—but to arrive unannounced and with a guy. His mother would have never dropped in on anyone.

But then Arlene Harper was nothing like his mother. All that big red hair. And she must have had a ring on every finger of her hand. Not to mention the makeup. He shook his head. It was amazing that he had even noticed that her skin had paled when she'd seen who Frannie was rolling around with on the couch.

No matter what Arlene said, Joe knew that his presence had disturbed her. Hell, he'd been shaken to see her, too. The last person he'd expected to find at Frannie's this afternoon was the woman who might be his birth mother.

He shook his head. It wasn't true. It couldn't be true. He'd had a mother—one who'd been the center of his life for eleven years. She was the only mother he'd ever wanted, the only mother he'd ever needed. That's why it didn't seem right that Arlene Harper, who was nothing at all like a mother should be, could be related to him.

Frannie thought he was afraid to find out the truth. Maybe part of him was. The part of him that felt loyal to the woman who'd held his hand on the first day of school, the woman who'd tucked him into bed at night, the woman who'd let him cry on her shoulder even though she knew his father would disapprove.

Joe had every right to be afraid of the DNA results. But not for the reasons Frannie expected. If he could be completely honest, he would tell her that the real reason for his fear had to do with losing a parent, not with finding one. The truth in this case could eventually take away the one other person he loved as much as he'd loved his mother.

The problem was, Frannie knew very little of the truth when it came to him and his father. She knew them as Joe Smith, Senior and Joe Smith, Junior. The Admiral and his son. Not as the Hawthorns, two men who'd created new identities to escape a past filled with accusations and threats.

If there were any investigations into what had happened at that naval hospital on Guam where both he and the Harper twins were born, it would only be a matter of time before it was discovered there'd been no Mrs. Joseph Smith at that hospital. There had been, however, a Mrs. Joseph Hawthorn.

With a little digging, anyone could find that Admiral Joseph Hawthorn's wife had given birth on the same night in the same hospital as the Harper twins. Admiral Joseph Hawthorn, the man who'd been tried and found guilty of treason by the media before his case ever got to the courts.

That's because the suspect had never made it to court. Joe had seen to that. As soon as he'd learned that his father's company was being investigated for selling the designs to classified military weapons to a foreign country, Joe knew that it had to be a setup. He accepted part of the blame for his father getting into such a situation.

Joe had been the one to encourage his father to seek employment after retiring from the Navy. Upon reflection, he knew he should have checked out the firm that had come courting his father's services. When the Admiral had told him how much money he was making for doing so very little work, Joe should have been suspicious, but he'd been absorbed in his own life. With his marriage crumbling, he'd focused his attention on his own problems.

It was only after his father had been charged with treason that Joe had realized his father's situation was not what it appeared to be. Even with the best of attorneys, there seemed little hope that the Admiral would be found not guilty.

And it wasn't simply the criminal charges that had threatened his father. A suspicious car accident led Joe to believe that if his father testified, his life would be in jeopardy. Unwilling to put his father's safety in the hands of those who'd already proven they were incapable of protecting him, Joe did the only thing he could do.

Now he needed to remember what they'd been through the past two years and not let his emotions undo everything he'd worked so hard to put together. Unfortunately, their safety had already been compromised, thanks to his involvement with Frannie. Now all he could hope for was that she would respect his wish to protect his father.

And he needed luck. A whole lot of luck.

FRANNIE TRIED not to think about Joe, but every time she looked at Arlene she was torn with uncertainty. She wanted to respect Joe's wishes and understood why he felt the need to protect his father, yet she also knew what it meant to be a mother.

If Arlene was surprised that Joe left, she didn't show it. Although she would have preferred him to stay, Frannie was a bit relieved he hadn't. With his departure went a tension that had made normal conversation difficult. Frannie knew that in the short time Joe and Arlene had been in the same room together, her mother-in-law had compared Joe to Dennis. It was a bit of déjà vu for Frannie, who had watched Alex do the same thing, only in a more obvious way.

Alex was the one person Frannie thought might mention his involvement with Joe. If he were to tell his grandmother about the DNA test, Frannie would either have to tell the truth about the results or lie.

To her relief, Alex didn't say a word. That's because as soon as he and Emma walked through the door, his grandmother said she had a surprise for them. Ted was sent out to the van to retrieve several large boxes. Inside were the components for a personal computer. Once the PC came into the house, Frannie didn't hear a word from the twins except for the litany of questions they asked Ted during dinner. To Frannie's relief, Ted not only was a nice man, but was proficient when it came to computers.

When Arlene offered to do the dishes so that Emma and Alex could spend time with Ted, who was putting everything together, Frannie didn't protest. She sent the twins into the living room, where they huddled with Ted around the monitor.

"I think Luke is feeling a bit left out. Maybe we should take him to the park," Arlene suggested as she dried the last of the dishes.

Frannie knew that once Luke heard the word *park,* there would be no changing their plans. He ran to the door to grab his shoes, his eyes wide.

"I think the park's a great idea," Frannie said, draping her wet dish towel over the back of a chair.

Although Frannie often complained to Lois about the size of her house and yard, she'd always appreciated its location. Around the corner was a park that had a small wading pool for the kids in the summer and an ice rink in the winter. As well as a baseball diamond and a basketball court, it had playground equipment that Luke loved. He'd climb and jump and run to his heart's content.

This evening was no different. While he played with several other toddlers from the neighborhood, Frannie and Arlene sat on a park bench just a few feet away. Frannie suspected her mother-in-law had suggested they come to the park so they could talk privately. She was right, only the questions weren't about Joe, but her boyfriend.

"So what do you think of Ted?"

"He seems very nice," Frannie answered honestly.

"Oh, he is. And he's smart."

"Does he live in Boise?"

"Uh-huh. But here's another coincidence. He's been thinking about moving to the Midwest because his children are here."

"He has children?"

She nodded. "Two sons. One's in Chicago, the other one's here in Roseville. So you don't need to worry about putting us up while we're here. We're going to stay at his son's place.''

''I'm hearing an awful lot of 'we's' when you talk about him,'' Frannie commented.

''It just seems so natural. I know to you it probably seems as if it happened really fast, but we never should have broken up all those years ago.'' She waved at Luke as he ran past, then said in a reflective voice, ''We almost got engaged our senior year in high school, but then his dad had a job transfer and he moved away, and next thing you know...'' She sighed. ''Well, there's no use crying over spilled milk, is there.''

''No, there isn't.''

''Isn't it strange how things turn out? I never thought I'd see him again and now...'' She had a dreamy look on her face.

''I hope it works out for you, Arlene,'' Frannie said sincerely.

''I do, too. It would mean I'd be part of a family again.''

Frannie reached out to cover her hand. ''You're a part of our family.''

She smiled and patted Frannie's hand. ''I know I am, and I love my grandchildren, but...''

''We remind you of Dennis,'' Frannie said quietly.

''Yes, but in a good way.'' She sighed. ''When I'm with Ted and I hear him talk about his sons, it reminds me of what I've lost. I have an adult son and I don't even have a relationship with him,'' she said sadly.

''That's true,'' Frannie said, thinking not of Dennis but of Joe.

"But that's the way it is. I can't make him want to be a part of my life," she continued.

Frannie knew that what she said applied to Joe, too. He didn't want to be a part of Arlene's life. Seeing the sadness that always came into Arlene's eyes when she talked about Dennis, Frannie made the decision to go against Joe's wishes and tell Arlene the truth. After all, she had a right to know.

"Arlene, there's something I have to tell you."

"And what is that?"

Frannie searched for the right words. "When Alex first found Joe Smith, he looked so much like Dennis that Alex refused to believe he wasn't his father."

"I can understand that," Arlene told her. "I have to admit, I did a double take when I saw him the first time. It's amazing how much he looks like Dennis. If I didn't know better, I would think they were related."

"Maybe they are." Frannie spoke so softly, she wasn't sure Arlene even heard her.

"What? You think he's a long lost cousin or something?"

"Actually I know he's related to Dennis. Because Alex refused to believe Joe wasn't his father, we had a paternity test done," Frannie stated carefully.

"And it showed that they were related? I didn't realize they tell those kinds of things with DNA. I mean, I knew you could tell if someone was a father to a child, but cousins?"

"He's not a cousin, Arlene."

Her face wrinkled in confusion. "Then, I don't understand."

She shifted uneasily. "Wasn't Dennis born in a naval hospital on Guam?"

"Yes. We were stationed there while his dad was in the Navy. Why are you asking that?"

"And you said he was a twin but that his twin brother died."

Arlene leaned away from her, regarding her suspiciously. "Why are you asking me these questions?"

Frannie knew there was no easy way to tell her. "Because according to the results from the DNA lab, Joe is Dennis's identical twin."

Arlene turned so pale, Frannie thought she was going to faint. She started to shake her head vigorously.

"No. He can't be. My baby died. I held him in my arms and he was gone."

Frannie put her arm around Arlene's trembling shoulders. "Maybe that baby you thought was your son belonged to somebody else."

"It's not possible. I gave birth to him...to both of them."

"Arlene, DNA results are accurate ninety-nine percent of the time. And if you don't believe them, just look at Joe Smith."

"Are you saying that someone made a mistake and gave me the wrong baby?" Her mouth was wide open at the possibility.

Frannie explained her theory about the babies being switched at the hospital. She also told her Joe's reaction to the information. "So you see, it's a complicated situation."

"Yes, it is," Arlene agreed.

"Then, you understand why we need to be careful how we investigate this."

Arlene nodded. "Of course."

"And you're okay with not pursuing this?" Frannie asked cautiously.

"I most certainly am not," she declared, rising to her feet.

Apprehensive, Frannie asked, "Please don't make any trouble for Joe."

"I'm not going to make any trouble. I'm going to pay him a visit."

CHAPTER ELEVEN

JOE RETURNED to Grand Marais feeling just as uneasy as he had when he'd left. Not only had he not ended his relationship with Frannie, but his reluctance to say goodbye to her had resulted in his meeting Arlene Harper. He wondered how long Nature's Hideaway would continue to be a safe harbor for him and his father.

The following morning, news came from the hospital that should have eased some of the tension knotting Joe's muscles. His father could come home because all the tests indicated his condition hadn't deteriorated since his last checkup. As relieved as Joe was to hear the doctor's report, he knew that his father faced another threat—an investigation into his past.

That night, while his father slept peacefully in his own bed, Joe tossed and turned, wondering if he had convinced Frannie not to search for answers as to what happened thirty-three years ago in a naval hospital in Guam. Needing to know for sure, he decided to call her first thing in the morning.

She wasn't home. A few hours later he learned why. She was in Grand Marais and she wasn't alone. She called from a pay phone to ask if he'd meet her and Arlene at one of the local cafés so the three of them could talk.

Joe knew Arlene wouldn't have come to Grand Marais if she didn't know about the DNA testing. Realizing that discussing the paternity test results was probably inevitable, Joe invited Frannie and Arlene to the lake, where there would be no danger of anyone overhearing them.

He waited outside for them, trying not to feel as if Frannie had let him down. He didn't want to make the assumption that she'd told her mother-in-law about the results of the DNA testing, yet other than her sister Lois, there was no one who knew the outcome. But he couldn't forget how she'd pleaded with him not to turn his back on the information.

As usual, the sight of Frannie unleashed a longing he was forced to keep at bay. As she climbed out of the car, he saw that she wore jeans and a red sweatshirt, reflecting the coolness of the late summer weather.

"Hi." She gave him a guarded smile.

"Hi. Where are the kids?"

"With Ted back at the lodge," she answered.

"You're staying overnight?"

She nodded. "Arlene wanted to bring the kids to the North Shore for Labor Day weekend. We're at a lodge near Lutsen."

"You're lucky you caught me at home. This is usually a busy weekend," he said, wishing the sight of her didn't make him feel so good inside.

"Arlene talked to the Admiral. He told us you'd be home."

He looked for the first time at the older woman. "You spoke to my dad?"

Some of his displeasure must have shown on his

face, for she said, "I only asked him if it might be all right if we visited. That's all I said."

Joe knew that she could have said much more. It was in her tone.

"Arlene's going back to New Jersey next week, Joe. She needed to talk to you before she left."

Frannie gave him a look that was a plea for understanding. He interpreted it as a sign that his assumption was correct. She'd told her mother-in-law the results of the DNA testing.

"Why don't we go inside?" he suggested, leading them toward the house. With one hand he held open the door, with the other he motioned for the two of them to go ahead of him.

"Would you like something to drink?" he asked as he showed them in to the living room.

"Not right now, thank you," Arlene replied politely, sitting down on the leather sofa. Frannie sat next to her, shaking her head in response to his offer.

Joe wondered what their reaction would be if he poured himself a good stiff drink. He could use one, but he resisted the urge. He glanced out the window. With a gray sky overhead and white caps rolling across the water, the lake looked as he felt—cold and irritated.

"I guess there's no point in pretending that I don't know why you're here," he said, trying not to sound uncivil.

Frannie sat with her hands folded in her lap, her back stiff. She was the one who began. "Arlene knows about the DNA test results, Joe."

"You told her." He knew his eyes were full of accusation. Hers were defensive.

"She would have found out sooner or later," Frannie argued.

"You know my reasons for wanting it to be later," he snapped at her.

"Don't be angry at Frannie." Arlene came to her defense. "She just did what she thought was the right thing."

Joe *was* angry. For two years he'd fought to keep a tight control on the events in his life. Now it was as if fate had yanked the reins right out of his hands. He hadn't asked for anyone to come looking for him, yet here was this woman sitting across from him full of questions he didn't want to answer.

"This isn't easy for any of us, Joe—" she said in a surprisingly calm voice.

But what was even more amazing was that it sounded comforting to Joe.

"You have my word. I would never do anything to jeopardize your father's health."

Again Joe looked at Frannie. "You told her about my dad?"

She nodded. "She understands he's frail."

Joe could feel both women's eyes on him.

Arlene said, "You look just like my son Dennis. And you have a way of tipping your head to one side just like he always did. And you have some of the same facial expressions. Alex told me—" She broke off as if suddenly embarrassed. "I'm sorry. This isn't getting us to the point, is it."

"And what is the point?" Joe asked, knowing perfectly well what the answer was.

She appeared to be calm, but when he looked at her hands he saw that she clutched her purse so tightly her knuckles were white. When his eyes met hers, she asked, "Do you believe the DNA report?"

He knew this was his chance to refute the lab results. All he had to do was pull out his driver's license and show her his date of birth. Neither she nor Frannie would know that it had been falsified. He didn't need to corroborate any of the information she'd told him.

He stared at the pale face of the woman sitting across from him. He could see the hope in her eyes— eyes that were the same chocolate brown as his. She was a stranger, yet she was familiar.

"I've talked with several different people at the lab and they all assured me that the report is accurate," he said quietly. He took a deep breath, aware that if he told them everything he knew about the night he was born, he would be no longer be able to contend that the DNA lab had made a mistake.

He paused, debating whether to admit he had the same suspicions as they did about his being Dennis's brother.

You strike me as the kind of man who puts truth at the top of the list. Frannie's words echoed in his head. Yes, the truth was important, but so was his father's safety. Did he have to sacrifice one for the other? Was he willing to risk finding out?

"Maybe you should tell me what you remember from the night your sons were born," he suggested, sure that he was slipping into muddy waters.

Arlene told him there had been a typhoon, the power had gone out for a short time, there'd been a rush of deliveries—more than they'd ever had in a single night.

When she'd finished, he knew the moment had

come. He could tell her he was born in November as his driver's license said, that there'd been no storms. But he looked at Frannie, whose eyes gazed at him with hope and compassion. Then he looked at Arlene and saw the desperation of a mother needing the truth.

So he said, "My father told me a similar story."

"There'd been a typhoon?"

He nodded.

"You were born at the naval hospital on Guam?"

Again he nodded.

"And the power had gone out?"

"Yes."

"Then—" she broke off, choked with emotion.

"If we are to believe what the DNA report tells us, I'm Dennis's twin brother."

"Oh, my goodness!" She pulled a tissue out of her purse to dab at the tears falling down her cheeks. Frannie leaned over to put an arm around her shoulder, but from the look on her face Joe could see that she thought he should be the one to comfort her.

Joe wasn't sure he was ready to embrace this strange woman. He went to her side, crouched at her feet. "Arlene?"

She looked up at him, her eyes brimming with tears.

"I know this is a shock for you," he said to her. "It is for me, too."

She reached for him then, wrapping her arms around him. "You're my son...all those years I could have had you and..." Hiccups and sobs drowned out the remainder of her words.

Joe let her cry, finding an unfamiliar but not unwelcome comfort in the warmth of the arms wrapped tight around his shoulders. Finally, when she'd finished crying, she pushed him away and stared at him.

"You're so handsome. Isn't he handsome?" she asked Frannie, who Joe noticed agreed with a smile. Arlene dabbed at her eyes again, saying, "I'm sorry. I promised Frannie I wouldn't make a scene, and here I am."

"It's all right," Joe soothed.

"Is it really going to be all right?" she asked him. That he couldn't answer.

She moved over on the sofa, patting the spot between her and Frannie, indicating he should sit there. "Tell me about your mother. Frannie told me she'd passed on, Joe. I'm sorry," she said, her eyes full of compassion.

He acknowledged her sympathy with a nod.

"She was a good woman. A schoolteacher, actually, although once she had me she gave up teaching, but she was always doing some type of volunteer work." He went on to talk a little bit about his childhood, answering all Arlene's questions patiently.

"She must not have known that you weren't the baby she'd delivered that night," Arlene commented.

Joe shook his head. "I'm sure she didn't."

"But, Joe, what about your birthday?" Frannie asked, then added for Arlene's benefit, "Joe was born on the seventeenth of November, not December as Dennis was."

Joe knew he needed to come up with an explanation that would satisfy them, yet keep anyone from discovering his ID had been faked. "Actually, my birthday is the seventeenth of December," he admitted. "When I applied for my Minnesota license, there was a typographical error when it came and I never bothered to have it corrected. It didn't seem important.''

He thought Frannie eyed him suspiciously, then realized he hadn't imagined it when she said, ''You didn't mention that to me when you showed me your license that day after the storm.''

''You didn't tell me when Dennis's birthday was, and I never imagined that we'd be even remotely close,'' he said, realizing that the tightrope he walked was a very unsteady one.

Arlene slowly shook her head. ''I still can't believe there could have been a mix-up, but it would explain why Daniel weighed so much more than Dennis.''

Another reason to believe it had to be true, Joe realized. He, too, had been a small baby. ''I remember my father teasing me when I was a teenager. He'd say, 'For a such a scrawny baby you sure turned out to be a big guy.'''

''Dennis weighed just under five pounds,'' Arlene reported.

''Me, too,'' Joe admitted. ''It still doesn't seem possible. Don't they tag babies when they're born? I remember my mother kept the little plastic thingy they had around my ankle in my baby book.''

''My kids had them, too, but the question is, when were they put on?'' Frannie interjected. ''And if there were more babies arriving than they had hands to take care of...and if the power went out before the tags were on...it's possible they mistook one baby for another.''

''So I went home with one baby that was mine and one that wasn't,'' Arlene concluded.

Again she dabbed at her eyes, and Joe said, ''Frannie told me one of your sons died as an infant. I'm sorry. That must have been very painful for you.''

She nodded. "He was called Daniel. He was such a good baby. He never fussed. Dennis could be screaming at the top of his lungs, and Daniel would just look around with those bright blue eyes of his.''

Joe looked at Arlene's brown eyes and was about to ask her if the baby's eye color hadn't raised her suspicions, when she said, "My husband had blue eyes and I thought the babies were fraternal twins. I had no way of knowing that there'd been some kind of mix-up at the hospital. If I had, I wouldn't have—''

Frannie said, "You can't blame yourself, Arlene. If Joe's parents didn't realize something was wrong, why would you?''

"All newborn babies look the same to me.'' Joe tried to ease her guilt. "Unless there was a birthmark or some other distinguishing characteristic, how would anyone know there'd been a mistake?''

"A mother should know,'' Arlene said, her voice full of remorse.

"Obviously no one knew,'' Frannie reminded her. "But that's not your fault or Joe's.''

"We need to find out how it happened and why,'' Arlene stated with determination.

It was something that Joe wanted to know, too, but he also knew that such an investigation could be disastrous for his father. "It was over thirty years ago. I doubt the hospital records will tell us much.''

"That doesn't mean we shouldn't look for answers,'' Arlene argued.

To Joe's relief, Frannie spoke. "Normally, I'd

agree with you, Arlene, but this involves other people, too. Joe's dad, for one.''

''I'd like you to meet him,'' Joe said, rising. ''He's resting in his room, but I'll go see if he's able to come say hello.''

Although Joe would have preferred not to wake the Admiral from his nap, he knew that if Arlene were to see for herself how fragile his father's health was, she'd have a better understanding of why he didn't want her searching old hospital records.

After a brief visit with his father, during which they had coffee and talked about naval life, Arlene announced it was time to leave. Joe left his father in the house sorting coins for his collection, while he walked the two women to their car.

''Your father is a sweet man, Joe. You don't need to worry about me. I wouldn't do anything to cause him heartache. There's been enough of that already,'' she told him. ''You have a wonderful relationship. I only wish my Dennis had had such a man for his dad.''

''Is he still alive—Dennis's father?'' Joe asked.

''It's been several years since I had any news of him, and then it was that he'd been seriously ill. Had cancer I believe.''

''You didn't mention that to me,'' Frannie commented.

Arlene shrugged. ''I wasn't sure you'd find it important, seeing as he was never a part of the children's lives.''

Frannie nodded in understanding.

Arlene said to Joe, ''If you have any questions about him, I'd be willing to talk to you about him. It's up to you, Joe.''

Joe looked out at the pines and clear blue water. "In time, maybe, but for now I don't see any reason to go digging into the past."

"I agree," Arlene seconded. "You have my word, Joe. I know it's not easy learning the past wasn't what you thought it was, but I do hope that now that we know the truth, you'll find a place for me in your life."

Joe knew this was his opportunity to say politely that he had all the family he needed. And he should have said that. When he'd moved his father to the North Shore, they'd broken ties with every member of both the Hawthorn and Delaney families, knowing that any investigation would start with their relatives.

When he didn't answer right away, Arlene said, "You don't need to tell me today, Joe. I know it's going to take a little time for you to get used to the idea of having more family."

He was grateful that she was making it easier for him. "It's not that I don't want you to be a part of my life, Arlene. It's just that I'm concerned about what this is going to do to my dad. I have to do whatever I can make sure he's not hurt by this."

"All of us can make that our priority, Joe," Frannie agreed.

Joe turned to Arlene. "So you understand if I want to take some time to get used to things?"

"Of course I do. I'm just so thrilled to discover that I have another son," she said, emotion choking her words. She gave him a quick hug, then climbed into the van.

Joe turned to Frannie. "This is all a bit overwhelming."

"It's going to be okay," she said, placing her hand on his arm.

He stared into her eyes and felt a longing for her that had nothing to do with sex. He took her fingers in his hand and gently squeezed them.

"The worms haven't scared you away?" he asked her, giving her a crooked smile.

"No, I can handle worms." She moved closer to him and said, "You can give me a kiss. Arlene's already seen more than that."

He pulled her into his arms and planted a tender kiss on her lips.

"I'll let that kiss go, but only today," she said with a mischievous smile. Then her face turned sober and she said, "What about Alex? What do we tell him? He thinks the DNA test was botched, and since we didn't do the second one, I know he's been putting two and two together and coming up with five."

"I really would like as few people as possible to know about this stuff," he said, rubbing a hand across his neck.

"You are his uncle," she reminded him.

He sighed. "Yes, and I should probably be the one to tell him that. You said you're spending the weekend at the lodge?" When Frannie nodded, he added, "Can you bring Emma and Alex over tomorrow afternoon?"

"You'll speak to both of them?"

"I am their uncle."

Frannie smiled. "Yes, you are."

He brought her fingers to his lips and kissed them. "Everything will be okay."

He only wished he believed that himself.

"SO WHAT'S THE DEAL? What's going on with you and Gramma?"

Joe answered Alex's question with a question. "What makes you think something's going on?"

Alex didn't see any reason to pretend he didn't know why Joe had suggested they fish off the dock. From the way his mother and grandmother had been acting, he knew something was up and he was determined to find out what it was. "That is why you brought me down here, isn't it? To tell me what the DNA test means?"

"You're pretty smart for a ten-year-old," Joe remarked.

"I'm almost eleven. Next week's my birthday."

Joe lowered himself onto the wooden bench, setting his tackle box at his feet. "Take a seat, and I'll tell you what you want to know."

Alex sat down beside him, eyeing him suspiciously.

Joe looked straight at him and said, "I'm not your father, Alex. I wish I were, because you're a kid any dad would be proud to call his own."

Alex jumped to his feet. "Don't say that! My mom says that all the time and it doesn't mean anything because I still don't have a dad."

"It's not your fault you don't have a dad, Alex," he said, his voice sounding all mushy as if he thought Alex was going to cry.

Joe didn't know Alex very well if he thought that. Alex didn't cry over a deadbeat dad. "No, it's your fault," he snarled, turning his back on Joe.

Alex felt a hand on his arm.

"Look at me, Alex."

Slowly, he turned around. Joe again looked him

straight in the eye and said, "I'm not Dennis Harper. Now, you can believe I'm telling you the truth, or you can go ask your mother or your grandmother and you'll get the same answer."

He thought about doing just that, but feared that they would tell him the same thing. "If you're not my dad, then why did Gramma want to drive all the way up here to see you?"

"This is where it gets complicated, but I know you'll understand because you're a smart kid." Joe patted the bench next to him. "If you sit down, I'll explain it to you."

Alex folded his arms across his chest and said, "I'd rather stand."

He was glad Joe didn't try to get him to change his mind.

"You love your mother, right?" When he nodded, Joe added, "And you would do anything you could to see that she didn't get hurt, right?" Again, Alex nodded. "In fact, that's why you hung the posters looking for your dad—because you thought his being gone was hurting your mother, right?"

"Yeah, so what?"

"I love my dad, Alex, the same way you love your mom. You've met the Admiral."

He nodded. "We played games the night of that storm."

"I'd do anything I could to keep him from getting hurt."

"Who's going to hurt him?"

"Not who, but what. In this case, information."

Alex wrinkled his brow. "What information?"

"That your grandmother is my mother. The reason

I look just like your dad, Alex, is that I'm his twin brother. I'm your uncle.''

"You can't be!" Alex had never heard such crap. "Uncle Daniel died when he was a baby. Just ask Gramma."

"Yes, your uncle died. But that uncle wasn't really your father's twin. I am.''

Alex listened as Joe explained how such a thing could have happened. To Alex, it sounded like something made up, but he knew his mom and his grandmother were pretty smart and that they wouldn't believe it unless it was true.

"So you can see how this information could really hurt my dad, can't you?'' Joe said to him when he'd finished telling him about the babies.

"The Admiral doesn't know you're not his son?''

"Oh, but I am his son," Joe insisted. "I may not have his DNA, but that doesn't mean he's not my father. What makes a man a father isn't necessarily genetics. A father is someone who's there for his son, who gives of himself without complaining and who loves unconditionally. You know what unconditional love is?''

Alex shook his head.

"It means that no matter how bad you screw up, your father understands.''

"Is that the way it is with you and the Admiral?''

Joe nodded. "And I've made some pretty big mistakes in my time. That's why I don't care what the DNA test shows. The Admiral is always going to be my father, but I'm worried that if he finds out what happened in the hospital all those years ago, he'll be hurt. And I don't want that to happen. You can understand, right?''

He nodded. "He's easily confused."

"Yes, he is."

"You want this to be a secret from him?"

"Yes. Will you do that for me?"

Again Alex nodded. "Mom knows about all of this?"

"Yes."

"Then, she's keeping the secret, too?"

"Yes, she is. And your grandmother, too."

He glanced back up at the house and saw his gramma sitting on the deck. She waved when she saw him, so he waved back.

"She's up there watching us," Alex said to Joe.

"It's been an emotional couple of days for her. It's not every day you discover you have another son," he said.

"How does it feel to have another mom?"

"A little strange, but I think once I get used to it, it'll be okay."

"Gramma's really cool."

"Does she know how to fish?"

"I do," he boasted, picking up one of the fishing rods. "What can we get off the dock? Pan fish?"

"I've been known to snag a walleye or two," he answered, reaching for the other rod. "This is a first for me, though. I've never fished with a nephew before. Actually, I've never had a nephew before."

"So are you going to come around a lot?"

"I'd like to."

He looked sideways at Joe and said, "Because of Mom?"

"A little. I like being with your mom, but I also like being with you and Emma and Luke. I know I can't replace your father, Alex, but I think I can be a pretty darn good uncle if you let me.''

Alex believed he would be, too.

"MOM! LOOK AT THE FISH I caught!'' Alex reached for the chain wrapped around the dock post and pulled a long, slender fish out of the water. ''It's a northern! Joe said it's the biggest one he's ever seen anybody catch off a dock.''

Frannie kept her distance from her son as the fish wiggled and flapped about on the end of the stringer. ''Is that dinner?''

''Maybe, if we get a couple more,'' Joe answered. ''That one's just barely over the size limit.''

''Are we staying for dinner?'' Alex asked as he lowered the fish back into the lake.

Frannie suddenly felt self-conscious, as if she'd invited herself to stay. ''I don't know. We'll have to see if your grandmother has made any plans.''

''I bet she'll want to eat with Uncle Joe,'' Alex declared. ''You want me to go ask her?''

Frannie was about to say that it wasn't necessary when Joe said, ''That's a good idea, Alex.''

As soon as he was gone, Frannie said, ''I came to see how things had gone, but I guess I don't need to ask.''

''I think he's okay with everything. What about Emma?''

She sat down beside him on the bench seat. ''She's more than okay.''

''What did she say?''

Frannie mentally debated whether she should tell him. ''That she's glad you're her uncle and not her father because that means you won't leave.''

"She's right. I won't leave." He didn't look at her, but stared out at his line.

"But the other day—" she began.

"That was the other day. Things have changed."

He looked at her then, and she was glad she was sitting down for she was certain the weakness in her legs would have caused her to fall.

"I'm not leaving, Frannie."

"The kids, or me?" she found the courage to ask.

"Neither. I think we should take things slowly, especially after everything that's happened these past few days."

The way he was looking at her made her breath catch in her throat. "It's okay with me as long as you intend to stick around."

He smiled, the most wonderful smile she'd ever seen on his face.

"Are you saying you're willing to take a chance on a guy who can't promise you anything except that he won't leave when things get tough?"

"That's enough for now," she replied simply.

"I'd seal the deal with a kiss, but even though I know Alex is comfortable with me being his uncle, I'm not sure he's ready for me to be anything more."

She knew he was right. "I should warn you that courting a mother of three does not leave for many quiet, romantic moments."

"If you're telling me I have to sneak my kisses, I should tell you that I'm a man who knows how to make the most of his opportunities," he retorted.

IN THE WEEKS that followed, Frannie discovered that Joe was true to his word. The more time she spent with him, the less satisfied she was with stolen moments.

Frannie was amazed at how easily he fit into their life. It seemed natural for him to be there for Alex and Emma's birthday, to carry Luke around on his shoulders, to repair the broken screen on the kitchen door. While he listened patiently to Arlene as she tried to say in a few days what she'd missed over the past three decades, Frannie fell even more deeply in love with him.

Everyone was happy that Joe was a part of their lives—everyone except Lois, who couldn't understand why Frannie wasn't bothered by the fact that her ex-mother-in-law was also the mother of her boyfriend—a boyfriend who looked exactly like her exhusband. Frannie tried to explain to her sister that Joe was nothing like Dennis, but she could see that Lois didn't trust him.

That's why she wasn't surprised when Lois showed up on her doorstep one afternoon waving a manila folder and saying, "You're not going to like what I found out about your boyfriend."

"Why would you have found out anything? I didn't ask you to go looking for information," Frannie said, as her sister stepped past her into the house.

"Where's Luke?" she asked, looking around for signs of the toddler.

"Taking a nap."

"Good. You better sit down," Lois instructed, taking a seat on sofa.

"You didn't answer my question. Why would you check up on Joe?"

"Because Arlene is my client and I always look after my clients' interests," she answered.

Frannie had an uneasy feeling in the pit of her stomach. "What interests?"

"That's privileged information," her sister answered in an annoying professional voice.

"Are you telling me that because Arlene came to you to discuss what happens now that she's discovered she has another son, you took it upon yourself to investigate Joe's background?"

"I did what any good lawyer would do."

Frannie put her hands on her waist. "Wait a minute. Aren't you forgetting something? Joe didn't come looking for Arlene. We found him. If you're trying to imply that he's some gold digger out to capitalize on a middle-aged divorcée, you're way off base."

"I only took steps to make sure that legally he is her son."

"Of course he's her son! You saw the DNA report."

"And I heard the story of the crowded conditions at that overseas hospital and the power shortage and the assumption that the babies had been switched," she stated flatly.

"What more proof do you need? Anyone can see by looking at him, he's Dennis's twin," Frannie argued.

"I wanted to have as much evidence as I could find."

"I thought Arlene explained to you that she didn't want to go digging into anyone's past."

"Yes, because *Joe* didn't want her to. When I heard that, I figured he had something to hide."

"What he has is a sick father, a very good man whose heart could be broken if the whole truth is revealed.'' She could feel her cheeks heating, and her voice had started to wobble.

"I'm sorry his father's not well, but that doesn't change the facts. If you'd stop pacing the floor and sit down, you'll see what I'm talking about."

Frannie didn't want to sit. She didn't want to look at what Lois had uncovered about Joe, because it didn't matter. Maybe he hadn't exactly been a Boy Scout, but he was a good man. In her heart she knew that. *But you thought that about Dennis, too.*

Her heart banged against the wall of her chest and her mouth felt dry as she sat down next to her sister.

Lois handed her a piece of paper with a hospital logo across the top. "Before you go giving him the farm, I suggest you take a look at this."

Frannie looked at the list and saw Arlene's name, as well as those of her sons, Dennis and Daniel.

"You'll notice there's no Joseph Smith or any woman named Smith," Lois said.

Frannie frowned. "Maybe his mother went by her maiden name."

"Which was?"

Frannie shrugged. "I don't know."

"What about her first name?"

"I think he said it was Kathleen."

"Do you see a Kathleen on that list?"

Frannie looked it over. There was one. A Kathleen Hawthorn.

"There's only one Joseph on that list. A baby boy named Joseph Hawthorn, mother Kathleen Hawthorn," Lois rattled off.

Frannie met her sister's eyes. "You think that's him?" she asked weakly.

"There are no other baby boys with that name."

"I don't get it. Why would he say his name is Joe Smith if he's..." She didn't want to think of what the answer to that question might be.

"If you were going to pick an alias, Joe Smith would be a good one," Lois told her. "There are a ton of them."

"You think Joe's using an assumed identity?"

"Sure looks that way to me."

Frannie couldn't believe what she was hearing. "It doesn't make any sense."

"To someone on the run it does."

"Are you saying you think Joe is a fugitive?"

"Why else does a man change his identity? Unless he's like your ex-husband—running from bad debts and responsibilities."

Frannie put her fist to her mouth, determined to push back the tears that threatened to fall. *Just like her ex-husband.*

No! Joe was nothing like Dennis. *Nothing.*

She looked at Lois. "You've met him. He's nothing at all like Dennis." Silently she begged her sister to agree with her.

"He's not who he says he is," her sister stated grimly. "There's a reason why he was so emphatic about your not looking into his past. He said it was because of his father's health, but that wasn't the only reason."

"You think he's a criminal, don't you." The roller coaster had reached the top and was on its descent, and there was no way for Frannie to stop it.

"I'm not sure, but I intend to find out. I've got someone working on it right now. Checking records, running traces."

Frannie sank down onto a chair, feeling defeated. "Have you told Arlene any of this?"

She shook her head. "Not yet. Until we know what it is that Joe's hiding, I don't want to cause her any more pain than she's already had."

Pain? Frannie almost asked, "What about my pain?" But she didn't. She couldn't admit to her sister just how badly she hurt inside.

"Are you going to be all right?" Lois asked.

"No."

"I'm sorry, Frannie. I know you think I don't like Joe, but the truth is I do believe he is a good man. It's just that ever since I met him I had this feeling that he was hiding something."

"I can't believe this," she said, choking back the emotion that threatened to clog her throat.

Lois reached across the table to cover her hand. "It's going to be okay, Frannie. You'll get through this."

Frannie almost laughed out loud. This morning she'd been planning a lifetime with him. Now she was wondering what horrible things he had done to warrant his going into hiding. She shivered at the possibilities that raced through her mind.

"What happens next?" she asked.

"We wait to see what information I collect."

We wait. Frannie didn't want to wait for anything. She wanted to call Joe and find out for herself what was going on. But her sister's warning stopped her.

"Whatever you do, Frannie, don't call him and tell him the authorities are onto him. You can't do that. You understand?"

Oh, yes, she did understand. After years of trying to find Dennis, she knew how slippery a fleeing man could be. If Joe Smith had done something wrong, she wanted him to pay. Not for the crime, but for breaking her heart.

Because it was broken so badly she didn't think it would ever mend.

CHAPTER TWELVE

"HI, ALEX. It's Uncle Joe. Can I talk to your mom?"

"Umm…she can't come to the phone. She's painting the kitchen."

"She's still working on that?"

"Yup."

"You did tell her I called yesterday, didn't you?"

"Yes."

"And you will tell her I called today, right?"

"Sure."

"Alex, is everything okay?"

"Yeah." Alex glanced nervously at Josh. "I gotta go. My friend Josh is here. We're playing a game on my computer."

"No problem. Ask your mom to call me back when she can come to the phone, okay?"

"I will. Bye."

As Alex hung up the phone, Josh asked, "Was that him again?"

Alex nodded. "He's called like six times and my mom won't talk to him." He kept his voice low deliberately, knowing that his mother was just around the corner.

He was glad he had, because she stuck her head into the family room and asked, "Who was on the phone, Alex?"

"It was Uncle Joe."

"Oh." She quickly disappeared into the kitchen again.

"See? I told you," Alex whispered when she'd gone.

Josh shrugged. "She's painting the kitchen. It's no big deal if she doesn't want to answer the phone."

"Oh yeah? So how come she told me she'd talk to Auntie Lois if she called?"

"You think she doesn't want to talk to him?"

"I know she doesn't."

"Why not?" Josh asked. "I thought you said everything was going to be really cool now that you'd found your uncle."

Alex shoved a finger to his mouth. "Shh. You're not supposed to know he's my uncle. You haven't told anybody, have you?"

"No way! I said I wouldn't and I keep my word."

Alex sighed. "You better. Things are messed up enough."

"You mean because your mom's mad at him?"

He nodded. "It's probably over something really dumb."

"Maybe he forgot to bring her flowers," Josh suggested.

Alex frowned. He knew it had nothing to do with flowers. In fact, a delivery truck had brought some yesterday and his mom had taken one look at the card and given the flowers to old Mrs. Greenley across the street. That wasn't a good sign. The other times Uncle Joe had sent his mom flowers, she had practically drooled over them, getting a really mushy look on her face every time she looked at them.

"I wish I knew what was going on," Alex said, voicing his uncertainty.

"Can't you just ask her why she's mad?"

"I did, but she got all emotional and started telling me how this was a difficult situation for everyone and that I shouldn't ask questions she couldn't answer."

"Well, at least if they break up, he's still going to be your uncle," Josh stated pragmatically. "You'll still get to do cool stuff with him."

Alex wasn't so sure. What he didn't tell his best friend was that he'd overhead his mom and his aunt talking. Auntie Lois didn't trust Uncle Joe. She'd warned his mother that Joe might be more like his dad than anyone wanted to believe. He could drop out of sight and never be heard from again.

That wasn't what Alex had wanted to hear. Ever since he'd seen his mom and Joe kissing, he'd started thinking about what it would be like if Joe were to marry his mom. Then Joe wouldn't just be his uncle, he'd be his dad.

Alex thought Joe would make a good dad. Joe liked to do things with Alex and his brother and sister. And he was always interested in hearing about school. And he was smart. He even knew more stuff about computers than Josh did. And he didn't care if Luke got crabby and cried all the way home in the car.

The more Alex thought about it, the more he was sure that Auntie Lois was wrong. Uncle Joe was not like his father at all. He wouldn't abandon his family.

JOE WAITED ALL DAY for Frannie to return his call. He pictured her on a ladder, with paint splattered across her face, doing a job he'd offered to do for her but that she'd insisted on doing herself. The fact that she was self-sufficient was one of the reasons he'd fallen in love with her, yet that didn't keep him from wanting to ease some of the load she carried so proudly on her shoulders.

As often as she'd told him she didn't need a man, he wanted to believe that she needed him. Not to take care of her, but to be with her as friend and lover. He knew that her first marriage had made her reluctant to trust any man. He was willing to wait, to give her time to discover that she could count on him. He wasn't going anywhere.

He couldn't imagine any man turning his back on Frannie. In a very short time she'd become such a big part of his world that he found it difficult to think of life without her. If a day went by when he didn't get to talk to her, he felt as if something was missing.

That's why he was so frustrated tonight. He'd been trying for two days to reach her, yet every time he called he got the same message, either from Emma or Alex. She couldn't come to the phone because she was painting the kitchen. The task hadn't surprised him, but he couldn't understand why she hadn't returned a single one of his phone calls. It was almost as if she was avoiding him.

He wasn't about to make that assumption, however. Not when it came to Frannie. Knowing her the way he did, he was confident that if she were upset with him, she'd tell him. It was another quality he admired—her directness.

And the memories of the last time they'd been together refused to let him think that anything could be wrong. She'd cooked dinner for the two of them after the kids had gone to bed. It had been a wonderful evening filled with soft music and intimate conversation that had been the instigation for the plans they'd made for a weekend getaway without the children. Aside from giving them time alone without any interruptions, Joe knew it would be a chance for the kind of intimacy they both wanted.

Thinking about what a weekend away would mean had Joe wondering if maybe that wasn't the reason Frannie hadn't returned his calls. Was she feeling as if things were moving too quickly? She was a mother with three children, a woman who'd been hurt badly. He could understand why she'd be a little gun-shy when it came to love the second time around. If that was the case, he needed to talk to her, to assure her he could wait until she was ready.

First thing in the morning he dialed her number, hoping to catch her before she left for work.

Once again when he phoned, Alex answered.

"Hi. It's Uncle Joe. Can I speak to your mom?"

"She can't come to the phone because—"

"She's not painting at this time of morning, Alex," he said a bit impatiently.

"No, she's in the bathroom."

Joe grinned. "Tell her I'll wait. It's important."

He heard a *clunk* as Alex set down the phone. Joe wasn't sure how long he waited. He heard a door slam, Emma warn her brother he was going to be late, another door slam. He waited so long that he was beginning to think that he'd been forgotten and that the entire crew had left the house with the phone sitting off the hook.

He was just about to hang up when he heard Frannie's voice.

"Joe, this isn't a good time. I have to get Luke to

day care and I'm already late for a meeting at the paper.''

There was no warmth in her voice, only impatience. His nerves tingled a warning. ''I don't want to make you late. I just wanted to hear your voice. I missed talking to you this weekend.''

She didn't say, ''I missed talking to you, too,'' or ''It's good to hear your voice.'' Gone was the affection he normally heard when they talked on the phone—that husky, seductive quality that made him ache with longing for her. She easily could have been talking to the neighbor next door, so impersonal was her tone.

''I painted the kitchen. It looks much brighter in here. I got rid of the dinginess.''

''I'm sure you did a good job.''

''I hope so. Look, this really isn't a good time for me, Joe. Luke's fussing.''

He couldn't hear any whining in the background. ''Frannie, is everything okay?''

''It won't be if I miss my meeting,'' she said tersely.

So he hadn't imagined the distance she'd put between them. ''Why don't I call you tonight? What would be a good time?''

She sighed. ''Alex and Emma have an open house at their school. I'm not sure what time we'll be home.''

''Maybe you should call me then?'' he suggested.

''If it's not too late,'' she said, and then abruptly ended the conversation, leaving Joe staring at the phone.

Everything was definitely not okay. Joe didn't know what was going on, but he was determined to find out. He paced the kitchen floor, watching the clock, waiting for time to pass. When he knew he'd given her enough time to get Luke to day care and herself to the newspaper, he tried her number at work. He was not surprised to find her at her desk instead of at a meeting.

"Frannie, we need to talk," he said as soon as he heard her voice.

"Joe, I'm at work," she said on a note of exasperation.

"Just answer one question. What's going on?"

She sounded nervous as she said, "I don't know what you're talking about."

"Last Thursday we practically made love on your sofa. Today you're treating me like one of those people who call during dinner trying to sell you new windows."

"Because I'm at work."

"We agreed we wouldn't play games, Frannie," he reminded her. "Give me a straight answer. What changed between last Thursday and now?"

"Joe, I really don't want to get into this now," she said with a plea in her voice.

"Get into what? Are you unhappy with the plans we made for next weekend?"

"I'm just unhappy!" she finally spat out.

"With me?" He hated to ask the question, but had to know the answer.

"Yes."

A pain knifed through him, tightening his chest so that he found it difficult to breathe. "Is it something I've done?"

"It's…" She paused. "It's just not going to work out between us," she said, her voice breaking with emotion. "I'm sorry, Joe. Please don't make this any more difficult than it is."

In other words, don't ask me why it won't work. Just get out of my life. Joe felt as if he'd just jumped out of a plane, only to discover his parachute wouldn't open.

"Frannie, you're not serious." He didn't know what else to say.

"Yes, Joe, I am. I'm sorry."

There was a finality in her voice that sent a chill through him. He wanted to ask her what had changed, to tell her how he felt about her and try to persuade her that she was wrong. It *could* work between them. They *were* good for each other. And a million other reasons why she couldn't be saying what she was saying.

Fortunately, his pride asserted itself.

"If that's the way it is," he said with as little emotion as possible, "I won't bother you again." And without waiting to hear if she had any response, he hung up the phone.

As usual, when he needed to think, he went down to the dock. He didn't bother grabbing a jacket or a sweatshirt, needing to feel the sting of the brisk autumn air. It was how he felt inside—as if a good strong wind had knocked all the warmth out of him. How long he sat outside he wasn't sure. When he finally made his way back up to the house, his father greeted him at the door.

Joe hoped the Admiral was going to say that Frannie had called and wanted Joe to call her back right away. He didn't. He said, "You trying to catch a cold sitting out there without a coat?"

Joe didn't answer, and the Admiral said, "Oh—

almost forgot.'' He shuffled over to the kitchen counter and picked up a piece of paper. ''You had a phone message while you were out.''

Hope that it was from Frannie had Joe's heart beating erratically. He reached for the slip of paper and frowned. It was a message from the dentist reminding him it was time for his checkup.

In the days that followed, Joe jumped whenever the phone rang, hoping that it would be Frannie. It wasn't. When his father asked him why he was moping around the place, Joe answered him honestly, telling him in as few words as possible that his relationship with Frannie was over.

With a pat on his shoulder, his father said, ''I know this isn't what you want to hear, son, but it's for the best. Women get you into trouble. Look at me.''

Joe knew his father referred to the fact that he'd been forced into retirement due to an affair he'd had with another officer's wife. That had eventually provided a motive for the treason charges made against him. But Joe didn't think that it was a mistake to be in love with Frannie.

''You were taking a risk seeing her, especially with her sister being a lawyer,'' his father continued. ''I'm not worried about me. I'd go to jail in a minute if it meant you could have a wife and kids, but the problem is that if they catch me, they catch you. And I couldn't bear the thought of your going to prison because of me.''

Joe looked at his father. ''We're not going to prison, Dad. I won't let that happen.''

''I know.'' Again the hand patted his shoulder.

"You're a good son. Have I told you how proud I am of you?"

Joe smiled. "Yes, Dad, you have."

The Admiral sighed as he sank down into his recliner. "I only have two regrets about the way we live. One is that you can't have a woman like Frannie in your life. The second is you have to deny who you are. You're a Hawthorn, not a Smith, and I'd like to shout that to the world. I feel as if I've robbed you of your birthright."

This time it was Joe who got up out of his chair to place his hand on his dad's shoulder. "You haven't, Dad. We both know who we really are." As he spoke, he thought how ironic those words were.

"We're safe here, Joe, aren't we?"

"Yeah. Why do you ask that?"

"Someone called when you were gone and asked Letty all sorts of questions."

Joe felt the hairs on the back of his neck stand up. "What kinds of questions?"

"I think..." he began, then stopped.

"What kinds of questions, Dad," Joe prodded him gently.

"I can't remember," he said with a blank look on his face. "I'm sorry."

"It's okay, Dad, it was probably just one of those telephone surveys," Joe said, but made a note to call Letty tomorrow and talk to her.

Only, he never had the chance. Shortly after breakfast three official cars pulled into his drive. Through the kitchen window Joe watched uniformed sailors climb out of one of the cars, the *SP* on their armbands identifying them as the Navy's Shore Patrol.

From another car emerged a couple of men in dark suits.

Joe thought about grabbing his father and making a run for it. His seaplane was out front. However, one look at his father rocking in his chair made him realize what a futile effort it would be. In his condition, the Admiral would never be able to run from men half his age.

Joe knew his worst nightmare had come true. They'd been found.

"YOU LOOK AWFUL," Lois remarked from the doorway of Frannie's office.

"Thank you. It's nice to see you, too," Frannie said sarcastically, as her sister walked into the tiny cubicle.

"I'm serious, Frannie." Lois came around the desk to feel her forehead. "You're warm, too. How's your throat?"

"A little dry, but it always is this time of the year. I have allergies, or have you forgotten?"

"You're probably coming down with something," her sister speculated.

"It wouldn't surprise me. Once the kids are back in school the crud usually ends up at our house. If I promise to take two aspirins and call you in the morning, will you quit looking at me like I'm something your cat threw up?"

Lois took a chair across from her. "I'm sorry, but you really do look miserable. Even your eyes are swollen." She continued to stare at her. "Have you been crying?" When Frannie didn't deny it, her sister said, "Frannie! You don't look like this because of Joe, do you?"

Frannie was too worn out to try to pretend she wasn't. "How am I supposed to look? I just broke up with a guy I thought…" She stifled a sob. "Oh, what does it matter what I thought."

"I didn't realize he meant that much to you," Lois said, handing her a tissue.

Frannie dabbed at her nose. "He doesn't," she lied. "I'm just mad because not only do my kids have a deadbeat dad, but now they've got an uncle who's a big, fat liar. Lois, you know I'm not a dumb person. Shouldn't I at least be able to recognize when a man is lying to me about who he is?"

"I'm not sure he was lying about who he was. He may only have been lying about what name he was using."

That brought Frannie's head up with a jerk. "What are you talking about? Did you find out why he had an assumed identity?" She could see by the look on her sister's face that she had, and quickly added, "Please tell me it wasn't because he has a wife and kids somewhere and he didn't want to be responsible for them."

"No, he doesn't have a wife and kids. I suspect that most everything he's told you about himself is true."

Frannie felt as if a great weight had been lifted off her chest. "Then, why is he using an assumed name?"

"Because of his father."

"The Admiral? What could he possibly have done?"

"He's accused of defrauding the government out of millions of dollars."

Frannie gasped. "The Admiral?"

She nodded soberly. "He claims he isn't guilty of anything but trusting the wrong people." Lois pulled a folder out of her briefcase and set it on the table. "I wasn't going to show you this until I had more details."

Frannie winced as she opened the folder and saw a picture of Joe next to his father on the front page of an old newspaper with the headline "Accused Spy Missing."

"It gets worse, Frannie. I just heard that the authorities have found them. They're no longer in Grand Marais."

Frannie couldn't believe what she was hearing. She needed to know more so she flipped through the articles in the folder.

Lois finally said, "As you can see the media has pretty much tried the Admiral and found him guilty."

"Is that what you think?"

"No, I think he may be innocent, as he claims," Lois replied.

"Of course he's innocent," Frannie declared emotionally. "Isn't there something you can do?"

"I'm not sure Joe would want me doing anything, considering the circumstances," Lois said.

"No, you're right. You've been so unfair. It's not like you."

Lois held up her hands. "I plead guilty and I'm sorry. Now, before you read me the riot act, let me tell you what I did do. I've made some phone calls—at Arlene's request—and found out that there are other people who think he was framed.

"Apparently he didn't retire from the military

willingly. He was forced to resign because of an indiscretion with the wife of another officer.''

"He committed adultery? Isn't that grounds for court martial in the military?''

"Yes, but proving adultery can be tricky, and when you're a distinguished Admiral with so many years of service, punishment is usually forced retirement.''

Frannie sifted through the clippings and saw nothing about any adulterous affair. "So what does the affair have to do with his being a suspect in the fraud case?''

"Apparently after retiring, the Admiral became a consultant to one of the largest defense contractors in the country. On a tip from an insider, the Navy investigated the company and found millions of dollars had been illegally funneled through kickbacks and bribes. The Admiral was accused of playing a major role in the fraud. What better way for someone to get revenge than to turn around and make his former employer pay?''

"That doesn't sound like the Admiral I know. He's a sweet, gentle man who doesn't seem to have a mean bone in his body.''

Lois lifted her brows. "You could be right. From the start the Admiral claimed his innocence, saying that he'd been set up. The government would only consider reducing the charges if he were to testify against other members of the company.''

"And he wouldn't do it?''

"He was going to do it. But before the case went to trial, he was in a bad accident. Apparently Joe had warned the government that his father was a threat to some very powerful people and had asked for protection.''

''It was denied?''

''No, but even with the protection, the Admiral was injured by a hit-and-run driver. That's when Joe took matters into his own hands, and they fled. Not trusting the authorities to keep his father safe, he moved and took another name.''

Frannie swallowed the lump in her throat. ''That's why he didn't want me or Arlene looking into the birth records. He was trying to keep his father safe.''

Lois nodded. ''You didn't fall in love with a loser, Frannie. Just a man who loves his father so much that he was willing to give up everything he had to protect him.''

''And I told him to get lost.'' She hung her head in self-recrimination. ''How could I have been such a fool?''

''Because you listened to your big sister. I'm sorry, Frannie.'' Lois reached across the table to cover her hand. ''You were just a mother who was trying to look out for her kids. How could you have known any of this? You did what you thought you needed to do, based on the information I gave you.''

Frannie could only shake her head. ''I hurt him, Lois. You didn't hear his voice the day I told him it was over between us.'' She choked back a sob. ''I knew he was a good man. I should have trusted him, talked to him. Instead I let you go dig up all that information—and now look where he is.'' She slid the folder across the table in her sister's direction.

''You think I informed the NCIS of his whereabouts?''

''You had him investigated,'' she accused.

''Yes, and that led to nothing. Frannie, I'm not the one responsible for the NCIS finding them.'' Lois put the folder back into her briefcase.

Frannie frowned. ''Then, who is?''

''Harold Gallivan.''

''Josh's father?''

She nodded. ''You know how Alex is always bragging about what Josh can do on the computer? Well, he's right. That kid went on the Internet and found the NCIS site where they post their wanted fugitives. The Admiral's picture was there. Apparently Josh showed his dad. Good old Harold did his patriotic duty. All it took was one click of his mouse and the NCIS had their tip.''

''Oh, good grief!'' She sat stunned for several seconds. Frannie could hardly believe what she'd just heard. Her own son may have unknowingly taken his uncle out of his life. ''Nothing's going to happen to Joe, is it?''

''Not if I can help it. Arlene's asked me to fly to Washington to see if there's anything I can do,'' she said, snapping her briefcase shut. ''I can't legally represent either of them, but I can offer my services behind the scenes.''

''I want to go with you,'' she said, getting to her feet.

''What about the kids?''

''I'll ask Lisa if they can stay at her place for a couple of days,'' she said, gathering her things together.

''Why don't you wait until I find out what the situation is there?''

''No, I can't,'' she said, reaching for her jacket. ''I have to explain why I said the things I did.''

"Frannie, I have to warn you. There's a good chance that this mess isn't going to go away. When the government builds a case against someone…"

"Then, we'll find a way to prove Joe and his father innocent. My kids are not going to have their uncle in jail."

CHAPTER THIRTEEN

NEITHER JOE NOR HIS FATHER was in jail when Frannie and Lois arrived in Washington. They were at a hospital where the Admiral had been admitted because of an irregular heartbeat.

Frannie found Joe in a small lounge outside the Cardiac Care Unit. He sat on a blue vinyl sofa, his head in his hands. When he heard footsteps, he looked up, and she saw what the past few days had done to him. He looked tired, his chin dark with stubble, his face lined with worry. As she and Lois approached him, he rose.

"What are you doing here?" The question was directed at Frannie, his tone indicating he was not happy to see her.

"She came with me." Lois stepped around Frannie, extending her hand in a professional greeting. "How are you doing, Joe?"

"I have an attorney," he said with even more coolness than he'd shown Frannie.

Lois nodded. "I know. I'm here because Arlene asked me to come, but if you'd rather, I can leave." She looked to him for approval.

He looked as if he might ask her to go, but then he shrugged and said, "It's all right."

"I'm glad you said that because I want to do whatever I can to help. Before I do anything, I need to grab some coffee. Anyone else want some?'' She looked first at Frannie, then at Joe. Both shook their heads, and she slipped out.

Frannie knew her sister had left to give her time alone with Joe, although judging by the look on his face, she wasn't sure it was what he wanted. He gave no indication that he was pleased to see her. Suddenly she was plagued with doubts. Had she made a mistake accompanying Lois to Washington?

''How's your father?'' she asked, wishing Joe wouldn't look at her so coldly.

''His heartbeat's back to normal but they're running some tests to determine what the underlying problem is.''

She nodded. ''What about you? Are you okay?''

''Do you care?''

She figured she deserved that, after the way she'd talked to him last. ''Of course I care.''

''You shouldn't have come, Frannie,'' he said, his eyes looking tired and defeated.

''I had to. I needed to tell you how sorry I am.''

He chuckled without humor. ''Sorry doesn't do much good, does it? I mean, the damage has been done. My father's in the hospital, and when he's well enough to get out...'' He let her draw her own conclusion.

Wanting to ease the pain she saw on his face, she said, ''Lois says there are lots of people who believe your father is innocent.''

''Lois says that, does she?'' he said with more than a hint of sarcasm.

''She wants to help, Joe.''

''What one sister pulls apart, the other one tries to put back together. Such teamwork.''

Frannie winced at the anger in his voice. "There are some things you need to know. Please let me explain."

"Explain what? Why you couldn't respect my wishes and leave well enough alone?" His eyes darkened as he stared into hers. "My dad wasn't a threat to your kids."

"You think I turned him in? Joe, it wasn't me!"

"The NCIS said they had a tip from a civilian."

"Yes. Harold Gallivan. You've met Alex's friend, Josh. His father." She relayed the information her sister had given her, ending with "Joe, I would never do anything to hurt your father. Neither would Alex."

"Does Alex know what's happened?"

She nodded. "It's been in the papers. He's feels bad, Joe."

He rubbed a hand across the back of his neck and made a sound of frustration. "This is incredible. For two years I manage not to raise a single eyebrow of suspicion, even though I come into contact with cops, private investigators, and lawyers—all wanting to go fishing in the wilderness. But a ten-year-old kid can go exploring on the Internet and stumble onto the NCIS site…" He shook his head in disbelief.

"Alex knew he wasn't supposed to talk about the results of the DNA test with anyone," Frannie said apologetically. "I think he was just so proud to have an uncle in his life that he had to share it with his best friend."

He waved away her apology. "It's not Alex's fault, Frannie. The truth is, I've no one to blame but myself."

"How can you say that? You did everything you could to protect your dad."

"I didn't stay away from you, did I." He fixed her with a gaze that was full of guilt.

"You're thinking none of this would have happened if you hadn't met me, aren't you."

His silence was his answer.

Frannie felt her hopes slipping away. What kind of a future could they have if he thought their happiness came at the expense of his father's freedom?

"I can't change what's happened, Joe. I wish I could, because the last thing I want is for your father to suffer because I wanted my children to get to know their uncle." She had so many things she wanted to say and so much love she wanted to share, yet he kept her at a distance. All she could say was "I'm sorry, Joe."

"You came a long way just to apologize," he commented, eyeing her suspiciously. "You could have called."

"I thought..." She wondered if there was any point telling him how she felt when there was so little hope that the two of them would have a future together.

"You thought what, Frannie?"

She shook her head. "It doesn't matter."

He reached for her hand. "It matters to me. What could you possibly have been thinking that made you leave your kids, get on a plane and fly all this way to see a man who'd lied to you from the very beginning?"

"I was thinking that I needed to tell that man that I understood the reason why he hadn't been totally honest with me—that no matter what anyone might say about him, I thought what he did for his dad was heroic, not criminal.''

He studied her hand, running his thumb over her fingers in a caressing motion. ''I'm not a hero, Frannie.''

''You are to me,'' she said quietly.

He raised his eyes to hers. ''But I don't make you happy.''

She knew she had hurt him the day he'd called her at the newspaper. ''Oh, yes, you do. What I said that day you phoned me...it wasn't the truth, Joe. I was scared.''

''Of me?''

She shook her head. ''No, of feeling so much for someone who'd changed his identity. Lois had shown me there weren't any Smiths in the hospital on the day you were born.''

''And you wondered why,'' he surmised.

She nodded. ''Instead of asking you about it, I went ahead and assumed you were just like my ex-husband.''

''I'm not Dennis, Frannie,'' he said soberly. ''I didn't leave my wife. She left me.''

''Foolish woman,'' she said, looking him directly in the eye.

He shrugged. ''I couldn't give her what she wanted.''

''And what was that?''

''To be the wife of an officer in the Navy. When I left the military, she found someone who could give her what she wanted.''

''You can give me what I want, Joe.''

''I want to believe that.''

''You can, Joe. I'm sorry for saying I didn't think

it would work between us, but I was confused. I didn't know what it was that had made you run.''

"This business with my father...it's not like running away from creditors. There's a man in a uniform outside my father's door.'' His voice held a warning.

"I know how serious this is, Joe.'' She needed to let him know she wasn't going to give up on him without a fight. "I want to be with you, Joe. What we have is special and I don't want to lose it. But if you don't want me to be here, just say so, and I'll go back to Minneapolis.''

His eyes probed hers. She could see he waged a silent battle within himself, his face reflecting his confusion. Then suddenly he opened his arms, and she didn't hesitate to go into them.

"Oh, Frannie, I've missed you,'' he said close to her ear.

"I've been so miserable without you,'' she said, tears pooling in her eyes.

They didn't kiss, but simply stood comforting one another, saying without words how much they needed each other. Finally, he released her, wiping away the tears and then kissing each cheek.

"I should have told you what you were getting into with me,'' he said, his voice full of regret.

"You did what you thought was best for your father,'' she replied, still amazed at the sacrifices he'd made. "I'm the one who should have trusted you. I knew in my heart you couldn't be a criminal, yet I was scared to find out what it was that had made you leave your past behind.''

He outlined her lips with his thumb. "And now you know what it is.''

"Yes, and I'm not afraid." She placed a kiss on his thumb.

"You should be," he warned, again stepping away from her. "I'm not sure what's going to happen here, Frannie. One thing I do know is that I don't want you or the kids getting involved in this mess."

"You can't expect me to leave you to go through this alone," she said, although she suspected that was exactly what he wanted her to do.

He confirmed her suspicions when he said, "Until this is cleared up, I want you to do just that."

She wanted to ask, "And if it isn't cleared up?" but she didn't dare voice her fears. Suddenly she felt as if she'd been given heaven only to have it snatched away again.

"You understand why I'm saying this, don't you, Frannie?"

She nodded and managed to ask, "And after this is all over?"

He smiled then, that special smile that made her think anything was possible as long as he was at her side.

"Maybe we can finally get that weekend away. One thing I do know, Frannie, is that I don't want there to be any more secrets between us."

"Me, neither," she agreed.

His finger moved across her jaw. "Don't look so sad. We will be together," he said with an optimism she knew he wasn't feeling.

She gave him a smile and hoped he was right, because if he wasn't, Frannie didn't think she could bear the consequences.

WHEN FRANNIE SAW Lois making her way through the office toward her cubicle, she knew there was only one reason she'd come. She had news about Joe and his father.

Frannie held her breath as she waited for her sister to reach her door. When Lois saw her, she smiled and Frannie's heart began to race.

"Well?" she prodded.

"All charges have been dropped," Lois reported with a victorious grin.

Frannie grabbed her sister and hugged her, jumping up and down as she said, "I knew he was innocent. Thank you for everything."

"I didn't do much. He had a very good team of attorneys working on his behalf," Lois said, when Frannie released her.

"I'm glad you were there. You said you thought the charges would be dropped."

"Considering the Admiral's mental state and the fact that he would no longer be a credible witness, it wasn't a difficult prediction to make," she said, shrugging out of her coat. "Sit down and I'll give you the details."

Frannie was an attentive audience as her sister relayed what the courts had decided and why. By the time she'd finished, there was only one unanswered question.

"So when are they coming home?"

"I believe they should be back in Grand Marais tomorrow night. Are you going to go up there to give them a welcome home party?"

Frannie wished she could say yes, but the truth was that she felt she needed an invitation to go see Joe. "No. I'll wait. I'm not sure Joe will want me there."

Lois rolled her eyes. "Are you nuts? The guy's crazy about you."

"It's not that simple," Frannie said.

And she found out how true that was, later when Joe called her from Washington.

"I suppose Lois told you," he said.

"Of course. That's wonderful news, Joe. You must be so relieved."

"I am. I'm bringing Dad home tomorrow."

She knew they'd be flying on a smaller airline that used the Minneapolis-St. Paul airport for its connecting flights, which was the reason she said, "Why don't I come to the airport, and we'll grab a quick drink to celebrate your homecoming while you wait."

"I don't think there's much time between flights," he answered. "And I'd hate for you to have to drive through evening rush-hour traffic if we're only going to have ten or fifteen minutes."

"It'd be worth it," she replied.

"I believe it would be," he said in a voice that made her long to be in his arms.

"Then, let me come. I'm so happy, Joe, I could jump over the moon. I need to share this feeling with you!"

He hesitated, then said, "I think the celebration should wait."

Disappointment flowed through Frannie. "All right. If that's what you want."

"It's not really what I want, but there are some loose ends I need to tie up."

"Can you tell me what those loose ends are?"

"I'd rather talk to you about it after I've taken

care of them. You trust me, don't you, Frannie? You know I'd never do anything to hurt you.''

"Yes, I do,'' she answered honestly.

"It's good to hear you say that, because I need to sort through some things and I really need to do it on my own.''

Her intuition had her skin prickling. "This is about Dennis, isn't it.''

"Yes. Can you trust me to do what's best for us?''

Her first inclination was to plead with him to tell her what was troubling him, but she also knew that it couldn't have been easy coming to terms with everything he'd discovered in the past few months. As much as she wanted to help him cope with the changes that had occurred in his life, she knew that only he could resolve the issues surrounding his newly discovered family.

"I do trust you, Joe, but I also want you to know that I'm here for you,'' she said.

"Thank you, Frannie. Everything is going to be all right. You'll see. Just have a little patience and faith, okay?''

"Okay,'' she told him, although it was easier said than done.

When she had lunch with her sister sometime later, she received the same advice. She bemoaned the fact that Joe had been back from Washington for over two weeks, yet she still hadn't seen him, and Lois looked at her and said, "He just needs a little time to adjust to everything that's happened.''

"How much time?'' she asked, knowing she was sounding rather churlish but unable to stop herself.

"Frannie! Look what he's been through. Have you forgotten that he not only nearly lost his father, but discovered he has another mother?'' she said in between bites of her salad.

"And a brother," she mumbled irritably.

"He knows where Dennis is?" Lois looked surprised.

"I didn't ask him, but I have a feeling he does."

Lois jabbed at the air with her fork. "Now, that would be something, but I suppose it shouldn't surprise me. He did work in naval intelligence and he was able to stay underground with his father for two years. Is that what has you so irritable? The possibility that he might see Dennis?"

"It does make me nervous."

Lois chuckled. "He's not going to see him and become his evil twin or anything."

"I know that," she said impatiently.

"He probably just needs to see for himself who his brother is." She raised her brows. "Poor Joe. I sure wouldn't want to discover I had a twin like Dennis."

"Thank you very much." Frannie threw her napkin down in disgust. "As if I wasn't worried enough."

"You still haven't told me why you are so worried. Joe loves you. Meeting his brother isn't going to change that."

Intellectually, she didn't believe it would, but emotionally Frannie couldn't seem to dispel the fear that somehow Dennis would screw up her relationship with Joe.

"Frannie, have a little faith in the man," Lois urged. "I do."

"I'm glad to hear that, because he's important to me."

Now, all Frannie had to do was trust that she was as important to him.

INSTEAD OF RETURNING to Grand Marais, Joe decided to go straight from Montana to Minneapolis. He didn't want to wait one more day to see Frannie, and finally he felt as if he could go to her with nothing standing between them. He no longer had to worry about his father's safety, and now he'd resolved the issue of his brother.

It had all seemed rather surreal—the brother he didn't know he had was the same man who'd abandoned the woman he loved. But it had all become very real once Joe found Dennis Harper.

Now, as he landed the Cessna on the small airstrip in suburban Minneapolis, he contemplated how he would tell Frannie what had happened on his trip.

By the time he'd called a taxi to take him to Frannie's place, it was after ten. The tiny house was dark except for one light in the kitchen. Joe paid the driver and went up to the door.

Just seconds after he rang the bell, the porch light came on. Frannie's head peaked through the square pane of glass in the door, her mouth dropping open at the sight of him. She yanked open the door.

"Joe! Is something wrong?" she asked as she pulled the edges of her robe together to ward off the cold air.

"No, everything's right," he said, stepping into the house. He closed the door behind him and stared at her. Her face had been scrubbed clean, her hair pushed away from her forehead and secured with a headband. She looked ready for bed, which made him ache with longing—a longing that grew more intense each time he saw her.

He wanted to pull her into his arms and kiss her until she moaned with pleasure. He didn't. He simply said, "I love you, Frannie."

She looked a bit taken aback by his declaration, but said, "That's good because I love you, too, Joe."

"You do?"

She nodded and grinned. He pulled her into his arms and kissed her until she was breathless. "My God, I've missed you," he said, inhaling the fresh scent of her shampoo.

When he gently eased away from her, she asked, "Where have you been?"

He led her by the hand into the family room, where he pulled her onto his lap as he sank down onto the sofa, planting several more kisses on her lips before saying, "I need to tell you something. I found Dennis, Frannie." He watched her face closely to see her reaction.

"Where is he?"

"Do you really want to know?"

She shook her head. "No, I don't think it matters anymore."

Joe felt a huge wave of relief. "I think you're right about that."

"Why didn't you call to tell me you'd found him, Joe?"

"I think you know the answer to that," he said softly, but he could see by the confusion in her eyes that she really didn't. "He's my brother and your ex-husband. I wanted to keep the two things separate."

"And can you?"

"Yeah, I can," he said, still a bit amazed that it

was true. "It felt really weird, Frannie. I mean, this
person I'd never met before and yet I had this connection to him. You were right. We *are* alike in many
ways, yet we don't share the same goals, the same
values."

"Did you tell him the whole story of how you
found out he was your twin?"

He nodded. "I didn't see any point in lying." He
fingered her hair. "He knows I'm in love with you.
I told him he didn't need to worry about taking care
of his children. That I'd do it…that I wanted to do
it."

Her eyes darkened with emotion and she kissed
him deeply. "That's for being such a wonderful
guy," she said, her expression full of the love she
felt for him. Then she asked, "Did he say anything
about seeing the kids again?"

He shook his head. "He's remarried, Frannie. In
fact, his wife is pregnant." He watched her to see
what reaction the news would produce, but there was
no anger, no pain.

She simply said, "I guess that doesn't surprise me.
Did you tell him about Arlene…how she misses
him? I hope you told him he should contact her even
if he wants nothing to do with us."

"It wouldn't bother you if they had a relationship
again?"

She didn't answer immediately, but finally said,
"No, it really wouldn't. I can imagine how I would
feel as a mother if I couldn't see one of my children."

He kissed her again, a tender brushing on the
mouth that told her how much he admired her. "I

don't know what the future will bring, Frannie. I only know that I want you in it.''

''I want that, too, Joe, but there are obstacles.''

''You mean Dennis?''

''No, I mean you live in Grand Marais and I live in Minneapolis,'' she said, slipping her fingers inside his jacket.

He grinned. ''That's not an obstacle. My home can be anywhere you want it to be,'' he told her, his body heating up at the touch of her fingers.

''Then, I guess there's nothing standing in our way now, is there?''

''Not a thing,'' he agreed.

A tiny voice interrupted their kiss. ''Mommy, I need a drink o' water.''

''Just little obstacles,'' Joe said with a twinkle in his eye. When Frannie would have gotten up to get Luke a drink, he stopped her. ''You wait here. I can handle this one.''

Frannie simply smiled and said, ''I believe you *are* just the man I need.''

HARLEQUIN *Super*ROMANCE

CREATURE COMFORT

A heartwarming new series by

Carolyn McSparren

Creature Comfort, the largest veterinary clinic in Tennessee, treats animals of all sizes—horses and cattle as well as family pets. Meet the patients—and their owners. And share the laughter and the tears with the men and women who love and care for all creatures great and small.

#996 THE MONEY MAN
(July 2001)

#1011 THE PAYBACK MAN
(September 2001)

Look for these Harlequin Superromance titles coming soon to your favorite retail outlet.

HARLEQUIN®
Makes any time special ®

Harlequin truly does make any time special. . . . This year we are celebrating weddings in style!

To help us celebrate, we want you to tell us how wearing the Harlequin wedding gown will make your wedding day special. As the grand prize, Harlequin will offer one lucky bride the chance to **"Walk Down the Aisle" in the Harlequin wedding gown!**

There's more...

For her honeymoon, she and her groom will spend five nights at the **Hyatt Regency Maui.** As part of this five-night honeymoon at the hotel renowned for its romantic attractions, the couple will enjoy a candlelit dinner for two in Swan Court, a sunset sail on the hotel's catamaran, and duet spa treatments.

To enter, please write, in, 250 words or less, how wearing the Harlequin wedding gown will make your wedding day special. The entry will be judged based on its emotionally compelling nature, its originality and creativity, and its sincerity. This contest is open to Canadian and U.S. residents only and to those who are 18 years of age and older. There is no purchase necessary to enter. Void where prohibited. See further contest rules attached. Please send your entry to:

Walk Down the Aisle Contest

In Canada
P.O. Box 637
Fort Erie, Ontario
L2A 5X3

In U.S.A.
P.O. Box 9076
3010 Walden Ave.
Buffalo, NY 14269-9076

You can also enter by visiting www.eHarlequin.com
Win the Harlequin wedding gown and the vacation of a lifetime!
The deadline for entries is October 1, 2001.

Makes any time special ®

HARLEQUIN WALK DOWN THE AISLE TO MAUI CONTEST 1197
OFFICIAL RULES
NO PURCHASE NECESSARY TO ENTER

1. To enter, follow directions published in the offer to which you are responding. Contest begins April 2, 2001, and ends on October 1, 2001. Method of entry may vary. Mailed entries must be postmarked by October 1, 2001, and received by October 8, 2001.

2. Contest entry may be, at times, presented via the Internet, but will be restricted solely to residents of certain georgraphic areas that are disclosed on the Web site. To enter via the Internet, if permissible, access the Harlequin Web site (www.eHarlequin.com) and follow the directions displayed online. Online entries must be received by 11:59 p.m. E.S.T. on October 1, 2001.

   In lieu of submitting an entry online, enter by mail by hand-printing (or typing) on an 8½" x 11" plain piece of paper, your name, address (including zip code), Contest number/name and in 250 words or fewer, why winning a Harlequin wedding dress would make your wedding day special. Mail via first-class mail to: Harlequin Walk Down the Aisle Contest 1197, (in the U.S.) P.O. Box 9076, 3010 Walden Avenue, Buffalo, NY 14269-9076, (in Canada) P.O. Box 637, Fort Erie, Ontario L2A 5X3, Canada.

   Limit one entry per person, household address and e-mail address. Online and/or mailed entries received from persons residing in geographic areas in which Internet entry is not permissible will be disqualified.

3. Contests will be judged by a panel of members of the Harlequin editorial, marketing and public relations staff based on the following criteria:

   * Originality and Creativity—50%
   * Emotionally Compelling—25%
   * Sincerity—25%

   In the event of a tie, duplicate prizes will be awarded. Decisions of the judges are final.

4. All entries become the property of Torstar Corp. and will not be returned. No responsibility is assumed for lost, late, illegible, incomplete, inaccurate, nondelivered or misdirected mail or misdirected e-mail, for technical, hardware or software failures of any kind, lost or unavailable network connections, or failed, incomplete, garbled or delayed computer transmission or any human error which may occur in the receipt or processing of the entries in this Contest.

5. Contest open only to residents of the U.S. (except Puerto Rico) and Canada, who are 18 years of age or older, and is void wherever prohibited by law; all applicable laws and regulations apply. Any litigation within the Provice of Quebec respecting the conduct or organization of a publicity contest may be submitted to the Régie des alcools, des courses et des jeux for a ruling. Any litigation respecting the awarding of a prize may be submitted to the Régie des alcools, des courses et des jeux only for the purpose of helping the parties reach a settlement. Employees and immediate family members of Torstar Corp. and D. L. Blair, Inc., their affiliates, subsidiaries and all other agencies, entities and persons connected with the use, marketing or conduct of this Contest are not eligible to enter. Taxes on prizes are the sole responsibility of winners. Acceptance of any prize offered constitutes permission to use winner's name, photograph or other likeness for the purposes of advertising, trade and promotion on behalf of Torstar Corp., its affiliates and subsidiaries without further compensation to the winner, unless prohibited by law.

6. Winners will be determined no later than November 15, 2001, and will be notified by mail. Winners will be required to sign and return an Affidavit of Eligibility form within 15 days after winner notification. Noncompliance within that time period may result in disqualification and an alternative winner may be selected. Winners of trip must execute a Release of Liability prior to ticketing and must possess required travel documents (e.g. passport, photo ID) where applicable. Trip must be completed by November 2002. No substitution of prize permitted by winner. Torstar Corp. and D. L. Blair, Inc., their parents, affiliates, and subsidiaries are not responsible for errors in printing or electronic presentation of Contest, entries and/or game pieces. In the event of printing or other errors which may result in unintended prize values or duplication of prizes, all affected game pieces or entries shall be null and void. If for any reason the Internet portion of the Contest is not capable of running as planned, including infection by computer virus, bugs, tampering, unauthorized intervention, fraud, technical failures, or any other causes beyond the control of Torstar Corp. which corrupt or affect the administration, secrecy, fairness, integrity or proper conduct of the Contest, Torstar Corp. reserves the right, at its sole discretion, to disqualify any individual who tampers with the entry process and to cancel, terminate, modify or suspend the Contest or the Internet portion thereof. In the event of a dispute regarding an online entry, the entry will be deemed submitted by the authorized holder of the e-mail account submitted at the time of entry. Authorized account holder is defined as the natural person who is assigned to an e-mail address by an Internet access provider, online service provider or other organization that is responsible for arranging e-mail address for the domain associated with the submitted e-mail address. **Purchase or acceptance of a product offer does not improve your chances of winning.**

7. Prizes: (1) Grand Prize—A Harlequin wedding dress (approximate retail value: $3,500) and a 5-night/6-day honeymoon trip to Maui, HI, including round-trip air transportation provided by Maui Visitors Bureau from Los Angeles International Airport (winner is responsible for transportation to and from Los Angeles International Airport) and a Harlequin Romance Package, including hotel accomodations (double occupancy) at the Hyatt Regency Maui Resort and Spa, dinner for (2) two at Swan Court, a sunset sail on Kiele V and a spa treatment for the winner (approximate retail value: $4,000); (5) Five runner-up prizes of a $1000 gift certificate to selected retail outlets to be determined by Sponsor (retail value $1000 ea.). Prizes consist of only those items listed as part of the prize. Limit one prize per person. All prizes are valued in U.S. currency.

8. For a list of winners (available after December 17, 2001) send a self-addressed, stamped envelope to: Harlequin Walk Down the Aisle Contest 1197 Winners, P.O. Box 4200 Blair, NE 68009-4200 or you may access the www.eHarlequin.com Web site through January 15, 2002.

Contest sponsored by Torstar Corp., P.O. Box 9042, Buffalo, NY 14269-9042, U.S.A.

PHWDACONT2

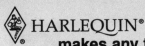

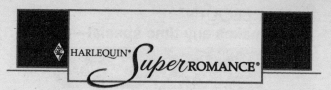

HARLEQUIN *Super*ROMANCE®

Welcome to Montana

Home of the Rocky Mountains, Yellowstone National Park, slow-moving glaciers and the spectacular Going to the Sun Highway.

BIG SKY COUNTRY

Set against this unforgettable background, Harlequin Superromance introduces the Maxwells of Montana—a family that's lived and ranched here for generations.

You won't want to miss this brand-new trilogy— three exciting romances by three of your favorite authors.

MARRIED IN MONTANA
by Lynnette Kent on sale August 2001

A MONTANA FAMILY
by Roxanne Rustand on sale September 2001

MY MONTANA HOME
by Ellen James on sale October 2001

Available wherever Harlequin books are sold.

HARLEQUIN®
Makes any time special ®